THE GRAND MISTLETOE ASSEMBLY

A REGENCY ROMANCE COLLECTION   SARA ADRIEN

NINA JARRETT   TANYA WILDE   PAMELA GIBSON

JEMMA FROST   EDIE CAY

Sara Adrien

ROGUE
PRESS

CONTENTS

Miracle on St. James's Street by Nina Jarrett   v

Chapter 1   1
Chapter 2   11
Chapter 3   16
Chapter 4   27
Chapter 5   34
Afterword   41
About the Author   43
A Daring Mistletoe Kiss by Tanya Wilde   45
Chapter 1   46
Chapter 2   50
Chapter 3   56
Chapter 4   62
Chapter 5   69
Chapter 6   74
Chapter 7   80
Afterword   87
About the Author   89
Lily's Scandalous Secret by Pamela Gibson   91
Chapter 1   92
Chapter 2   97
Chapter 3   103
Chapter 4   108
Chapter 5   114
Chapter 6   120
Chapter 7   125
Chapter 8   131
Afterword   135
About the Author   137
Surprising Captain Davies by Jemma Frost   139
Chapter 1   140
Chapter 2   145
Chapter 3   150
Chapter 4   155

Chapter 5   159
Chapter 6   166
Chapter 7   171
Epilogue   176
Afterword   179
About the Author   181
The Footman's Mistake by Edie Cay   183
Chapter 1   184
Chapter 2   194
Chapter 3   202
Chapter 4   208
Chapter 5   219
Afterword   225
About the Author   227
Captured at the Ball by Sara Adrien   229
Preface   231
Chapter 1   233
Chapter 2   239
Chapter 3   246
Chapter 4   253
Chapter 5   258
Chapter 6   266
Chapter 7   271
Chapter 8   276

Afterword   279
About the Author   281
Ballroom Whispers: Bonus Book Download   283

MIRACLE ON ST. JAMES'S STREET
BY NINA JARRETT

Spice Level 🤍

CHAPTER 1

*T*he Honorable Mr. Cameron Bolton contemplated the ballroom with a critical eye, noting the expensive attire and exuberant expressions of the couples dancing. A mere spare for a rather insignificant baron from the far north, he barely made the cut to attend such an illustrious event. His recent service as an officer in His Majesty's army gave him slightly better credentials, but, nevertheless, he was uncomfortable surrounded by the elite of the *ton*. He had only attended this evening because his good friend, Mr. Brendan Ridley, who was the heir to a barony in Somerset, had insisted Cameron accompany him.

Just as Cameron was wishing he were back in his rooms reading a good book, his focus turned to the seating area usually haunted by shy wallflowers, disregarded companions, and elderly guests, and a ravishing young woman caught his eye, his gaze riveted to her sweet oval face framed by curling ebony locks. But that was not what held his attention. It was the book she hid in the folds of her gown, for she was ignoring the dancers and music to steal time to read. A woman after his own heart, her obvious love of reading trumped the sought-after entry to this ball.

After hesitating for some time, he made the decision to discreetly approach her despite the impropriety. Cameron did not know who she was, and he did not recognize the young noblewoman who stood nearby, clearly standing guard over her charge. The chaperone had unusual red-blonde hair and was with child. She looked to be the same age as the woman he was eyeing, but clearly had reached a different station in life as a wife and expectant mother. While the blonde chatted animatedly to a friend, the lady who had captured his interest took the opportunity to read surreptitiously.

Cameron could not shake the desire to approach the girl to find out who she was. If he could speak to her, he might find a way to be formally introduced. As it was, he barely knew anybody at this ball, so he had no inspiration for how to meet her. Ridley had vanished, presumably to engage in a tryst with one of the loose widows he was so talented at uncovering at such events, which left Cameron an outcast with no acquaintances at this fashionable gathering of society's most important members. He vaguely recognized a few faces from his time at Harrow, but no one he was confident enough to approach. What if he recollected their names incorrectly and made an arse of himself?

If he secretly spoke to the girl, he still might not find a path to meeting her, which accounted for his hesitation. But the intense bemusement on her face while she read drew him with an inextricable call. He had never encountered a woman so enamored with reading, which greatly intrigued him. Books had long been his friends on his lengthy and lonely campaigns in the army.

Compelled to know who she was, he affirmed his decision to risk speaking to her in the hopes that she might assist him in seeking an introduction to her chaperone and thus a formal introduction to the alluring young lady herself. If he failed to be formally introduced this evening, perhaps he could question her about her social engagements so he could meet her another night. There was no time to dally, for only a few events remained before the *beau monde* left London for their country estates to celebrate the approaching holidays.

Decision made, Cameron checked his cravat, straightened his tail-coat, and tugged at the cuffs to ensure he was prepared before he began to skirt the elegant ballroom illuminated by hundreds of candles reflecting off strategically placed mirrors to enhance the light.

* * *

ISABELLE TURNED the page of the book she had hidden upon her person. The only reason she attended these social events was because Papa, her true father, the man who had raised her, had insisted she seize the opportunity to ally herself with the current Earl of Saunton.

Over the years, Papa had held her as a child in his arms when she wept from the pain of skinned knees, lifted her high to touch the sky, and sang her whimsical ballads of bonnie lasses and strapping lads. He had encouraged her love of books and learning and taught her any subject that took her interest, despite her unfashionable thirst for knowledge as a young woman. A scholar and a tutor, Papa had married her mother to give her the protection of his name when the late Earl of Saunton had failed in his responsibilities as a father to his unborn child.

If Papa wanted her to cement her connection to the current earl, who had privately claimed her as his sister, she would obey. However, she was not obligated to like it. She would prefer to be at home with her parents and her father's pupils, discussing literature in front of the fireplace, than at this infernal ball attended by the wealthiest members of high society. She knew she did not truly belong here, although she appreciated the lengths her newly found elder brother had gone to, introducing her to important people and striving to secure her future with ties to the elite that would aid her rise in social status.

Papa had said it was essential to him that she be protected and safe, and that a link to a powerful earl and his friends would help her secure a better future than what he could provide her as a lowly scholar. Isabelle trusted her beloved parent, so she was cooperating despite her disbelief that she would find an interesting gentleman among the prideful lot at these high society events.

Living in her brother's unfamiliar household these past weeks still felt awkward. While she had been warmly welcomed there, she was uncomfortable among these people, and only her loyalty to Papa prevented her from packing her valise and finding passage back to Saunton.

Isabelle looked up to find her chaperone, Lady Saunton, chatting to her cousin, Miss Lily Abbott, whom she had met several times since coming to London. Satisfied that no one paid her any mind, she lowered her gaze back to her book.

"What are you reading?" a deep male voice asked. It came from her right, where columns created a well of shadow next to the bank of spindly chairs.

She flinched in surprise. An encounter with a strange man could ruin her, so she furtively glanced over to see who addressed her from the shadows.

* * *

CAMERON WAITED with bated breath to see how the young woman would respond to his audacious question, careful to stay positioned behind a Doric column covered in gleaming scagliola. He watched her freeze in alarm before she carefully stretched her neck to throw a hidden glance in his direction. After several moments, she unfurled an ivory and green fan and raised it to flutter in front of her mouth as if to cool her face.

"It is a book on etiquette," she responded in a low voice.

"You read etiquette at a lavish ball?"

Still fluttering the fan, she smiled as she watched the dancers pass by in a twirl of silk and wool. "I have only recently entered society and am still committing the rules to memory. It would not do to use the wrong fork or address a peer incorrectly."

"Surely you should have read the book before you attended a ball?"

She frowned, her slight scowl visible in profile. "Sir, this conversation is most improper!"

"I appreciate that, I do. Please be assured this is unusual behavior for me, but I caught sight of you reading and simply could not turn away without learning more about you."

The young lady cocked her head at an angle, careful to flutter the fan so no one would notice her untoward conversation with him. "I have read the book twice through, but I still have difficulty remembering the arbitrary rules by which high society conducts itself."

Cameron grinned. She was utterly charming, evidently as unimpressed with fashionable society as he. Seizing his chance, he spoke quickly before he could lose his nerve. "I must meet you! What, pray tell, is your name so I may find a mutual acquaintance?"

A becoming blush stole across her cheeks, and she subtly turned to look him over. He hoped he cut a fine figure, in her estimation, with his above average height, broad shoulders, flat stomach, and his legs long and lean in his fashionable trousers. Tanned from his years in the British Army, he knew his hair was streaked with blond. He did not often pursue the fairer sex, but he had enjoyed some success in his college days at Cambridge. Not the same level of success as his chum, Brendan Ridley, who had dragged him to this event, but enough to have developed confidence in speaking to ladies.

Palpitating the delicate fan in front of her mouth, the young woman responded, "Isabelle. Isabelle Evans."

Cameron silently sounded out the name. It suited her.

"And your name is …?" she prompted with a raised brow.

"I am the Right Honorable Mr. Cameron Bolton, second son of the Baron of Limpton. How would this lowly baron's son go about properly meeting such a lovely lady?"

Her lips curved up in pleasure. "I suppose you could have my … relations introduce us."

Cameron wondered why she had hesitated. "Who would that be?"

"The Earl and Countess of Saunton."

Cameron's stomach tightened, and he blinked slowly. *An earl?* How could he possibly aspire to such great heights? Not just any earl, but the much-lauded Earl of Saunton, who had expanded the wealth and power of his estates these past years. Certainly, they shared no acquaintances who could introduce him to the earl?

"That poses a problem. I suppose it would be unutterably gauche to simply walk up to your chaperone and present myself?"

Isabelle snorted charmingly in rejection. "In theory, you should be allowed to do so because this is a private ball, but in practice, it would be as poorly judged as Mr. Collins approaching Mr. Darcy at the Netherfield ball."

Cameron was elated to hear her reference to *Pride and Prejudice*. He knew it! Isabelle was a bibliophile like himself. His estimation and interest rose even further.

"I most assuredly would not want to offend your family. I have a friend who might know someone who could introduce us, but he has disappeared somewhere with a lady."

Isabelle's smooth forehead furrowed, her rosebud lips twisting in disquiet. "I hope the lady does not come to regret the choices she is making."

"I would never say anything against a fine woman of the *ton*—"

"No need. I have said it for you. I hope you are not here to try to lure me into a private tryst?" She quirked an eyebrow as she glanced at him playfully.

He laughed. The young lady was not only beautiful, but she was well read, with a wry sense of humor. Tonight's attendance had been a favor to his university friend, but Cameron was pleased he had agreed to accompany Ridley now that it had led him to Isabelle. They were two intelligent adults who simply needed to solve the obstacle standing in their way. It was high time he located his roguish friend and found a path to formally meet Isabelle Evans this very night. "Be assured I do not share my friend's tendencies. I recently sold my commission in the army after many years stationed in India, so there has been no opportunity for such pursuits, even if I was so inclined … which I am not, to be clear."

She quirked an eyebrow. "You were in the army overseas? You must be well-traveled. What brings you back to England?"

"I wish to settle down and open a bookshop."

Isabelle's head bobbed in reaction to this news. "Truly? That sounds wonderful!" She was genuinely intrigued, and so was he.

They talked for a bit, Cameron telling her a little of his career in the British Army. She told him of her parents residing in Saunton, and how her father was a tutor who hosted boys in their home to teach them classical subjects in preparation for Oxford. Her learning was evident, along with her appetite for books.

While they spoke, Cameron surveyed the ballroom, but Brendan Ridley was nowhere to be found. Feeling rather pressured, Cameron scrutinized faces for anyone he knew. Finally, he recognized an old acquaintance from their university set, one whose name he could recollect. "If you will excuse me, I see someone who might be able to introduce me to the countess."

Isabelle gave a barely perceptible nod, and Cameron once more skirted the perimeter of the overflowing ballroom.

Back at Cambridge, Hadley had run in the same circles as Brendan and Cameron. Too important to be welcomed by the middle-class students below them, and far too unimportant to be accepted by the sons of higher-ranking noblemen, the sons of barons had flocked together to form a club of sorts. Brendan Ridley was the only friend from that time whom Cameron had maintained a relationship with, but he boasted many baronial connections across the realm.

After several moments of discussion, Hadley revealed he had recently inherited the title, so he was now an actual baron and a member of the House of Lords. Relieved, Cameron waited for an opening and took the opportunity to swing the topic.

"Hadley, do you happen to be acquainted with the Earl of Saunton?"

"Of course. We serve in Lords together. An interesting fellow. A notorious rogue until he recently wed. Apparently, he has become quite the bore now, enamored with his wife and spending all his time with family."

Cameron's spirits lifted. "That is wonderful news. I am seeking an introduction to Lord Saunton and was hoping that you might do me the honor as I wish to meet a relation of his."

Hadley burst out laughing. "Dear chap, just last week, I voted against a bill that was quite dear to the earl. I am afraid he has not forgiven me yet, so if I were the one to present you, you would be most unwelcome in his domain. Nay, I will grant you a favor by *not* introducing you."

Cameron's spirits fell once more. He had never met a woman who captured his attention in the way that Miss Isabelle Evans had, but he was fast losing hope of finding a path to meeting her.

Where is blasted Ridley?

Cameron knew his friend's sister had married very well, but Cameron did not care much about the goings-on of the *beau monde,* so he had not paid much attention. Now he wished he could remember whom the young Miss Ridley had married. He had a hazy idea it was someone important. Someone who made Brendan Ridley well-connected since the esteemed wedding two years earlier. If he could just find his blasted friend, he was certain the man had the connections required to make an upstanding introduction that would allow Cameron to engage in a courtship. His own honor dictated that he must pursue the young lady in a proper manner, even if he briefly wished he could steal a page from Ridley's book and take what he wanted without thinking of the consequences—a kiss to taste the sweetness of Isabelle's rosebud lips.

* * *

ISABELLE WATCHED Cameron circulating the room, fascinated by the handsome young man who toiled to find someone to introduce them. She wanted him to succeed. In the many weeks since she had taken residence at Balfour Terrace, the earl's London home, her interest was finally engaged by someone. The homesickness that had plagued her had lifted, and she found herself enjoying the music and the twirl of dancers for the first time.

It was not only that he was handsome, which he was, but it was the conversation they had shared. He had demonstrated that he was a well-read young gentleman. Despite the breach of etiquette, he had displayed respect in their discussion before he excused himself to look for his friend who might assist them. Fortunately, the countess was in deep discussion and must have lost track of time, so she did not notice her charge's activities.

"I have traversed the room and can now confirm you are the most beautiful woman present tonight."

Isabelle felt her cheeks warm at his return.

"Did you find your friend?"

Cameron sighed deeply. "I am afraid he has vanished. I attempted to find another method to meet you, but I am afraid I failed. I wanted to return and talk to you before supper. And perhaps discover what social engagements you plan to attend, so I may have another opportunity to meet you."

"We are attending the Lawson musicale in a few days. Apparently, his daughters are quite talented, and he is holding another by popular request."

"I could be there. Lord Lawson was an army man once, although I do not know him personally. I may not be very important, but as a former officer, I daresay I could find one of his guests to invite me to the musicale."

"You are important to me ..." she said in a shy voice, unsure he could even hear her from where he stood in the shadows until she saw him smile from the corner of her eye, revealing a flash of white teeth in the dark.

Isabelle very much looked forward to meeting this young man. How wonderful to be courted by a gentleman who set her at her ease and shared common interests.

Cameron leaned against the column, out of sight, and continued their earlier conversation. She learned his father had passed away earlier that year, and subsequently, he had sold his commission in order to pursue his own dreams.

"Did you mean it—that you wish to own a bookshop?" Isabelle could not quell the excitement in her voice.

"I do. I discussed it with my brother, who is now the Baron of Limpton, and we agreed I may pursue a trade. His only request was that I do so far from his constituency, so I thought I might go south. I was surprised to find him so supportive, but he said the ways of the aristocracy were changing, and he did not mind if I went into a scandalous trade if I did so discreetly. It turns out my older brother is quite forward-thinking about the accumulation of income."

"I would dearly love to own a bookshop!"

"If I can find a way to court you ... perhaps you shall."

Isabelle could not deny the thrill that ran through her at his words. Earlier, she had wondered if this was an elaborate ploy to seduce her into an untoward tryst, but that concern had passed when she had watched him put so much effort into seeking an honorable means to approach her.

Damn these rules! Why did a simple introduction have to be so complicated?

CHAPTER 2

NOVEMBER 14, 1820

Isabelle sat, once again, in a spindly chair, scouring the guests within the crowded room, hoping to catch a glimpse of the tanned, blond man who made her giddy with anticipation. Had he managed to find entrance to this well-attended event? She had spent three days poring over her etiquette books for ideas on how they might resolve their problem, and she wanted to share the news of what she had found in case he had not yet found a solution.

Since they met, Isabelle had frequently wondered if her interlude with Cameron had been a dream or a figment of her imagination. It had been a moment of respite, interrupting the isolation she had felt since Lord Saunton had collected her from her papa's home in Somerset to bring her to London. Her new brother had instructed her to call him Richard, but she was having trouble thinking of her newfound relations as ... well ... family. To her, family meant Papa and cozy evenings reading or discussing their thoughts over dinner with his pupils, while Mama scolded them for inappropriate conversation.

Her new kin were friendly and did their best to welcome her, but their townhouse was so gigantic that Isabelle lost herself in endless corridors daily. Dinner was the time they came together, but the conversation in which they partook was unfamiliar to her small-town upbringing and felt like she was visiting a foreign land. From the fine clothing and fine dinners, to the lavish rooms and, most of all, the aloneness of being surrounded by strangers, Isabelle felt isolated in her new life and yearned for the cozy comforts of home.

Her friends and family were all so far away, and she had to pretend to be someone she was not—the distant cousin to an important earl—to protect her reputation and that of her parents. The role she played was simply that—a role. But Papa had insisted she take advantage of the benefits offered by her new brother, so she smiled and pretended she was at ease.

Until three nights earlier when Cameron Bolton had struck up a secret conversation with her at a ball, and she had made a friend. While they had talked, he made her relax and feel like her old self, and they found many common interests and ideas. The thought of seeing him tonight had made her shivery with nervous excitement. She had fussed over her appearance, wanting to look her best in anticipation of their next encounter.

Across the room, several men walked away from the laden refreshment table and, through the parting created, she saw Cameron watching her. Catching her eye, he gave a brief nod of greeting. She permitted a subtle smile in acknowledgment.

Turning to her brother, she placed her fingers on his arm to gain his attention. "Lord—Richard—I must visit the necessary. I shall return shortly."

"Would you like Sophia to accompany you?"

Isabelle shook her head. "Let her rest."

Lord Saunton smiled warmly, his brilliant green eyes reflecting the affection Isabelle was yet to grow accustomed to receiving from her sibling, before returning his attention to his wife, who was informing him what was in the program she held in her hand.

The countess was luminous with her rounded belly, and her

excitement over the evening's entertainment provided the perfect opportunity for Isabelle to speak with Cameron alone. Isabelle sprang to her feet and headed to the hall closest to the refreshment table.

* * *

CAMERON WATCHED Isabelle approach the hall to his right. She was breathtaking in her ivory dress trimmed with green ribbons that picked out the unusual color of her eyes. Silky locks framed her face, while the ivory gown offset her golden skin tone in a manner that made his mouth water at the prospect of tasting her smooth skin.

She made a point of not gazing in his direction as she entered the hall, but sensing her objective, he moved to lean against the archway. Swiveling his head as if to admire the room, he could see from the corner of his eye that she had flattened herself against the corridor wall—out of sight of the room but mere inches away from him.

"I have been thinking of you." Her satiny whisper sent a shiver of pleasure cascading down his spine to settle as a banked warmth in his loins.

"I have not stopped thinking of you for even a moment, Isabelle. You have haunted my dreams since we met." He heard a happy sigh emerging from the dimmed corridor. It was an agonizing delight to be so close yet so far. Slowly, he lowered his hand to rest against the wall and inched his fingers to the edge of the arch. If he could just touch her ...

With startled exhilaration, he felt her fingertips brush his.

"Did you find your friend? The one with the well-connected sister?"

Cameron drew a heavy sigh. "No, I suspect he is staying with a lady friend. I tried his home and his clubs, but he is nowhere to be found these past three days."

Silence ensued for several moments.

"I cannot stay long, but I wanted to inform you of a possible solution."

"Oh?" His response was inadequate to express his profound relief. Without Ridley, he had yet to think of anything.

"I have been researching the rules of introduction, and I confirmed a way to do it." She paused, evidently shy. "You may already be aware, but I had to verify that it held true in London, as it does in Saunton."

"What is it?"

"The final ball of the Season is on Saturday, a public assembly to benefit charity being held at Pearler House on St. James's Place. Do you know of it?"

"The Grand Mistletoe Assembly?"

"Yes, that is the one. Lord and Lady Saunton have informed me that we will be attending in order to make a sizable donation before we leave for the country on Sunday. I recalled that at a public assembly of this nature ..."

Cameron waited, but she did not elaborate. "What is it?"

"A gentleman could prevail on the Master of Ceremonies to make an introduction. If the Master believes them to share social parity, he may grant the request. You are the brother of a baron, and I am the"— she cleared her throat uncomfortably—"distant relation of an earl, so I believe an argument for parity could be made."

Cameron drew a sharp breath, exulted to finally be in possession of a plan, even if a ticket would cost an enormous price. "You are brilliant! That is how Catherine Morland and Henry Tilney met in *Northanger Abbey*! Why did I not think of that?"

"Shh ... someone will notice our conversation." He could hear the pleasure in her voice, despite the censure of her words. Gently, he squeezed her fingers to express his affinity.

"I will purchase a ticket and find you there, I swear it."

"I have thought of dancing with you ... I would very much like to do so."

Zooks, she was sweet. He thought of taking her in his arms, of one day pressing his lips to her soft pink mouth. Frustration at their restrictions coursed through his body like steam through one of those newfangled engines. "I can think of no greater pleasure." And it could not possibly happen a moment too soon.

"It …" She hesitated. "It will be our last opportunity to meet before I leave for the country the next morning."

"Rest assured, I will be there." He felt her gently squeeze his fingers in acknowledgment.

At that moment, Cameron noticed two giggling debutantes headed in their direction. With great reluctance, he released her hand. "Someone approaches. You must go, sweet Isabelle."

He knew the moment she left his side by the feeling of loss that assailed him as her gracious presence departed. He could only be thankful she had recalled the rules of public assembly, the answers to his prayers. With so much time spent away from England, the thought had not occurred to him. If everything went to plan, he would hold her in his arms while they danced the length of Pearler House's ball-room, and he would soak up every breathtaking moment of it to treasure before seeking permission to court her.

CHAPTER 3

The day of the ball, Isabelle found her excitement—and trepidation—mounting. Tonight, Cameron would be formally introduced, first to the countess and—heaven prevailing—then to her. Her insides were knotted in nervous anticipation as she ruthlessly sought a distraction from her thoughts.

Her nephew, Ethan, contemplated the chess set between them with his chubby little face screwed up in concentration while she waited in patient silence. The little chap loved to play, and daily, he would request a game from each family member in turn. Finally, he picked up the white queen and moved it into place.

"Checkmate!" His emerald eyes, a Balfour family trait, glowed in triumph.

Isabelle smiled. "Oh my, you have me cornered with nowhere to go."

His small chest swelled with pride as he beamed from ear to ear. "I finally beat you!"

"So you did. Well played, Master Balfour."

The little boy stood and gave an adorable bow. "Thank you, Miss Isabelle Evans. It was a pleasure to play with you." He whipped his head around to ensure no one could overhear him. "And thank you for showing me how to win," he whispered.

Isabelle stood to dip into a curtsy. "You are welcome. It was a pleasure, as always."

He beamed up at her before running off. Ethan well knew his governess would be seeking him after he had snuck off to find Isabelle.

Left to her own thoughts, she returned to her bedchamber. Walking over to the carved walnut closet, she opened the door to stare at the emerald ball gown hanging inside while her pulse beat out a nervous rhythm. Her imagination had been interrupting her several times a day with visions of courtship and a wedding ceremony, followed by establishing their bookshop together. She had even gone so far as to envision a healthy babe bouncing on her hip with Cameron's blond curls. If they had a child together, would he or she have her green eyes or his brown hue?

Tonight, I finally meet Cameron. He will take me in his arms, and we will dance a waltz together.

* * *

CAMERON KNEW it was unfashionable to arrive too early, but he had been waiting to meet Isabelle for an entire week. The green-eyed beauty who preoccupied his thoughts would arrive at the Grand Mistletoe Assembly at any time, and the sooner he was there, the sooner he could meet her.

Checking for the hundredth time that the ticket was still in his pocket, he pulled at the cuffs of his black evening tailcoat, fiddled with his pristine white cravat, and inspected his appearance in the mirror once more before donning his overcoat and beaver, pushing the hat to a jaunty angle before resolutely leaving his rooms.

Outside, the streetlamps cast a glow through the thick early evening fog cloaking the busy London streets. Noting the heavy traffic of horsemen and carriages clogging the roadway, Cameron decided to walk the few blocks to Pearler House rather than hire a hackney. His mind made up, he made his way over the cobblestones of St. James's Street.

Not long after, he reached St. James's Place to approach Pearler House, carefully avoiding the line of carriages delivering the early arrivals to the evening's event. He knew it was unlikely that the earl and his family would arrive early, but he wanted to seek out the Master of Ceremonies and introduce himself in good time to arrange his meeting with Lord and Lady Saunton as early as possible.

* * *

ISABELLE STOOD in front of the mirror. Fussing with her hair, she noted how her eyes shone. She was excited to wear a flattering gown and to attend a fashionable ball because Cameron would be there waiting for her.

He was wonderful. Charming, well-read, respectful, and ever so handsome, with his broad shoulders and bronzed skin. She had made a point of studying him as thoroughly as she dared under the circumstances of the night of their first meeting.

She had not expected to meet such an intriguing gentleman in London, but now that she had, he occupied her thoughts. The idea of the courtship they planned filled her stomach with the elated quiver of butterflies taking flight. She could not help but imagine that one day they might run his bookshop side by side and attend Sunday dinners at her parents' home. *Will he wish to live in Saunton?*

She recalled that he planned to open his shop somewhere in the south of England. Surely, she could persuade him to consider Saunton, a bustling town with a strong sense of community.

"You look ravishing, Isabelle. That color is very becoming on you."

She turned to smile at the counte—Sophia—*drat!* She needed to learn to call these fine new family members by their first names. "Thank you for your help selecting it, Lady—" Seeing the slight frown mar her chaperone's face, Isabelle corrected herself. "Thank you ... Sophia."

The countess smiled, her blue eyes sparkling despite the subdued lighting. "You seem more eager than usual."

Isabelle sought for an explanation. She was still getting to know this family she had only recently joined, and she was uncertain how receptive they would be to the fact that she had met a gentleman in an improper manner. "It is our final social event in London, and I have heard the Pearler House is very"—she grasped for a word before finishing weakly—"elegant."

"I am so glad to see you finally enter the spirit of things. I know this transition from tutor's daughter to an earl's ... relation ... must be difficult, but you will grow accustomed to it. And Richard is gratified to be hosting you, Isabelle. Family is very important to us, and after what the late earl did"—the countess shook her head—"well, Richard is just so grateful to have the opportunity to make it up to you."

Isabelle smiled at Sophia's hesitation. It would appear all of them had to adjust to the fact that she was the earl's secret sister, all the while introducing her as his distant relation to protect her reputation. She had to admit that her brother and his wife did not fit her concept of spoilt members of the peerage, and their consistent efforts to make her feel welcome could not be denied. As she contemplated the subject, an awful thought slipped into her head. *Will Cameron be repelled when he learns the truth of my relationship to Lord Saunton?*

The notion brought a sudden dip in her spirits before she scolded herself. He did not seem a capricious young man, and she could only take this courtship one step at a time. Formally, her parents were married, so she was not considered illegitimate despite her mother's abandonment by the nefarious, deceased earl. Besides, the next step was to actually meet before she could concern herself about the implications of her parentage.

"Shall we prepare to leave?"

The countess inclined her head. "After you."

* * *

Tugging at the fob tucked in his pocket, Cameron looked down to check the time. He had arrived at the assembly practically the moment the black front door of Pearler House had opened. He had been hovering under the gaslights for two hours but had yet to glimpse Isabelle or her family in the crowded room. Many notable families had arrived in fine silks and rich wool, but he had not heard Lord and Lady Saunton announced.

He loitered at the edge, watching the crush of guests mingle in the overcrowded ballroom and wishing he had managed to unearth Ridley. He had sought his roguish friend for days, but he was nowhere to be found. Cameron had planned to have his friend accompany him to the assembly to arrange the introductions, but to no avail. He would need to persuade the Master of Ceremonies of their social parity according to their new plan.

Standing too close to an archway, he was startled when a young lady approached the gentleman next to him, stretching on her toes to plant a kiss on the stranger's lips. Cameron stared at the couple for a moment, perplexed by their behavior, before looking up to find a festive sprig of mistletoe tied in ribbon, the white berries plump and shining in the gaslight. If Isabelle were here, he could have found an excuse to maneuver her into a playful kiss; a wishful thought if she did not arrive.

Stretching his neck to alleviate the tension in his shoulders, Cameron made to skirt the ballroom again in case he had missed her. His book-loving beauty had invaded his dreams, causing him to wake many times in sweat-soaked desire at the thought of tasting her lips. Minimally, he needed to hold her in his arms while they danced. His fingers itched with the need to touch her slender form and feel the sway of her curved body.

Blazes! What if she is not coming tonight?

* * *

ISABELLE TIED the tapes of her cape while the earl assisted Lady Saun —Sophia—with hers. The earl—her brother—*drat, Isabelle, you need to warm up to this new family of yours—*

From behind her, she heard the countess hiss in distress. Isabelle turned to find her sister-in-law clutching her rounded belly, pain contorting her usually composed face.

The earl dropped his beaver and gloves on the floor to stare at his wife, stark fear on his face. "What is it, Sophia?"

The countess failed to respond, whimpering in pain as she grabbed the banister.

"Radcliffe! Call for the doctor!" The earl shouted the demand to the stoic butler with ginger hair.

In a panic, Saunt—Richard—swept his wife into his arms and ran up the stairs two at a time.

Mouth agape, Isabelle nearly wept as her plans for the evening disappeared in the flurry of family crisis, before quietly berating herself for being selfish. The countess was several months along, and her health and the health of the earl's progeny took precedence over her own petty hopes and dreams.

She considered the time it would take for the doctor to come. And the ramifications if there were any issues with the countess. Her concern for the young woman who had hosted her warred with her desire to set off for the assembly to meet Cameron, but there was nothing to be done. Her last chance to meet him had just run up the staircase, and she wondered if she would ever see him again.

Would he be married when they finally met the following year? Another young woman taking her place to run their bookshop? Tears sprang into her eyes at the vision of her Cameron dancing with another young lady at the charity ball while Isabelle was constrained in her strange new home by expectations and duty.

She considered leaving on her own to find him, but she could not dishonor her parents. They had made so many sacrifices for her; she owed it to them to conduct herself with honor.

Drawing a deep breath, she blinked the tears away and followed the frantic couple upstairs to offer her assistance while they awaited the doctor.

* * *

CAMERON PACED the length of the ballroom yet again, watching the crowd intently while string music and chatter grated on his nerves. *Where is she?*

Impatience hummed through his veins as he sipped a glass of champagne. A young woman with brown hair entered the room. Straightening, he peered at her closely to see if his lovely Isabelle had finally arrived, but as she moved under a gas lamp, it became obvious her hair was lighter.

Thwarted, his eyes followed the young woman's path as she brushed past him in a graceful swirl of white skirts and purple lace. The lady seemed in a terrible hurry, tendrils of hair coming loose from the elegant pearl comb that held up her hazelnut curls as she swung her head back and forth to observe the room in a frantic sweep. He briefly wondered if she needed assistance, but she rushed away before he could form a thought to approach her. *Besides, you cannot approach any young woman without an introduction.*

The reminder salted the wound. He very much feared that Isabelle had been detained, and they would be forced apart until the following Season began in several months.

His chest tightened in dismay. It was time to walk through the rooms open for the assembly and look for her one more time.

* * *

ISABELLE SAT TENSELY in a plump armchair while she observed the portly doctor examine her sister-in-law. Contrary to fashion, the earl was in attendance, refusing to leave the countess's side although he had been forced to move a few feet back when the doctor had thrown a vicious glare at his intrusion after accidentally elbowing her brother in the ribs.

"My lady, it would appear you are simply suffering from an excess of gas."

The earl clutched his chest in relief. "Are you certain?"

The doctor ignored him to continue talking to the countess. "I would recommend you stay away from rich foods, and I will give you a tonic to assist with the bloating—"

"What of the babe?" The earl's frenzied and autocratic manner was visibly annoying the practitioner, who continued to ignore him.

"—I recommend you rest tonight, but I see no reason for concern. This is quite common for a woman in your condition."

"But—"

The countess's gentle tones cut the earl off. "Thank you, doctor. I do confess that a craving for cheese the past few days could be the cause of my ailment. I am not accustomed to the quantity I have recently consumed."

The doctor gave a nod of assent. "That would definitely cause it. Perhaps you could stick to broth for the next few days. Some dry toast and apples are quite beneficial for digestive complaints. Just ensure you eat sufficiently."

Both the countess and the doctor pointedly ignored the earl as he paced back and forth in agitation. "Thank you so much for coming so quickly, doctor. I hope we did not interrupt something important?" Sophia bobbed her head at his formal evening attire.

"I was headed to the charity ball at Pearler House when your footman found me." He pulled out a gold pocket watch to peer at the time. "There is still time to attend, I suppose."

"Oh, I do hope so. It is such a worthy cause."

Isabelle listened with pangs of regret causing an ache in her belly. She should be at the ball in Cameron's arms by now. The desire to leap from her chair and insist the doctor accompany her to the ball was overpowering, and she had to grip the edge of her seat tightly to prevent herself from making an embarrassing outburst.

Her brother looked like death itself. She knew he was besotted with his wife, and it was obvious he was still recovering from the shock because he had slumped into a chair to stare at the ceiling, pale-faced, while the conversation went on without him.

While the doctor was taking his leave, and the earl and his countess had conducted a hushed discussion with the lady reassuring her husband of her good health, Isabelle realized she was an interloper. Standing, she made to leave the room.

"Isabelle, I am so sorry I ruined your evening," the countess called from behind her.

Tears were welling in her eyes, but Isabelle blinked them back while keeping her head averted to the door. She could not reveal her scandalous interactions with Cameron Bolton by displaying untoward grief. There was no telling how the earl would react to the news of her inappropriate behavior, so she swallowed hard and steadied her voice. "I quite understand. Please rest and take care of yourself. There is nothing to be done about the ball, so do not concern yourself with it." Isabelle was proud of how cheery her tone sounded while she headed out the door.

Cameron would be at the ball, thinking she had not bothered to attend. He must be angry by now. Soon he would forget the troublesome wench who had disappointed him, and she would not blame him for giving up on her. Inside her chest, disappointment caused Isabelle's heart to weigh as heavy as a stone.

* * *

CAMERON LEANED AGAINST A COLUMN, a gaslight flickering above his head as he tapped his foot. Not in time to the music, but rather in time with his pulsing frustration to be thwarted so in his plans. He had spent a small fortune on a ticket to a ball, so he might stand about like a fool, pining after a woman he had never even properly met. And he still waited. He would wait right until supper because he still held out hope.

Isabelle was special. He might never meet such a woman again. She was beauty and grace and intelligence all wrapped up in a stunning green-eyed package, and he could not give up on her. On them.

He knew she was leaving for the country in the morning. Like an imbecile, he had not questioned her regarding where she would be staying during the holiday season nor the successive months. The only thing he knew for certain is that he could find her after Easter when the new Season began. *But by then she might be married to some wonderful young man she met during the holidays.*

Cameron clenched his jaw.

If only Brendan Ridley had shown up. He was sure his friend could have assisted him, but the reprobate was likely in the arms of a wicked widow these past days. If he could find the rogue, perhaps Ridley could offer a suggestion but, for all Cameron knew, he could be leaving Town for the country, too.

His pulse pounded in his ears, his turmoil having magnified over the past hours.

As if to mock him, he saw a server balancing a heavy platter, indicating it was nearly time for supper. Checking his pocket watch yet again, he confirmed that indeed, that time was quickly approaching.

A loud clatter jolted his attention back to the server. The silver platter was on the floor while the contents drenched the once deep orange skirts of a young woman standing with Corinthian John, the former prizefighting champion. Cameron gaped, momentarily forgetting his own problems to commiserate with the woman and the agonized footman as the crowd turned to stare.

His first impulse was to rush over to her and offer his help, but he observed how Corinthian John took charge and squashed the impulse to insert himself.

And that is my cue to leave.

There was nothing left for him to do. The woman he desired had not arrived, and the evening, at least for him, was over.

Cameron battled to draw breath into his constricted lungs to relieve the weight that had settled upon him. Fresh air and a walk would clear his thoughts. He might not know how to find Isabelle's family now that they were departing for the country, but the evening was just beginning for the gentlemen attending clubs. He would search for Ridley in every corner and crevice of London, pester the man's family butler again, or find someone else who could tell him where the earl's household would be headed when morning came.

Or where they are now.

Weaving his way through the crowd of elegant peers, Cameron headed for the hall that would lead him out of the stately home, scanning faces for anyone he might recognize. Blast, he had been gone from England for too long. Home no longer felt familiar.

Isabelle could rectify that, if I ever find her again.

He eventually emerged from the front door of Pearler House, brushing past a portly man on his way in. Once outside, he briskly walked along the quiet roadway of St. James's Place, heading in the direction of his rooms, all the while regretting the formal buckled shoes that pinched his feet in their tight embrace.

Turning onto St. James's Street, he stopped to observe the congested evening traffic of horsemen and carriages still clogging the busy street. Cameron stood under a street lamp, a well of defeat rising from his gut. He had been absent so long from the realm that he felt he barely knew anyone anymore. His absence from home had suited him at the time, but now he was discovering the consequences of being away for such a prolonged period. He had no inkling how to obtain information about the earl's household, or even where in the country he might head in the hopes of encountering Isabelle at a mutually attended event.

It might very well be next year's Season, which was months away, before they had another opportunity to be introduced. So much could happen between now and then, but this connection was so unique. For the first time, he was drawn to another person, and he could not shake the need to explore where it might lead.

If I do not find her soon, she might be married the next time I see her.

His shoulders slumped, Cameron finally admitted the truth of it to himself under the street lighting.

It will take a miracle to find Isabelle before the holidays.

CHAPTER 4

*S*till in the same spot several moments later, while he gathered his wits and attempted to plan his next steps, Cameron was startled to hear his name.

"Bolton!"

He raised his head to look back at the voice calling him. An elegant but aging carriage had come to a stop nearby, and a familiar face peered at him through the open door.

"Ridley?"

Brendan Ridley was a handsome young man with chestnut hair and brandy eyes, who never suffered a lack of female companionship. A chiseled jaw and athletic frame, he topped Cameron by a couple of inches. Although he could be immature, he had always been a good friend, so Cameron tolerated the man's excesses.

"I've been looking for you everywhere, Bolton! You're a hard man to find."

Cameron grimaced at the irony of the statement.

I am difficult to find?

He gritted his teeth. It would not do to display his impatience. Ridley had a younger sister who had married a powerful peer. A peer he might meet, and who, in turn, might know the Earl of Saunton. Ridley might have appeared too late, but he might open another opportunity, so forbearance was crucial.

Ridley pushed the steps down and clambered from the carriage to stride over.

"Why were you looking for me?"

"What are your plans for the holidays, Bolton?"

Cameron squinted in surprise at the abrupt switch of thoughts. "I don't know. It is my first time back in England in some years. Perhaps I will go home to visit my brother and his family, although that does not sound very appealing. He is quite a bit older than me, and we do not share many interests."

"I am thrilled to hear that. I have this holiday house party to attend at my sister's home, and I need a suitable companion lest I go mad. It is all families and couples and whatnot. My sister will pester me about my marital prospects, and I will need a respite. For obvious reasons, I cannot take a woman with me, so I thought of you, my good chum. Please say you will accompany me?"

It did not sound very appealing, but there was a possibility such an event could eventually lead him a step closer to Isabelle. "Remind me who your sister is?"

Ridley laughed. "Can you believe it? She married a duke? Annabel is a duchess. Of Halmesbury. Very influential family, what?"

Cameron's spirits rose. A duke? There were few earls and even fewer dukes. Surely a duke could introduce him to the Earl of Saunton? He would not usually be interested in such an introduction, but this situation with Isabelle made meeting such a high-ranking peer imperative.

"When do we leave?"

Ridley patted the pockets of his overcoat and withdrew a card. "Meet me at this address at first light. The family plans to leave *en masse* in the morning, so you must join us for breakfast before we embark for Avonmead." Observing his confusion, Ridley elaborated.

"Wiltshire, dear chap. We leave for Wiltshire directly after breakfast. You will be on time?"

Cameron nodded, pocketing the card. "It is a little early on for a holiday house party?"

Ridley grinned. "My sister is adamant we all head to Avonmead forthwith to prepare the plum pudding. And she wants us to assist her with a special event for the children of their estate. Something about Saint Nicholas Day. Her holiday arrangements will continue for weeks, so plan on being out of Town longer than the usual two weeks."

With another nod, Cameron assented. Whatever it took to please the duchess so he might prevail on the Duke of Halmesbury for an introduction to the earl next year. He would learn how to embroider holiday seat cushions like a debutante if the duchess willed it, just so long as it would somehow bring him closer to Isabelle.

"Can I drive you somewhere, Bolton?"

"No need, Ridley. My rooms are close by."

Ridley gave a wide smile and tipped his beaver in salute. "Until morning, then. I will leave you to pack." His friend walked back to the awaiting carriage until Cameron called out, remembering just in time why he had been looking for Ridley in the first place.

"Ridley, do you happen to know the Earl of Saunton?"

His friend turned back with a bemused expression. "Why?"

"I have been trying to meet him. Quite desperately, in fact. He has a relation … a young woman I am eager to meet."

A strange look flickered over his friend's face. Cameron had the impression Ridley was concealing a smile. "We shall ask the duke in the morning, shall we?"

Cameron suppressed his irritation. There was nothing for it but to wait until morning. Checking his pocket watch, he realized it was just gone midnight. It was a good thing he needed to pack because his misery at the way the evening had turned out would prevent him from sleeping a wink.

Hopefully, his introduction to the Duke of Halmesbury would ultimately straighten out this muddle with Isabelle, so he could learn more about her and her family in order that he might one day meet her.

* * *

CAMERON'S DILAPIDATED HIRED hackney stopped in front of the Mayfair mansion with a jolt just as the first ray of sunshine broke over the chilly autumn sky. As he descended to the roadway, the front door opened and two footmen rushed forward to assist him with his two trunks and valise.

After Ridley had warned him that the house party would be lengthy, he had given up his rooms for the duration and brought his meager possessions with him, including a heavy trunk of his favorite books that had accompanied him on his long journeys since leaving Cambridge.

Packing his things had reminded him of his hopes to settle down and put down roots now that he was his own man without a father to please. The notion had been so appealing, especially after encountering Isabelle a week earlier. But he could no longer summon the same optimism he had experienced after he had envisioned her presence at his side, assisting him to establish the new business venture.

Nevertheless, he had decided he would set off to explore Wiltshire, then head farther south to hunt for a suitable location to house his new bookshop, rather than mope around Town for the next few months awaiting Isabelle's return to London. He would travel back after Easter, when the new Season commenced, to find her.

God, what a depressing thought. How did I let her slip through my fingers?

Cameron consoled himself with his imminent introduction to the duke. Surely it would assist him when the next opportunity arose to meet Isabelle. Sighing deeply, Cameron followed the servants through the doorway into the duke's home with a decided lack of vigor in his step.

When he reached the entrance hall, he found Ridley engaged in conversation with two tall gentlemen. Noticing Cameron's arrival, Ridley's face split into a grin. "Bolton! You made it!"

Cameron nodded in greeting as his friend turned to one of the men. Blond, several inches past six feet with the broad, handsome features of a Viking god, the imposing gentleman turned toward Cameron.

"Your Grace, may I introduce the Honorable Cameron Bolton from Limpton, late of His Majesty's army and my closest cohort from my Cambridge days?"

As Cameron gave a bow, the duke stepped forward to shake his hand. "Ridley tells me you have returned from your adventures in India. Welcome back to England, Bolton. We are well pleased you will keep my reprobate brother-in-law in line during our holiday festivities." Despite his intimidating stature, His Grace had an amiable manner that immediately put Cameron at ease.

The second gentleman, a sable-haired man of about six feet with wide shoulders and a lean, muscular build, snorted as he glanced at Ridley and then turned to Cameron. "I never understood why your father insisted you attend Cambridge, Ridley. But then he never did like you very much."

Ridley laughed in a good-natured way at the jape. "Your Oxford snobbery is showing"—Ridley turned to Cameron to give him a mischievous wink—"Saunton."

Cameron came face-to-face with the dark-haired gentleman and looked straight into his emerald green eyes, skipping a beat in his chest. His mouth agape, he shot Ridley a questioning look.

"Saunton is the duke's cousin, Bolton. His family will be accompanying us to Wiltshire this morning."

Cameron snapped his jaw shut lest he appear to be a dullard, while a shot of joy ran straight through him. Shaking hands enthusiastically with the man he had sought to meet this past week, he thought about how he had wished for a miracle, and Ridley had delivered it. Did this mean Isabelle was close by?

* * *

ISABELLE WAS SIPPING tea and staring despondently at the garden through the window of the brightly lit breakfast room while her sister-in-law chattered with the duchess.

She had yet to sleep a wink after her disappointing evening, her mind chewing over the problem of how to get word to Cameron about … well … to get any word to him at all.

She could hardly ask one of the servants to deliver a message to an unknown man without causing a scandal. And what would it matter if she could devise a plan? They had already left Balfour Terrace for Markham House, and directly after breakfast, several carriages would draw to the front of the townhouse so that the Balfours, the Markhams, and numerous servants, including Ethan's governess and nursemaid, could embark to Wiltshire.

Leaving Cameron far behind without even a word of explanation.

She rubbed her neck to ease the tension building in her shoulders. Isabelle could not afford to display her sense of loss in front of all these strangers. They would require an explanation for her melancholy, which meant she needed to suppress her grief over what might have been if only she could have spent a little time with Cameron. To share a dance and clasp hands in a waltz, to feel the warmth of his breath on her cheek and the brush of his fingers against her ribs, or even to just engage in proper conversation without hiding in the shadows.

Instead, she had to repress the urge to shed tears over a relationship that had never truly begun and wonder if the gentleman was as regretful as she or if he had found another young lady to occupy his attentions when she had not arrived as promised.

Isabelle was distracted from her maudlin thoughts a moment later when the men reappeared, entering the room while the duke's cavalier younger brother-in-law stood in the doorway and spoke in a loud voice.

"Everyone, if I may have your attention, I would like to introduce my dear friend to you, who will be joining us in Wiltshire for the holidays."

The duchess sprang to her feet to join her brother as a familiar blond figure appeared in the doorway behind Mr. Ridley. Isabelle froze before choking back tears of happiness, discreetly running a hand over her face before patting her hair and smoothing her dress.

It was unbelievable. Was the friend Cameron had sought these past days the brother to the duchess?

After a few moments, the duchess brought the new arrival over, while Isabelle rose to her feet.

"Isabelle, may I present the Honorable Mr. Cameron Bolton? Miss Evans, Bolton and my brother are the only single guests of our house party, so I do hope you might find some time to spend together to keep each other entertained."

The young duchess gave a broad smile as she directed the final remark to the gentleman, a mischievous twinkle in her brandy eyes, and Isabelle got the sense that Her Grace was playing matchmaker. The duchess turned to give a knowing wink to her brother, confirming Isabelle's suspicions that Mr. Ridley had confided something about the situation. She would be mortified if she had not been overtaken with a rushing giddiness that made her feel unsteady on her feet.

Careful to hide her great happiness, Isabelle held out her hand which Cameron gathered up in his larger, gloved one to place a fleeting kiss on her knuckles as he bowed, sending a rush of warmth up her arm to settle in the region of her overflowing heart.

Straightening, Cameron's warm brown eyes found hers to stare into the very depths of her soul before he spoke in a deliberate and sincere tone. "It is my great pleasure to meet you, Miss Evans."

Isabelle smiled in delighted response.

And mine, Mr. Bolton. And mine.

CHAPTER 5

*C*ameron tugged at his burgundy wool cuffs and anxiously combed his hair with unsteady fingers while pacing in his black Hessians.

The duke's country seat was a grand honey-colored manor surrounded by ample parks, including the shimmer of a lake peeking through the trees on the horizon. The square-paned windows and arches of the Avonmead library formed a tapestry displaying the last rays of sunlight in washes of red, purples, and various strains of oranges reminiscent of steeped tea, but Cameron was too bemused to appreciate this view of the heavens.

Over the past two weeks while staying in the elegant home, Cameron and Isabelle had participated in activities together for most of the days and evenings, spending as much time together as they could manage.

Several times, Ridley had complained that bringing a friend along to keep him entertained had been a pointless endeavor because Cameron was perpetually taking part in family entertainments.

But Cameron did not care. He was going to steal every moment he could with the lovely young woman whom he adored.

The two had taken to secretly meeting before dinner each day in an alcove behind the spiral staircase in the library, where he now awaited her arrival. Their time together had been wondrous. They shared their thoughts, their favorite books, and their concerns. He knew she was the woman who would own his heart for the rest of his days because he felt truly happy in her presence.

However, in a few days, the Balfours would depart from the duke's house party and head to the earl's country seat in Saunton, while Cameron would be left behind unless ... unless their relationship progressed. He needed to secure Isabelle as his own before he found himself separated from her yet again.

The earl appeared to be amenable to their burgeoning relationship, and Cameron was confident he would be received favorably by the lord when it came time to request a private meeting.

At these runaway thoughts, he raked his fingers through his hair again while he pondered his impending proposal and awaited her delightful arrival. The conversation he planned this evening was more daunting than the eve before a campaign.

Cameron spun around when he heard light footsteps approaching. Receding into the alcove lest someone walk by, he watched appreciatively while Isabelle traversed the expansive library, weaving around the eclectic mix of furniture. She was utterly charming, her hair framing her face while her eyes reflected the last light of sunset. His eyes fell to the pink bow lips that were the subject of his frustrating nightly dreams, a wave of hot desire distracting him from his anxious anticipation.

Isabelle entered the alcove, a pretty blush washing her cheeks when she shyly rushed against him in an embrace of velvet and lace. Cameron traced the back of his fingers down the curve of her cheek, savoring her sweet fragrance of apple blossoms before wrapping his arms around her to lean down and claim her mouth with his own.

Her lips were warm and soft, molding to his until they were one. Two bodies, two souls, two hearts beating in perfect unison. She sighed gently, allowing him to sweep his tongue between her parted lips to caress her own in hungry ardor. His hand rested on her waist before creeping up from her waist as close as he dared to brush against the underside of her full breast.

Regretfully, he eased back, moving his hand up to cup and lift her chin so he might peer down into the fascinating green depths of her eyes.

"I missed you," he whispered.

"We were together not an hour ago assisting the duchess with an inspection of her plum puddings!" Isabelle protested.

"An hour too long," he growled.

Isabelle stared up at him in silence before responding with a fleeting smile. "I must admit, I could not stop thinking of this moment when I would join you in the library." Her face grew contemplative, and he knew she was thinking about her pending departure from Avonmead.

This was it. This was the moment when he must ask the question that had been on his lips for days and trust she was ready to hear it, or they would be parted yet again.

Drawing a deep breath, he shored up his courage—*Blast, why is this so intimidating?*—and slowly lowered himself onto one knee. She looked down at him in surprise as he claimed her hand and gazed up into her eyes.

"Miss Isabelle Evans, I admire you greatly. I wish to spend my life with you, to open my bookshop with you at my side, and to start a new family together. I humbly request your permission to speak with the earl to seek permission to request your hand in marriage?"

Isabelle looked nonplussed and then giggled. "Did you just ask my permission to seek the earl's permission to ask me to marry you?"

Cameron grinned. "I did."

A smile spread over her face, then suddenly, panic took its place, squeezing his chest. He had been too forward! She was not ready!

Oh my God, what have I done?

Isabelle carefully drew her hand away before stepping back, while Cameron found it difficult to draw breath.

She is rejecting me? Did I misread the situation?

Eyes downcast, Isabelle spoke in a tremulous tone that froze the blood in his veins. "Before I answer, I have something to tell you ..."

He scarcely dared to breathe as he waited for her next words.

"... I ... I am not the earl's distant cousin," she blurted out.

Cameron frowned, trying to make sense of the fresh path the conversation had taken. He slowly stood, but he could not see Isabelle's face. "I do not understand."

She turned to stare at the bookshelves, throwing a nervous glance his way before focusing on a shelf of leather-bound books while her fingers picked nervously at her skirts. "I ... Can you keep a secret? Even if it changes your mind and you decide to withdraw your request?"

Nothing she could tell him would change his mind. He loved this woman, and he could not walk away from a life with her even if she revealed she had a tail. Or six toes.

"On my honor, I will never speak to anyone about the words that have passed or will pass between us."

Isabelle raised a hand to trace a slender finger down the spine of a heavy tome, revealing her agitation which mirrored his own growing horror that she might turn him away.

"The earl ... he is not a distant relation ... he is my half-brother. The late earl is my true father ... or my sire ..." Isabelle lapsed into stricken silence, clearly attempting to gather her thoughts. "He abandoned my mother while she was with child. My father ... I mean, Horatio Evans, is a childhood friend who married her to protect her reputation. So ... you see ... I am ... illegitimate ... I suppose."

Cameron struggled to comprehend the mumbled explanation. He gathered his thoughts together to pose his response. "Your parents married before you were born?"

Isabelle blushed a fierce red, her ears a deep rouge as she continued to look away from him. "Yes."

"Well, then, you are not illegitimate. Mr. Evans is your lawful father."

"Um ... yes. He is my true father. He has always been a very considerate parent." She sounded defensive, not quite gathering Cameron's point in her embarrassment.

Cameron ached for his beloved and the shame she felt. "And the earl—the current one—he has ... claimed you as his sister?"

Isabelle slowly nodded. "Privately, yes. He wishes to make it right ... but he also wants to protect me and my parents from scandal. He sought us out a couple of months back, and Papa said it was a wonderful opportunity to secure my future. The earl is ... very kind. We agreed to present me as a distant relation."

"Excellent. Do I have your permission to approach the earl regarding you?"

Isabelle's head spun back in surprise, jaw agape as she stared at Cameron. "You do not care about this matter?"

"I do not. Even if your parents were not wed, I would still desire this match. If you are amenable, I will approach your brother and then follow you to Saunton to speak to your parents."

"But ... but ... someone may find out about me. Your reputation might be ruined!"

Cameron rubbed his neck to ease his discomfort. Swiping a hand over his face, he sighed deeply. "I have never shared this with anyone."

Isabelle gazed at him quizzically. Proposing was daunting enough. Now he was forced to share the darkest secret in his soul, which he was ill-prepared to do. How did one speak of a matter after so many years of pretending the situation did not exist?

Isabelle just bared her darkest secret to you. It is your turn to demonstrate your respect for the young lady and humble yourself in the same manner.

"I do not resemble anyone in the Bolton family, although no one ever spoke of it." Cameron halted, seeking the words to explain the situation that had never been discussed. When he had his own family, he would make certain that communication was a fundamental component of their relationships because he would never wish to have a wife or children experience the isolation that had accompanied him his entire life because of the subjects that were strictly forbidden.

Isabelle's parents had clearly discussed the matter of her parentage with her in a loving manner, as evidenced by their current conversation. He wished his own parents had aired the topic with him, instead of the repressed silence that had haunted their home.

"My mother had an affair. The whole family pretended I was my father's son, but it was patently obvious that I did not ... match. In fact, I look eerily similar to the family butler, who now serves my mother in her dowager household. For years, I felt like an outsider—I did anything I could to appease the baron, who never complained. Nor was he cruel, but his disappointment was ever palpable. I have never truly felt that I belonged anywhere. Cambridge was something of an escape, but even there I felt like an impostor—the baron's apparent son, who was far more likely the son of a servant. But as we have never spoken of it ... hell ... it could be all in my imagination. So, you see, I do understand your position."

Isabelle stared at him before rushing into his arms to embrace him tightly against her, arms wrapping around his neck. "Oh, Cameron, I am so sorry. You—you will always belong with me!"

Cameron tucked his head over hers to breathe in the floral apple fragrance of her silky hair. "I know. For the first time in my life, I feel truly engaged with another person. I ... I love you, Isabelle."

A small sob escaped the lips pressed into the crook of his neck, and he felt her smile as he banded his arms around her to pull her even closer.

"And I love you, Cameron."

Her words melted him to the core. It was the first time in his entire life that anyone had voiced the sentiment to him, and he found himself blinking back inexplicable moisture in his eyes. He had finally found his home, here in Isabelle's arms, and he looked forward to building a bright future with her.

Isabelle mumbled into his collar.

"What is that?"

She pulled back slightly to repeat her statement. "I would very much like to provide my permission to seek out the earl and ask his permission to speak with me about marriage."

Cameron chuckled. "We have conducted a rather complicated courtship, have we not?"

"I would not have it any other way."

She reached up on tiptoes to press her soft lips to his. Passion ignited across his body as he pulled her back in his arms to ardently kiss her sweet mouth, a vision of their forthcoming wedding night in his mind as he pressed her womanly shape against his hardening body.

With Isabelle at his side, he would have everything he had ever dreamed of since he was a small lad and had realized something was not right in his household.

But that was the dismal past, while the future now beckoned with open arms. He was so utterly grateful that Ridley had found him that night on St. James's Street. Being reunited with Isabelle was his very own Christmas miracle.

* * *

Uncover more family secrets in the Inconvenient Brides series, which begins with The Duke Wins a Bride.

AFTERWORD

I hope you enjoyed my tale of Regency etiquette, expectations, and enduring passion.

You can uncover more of the Balfours' scandalous family secrets in Inconvenient Brides, a steamy Regency romance series.

Brendan Ridley will return in Long Live the Baron, when he stands accused of murder and a young maiden of the *ton* comes to his rescue.

Subscribe to my email newsletter for two free novellas at nina-jarrett.com/free

* * *

INCONVENIENT BRIDES

- Book 0: Friends of the Duke
- Book 1: The Duke Wins a Bride
- Book 2: To Redeem an Earl
- Book 3: My Fair Bluestocking
- Book 4: Sleepless in Saunton

- Book 4.5: Miracle on St. James's Street
- Book 5: Caroline Saves the Blacksmith

INCONVENIENT SCANDALS

Brendan Ridley will return, along with the Balfour family, in a new romantic suspense series.

- Book 1: Long Live the Baron
- Book 2: Moonlight Encounter
- Book 3: Lord Trafford's Folly
- Book 4: Confessions of an Arrogant Lord
- Book 5: The Replacement Heir

ABOUT THE AUTHOR

Nina started writing her own stories in elementary school but got distracted when she finished school and moved on to non-profit work with recovering drug addicts. There she worked with people from every walk of life, from privileged neighborhoods to the shanty towns of urban and rural South Africa.

One day she met a real-life romantic hero. She instantly married her fellow bibliophile and moved to the USA where she enjoyed a career as a sales coaching executive at an Inc. 500 company. She lives with her husband on the Florida Gulf Coast.

Nina believes in kindness and the indomitable power of the human spirit. She is fascinated by the amazing, funny people she has met across the world who dared to change their lives. She likes to tell mischievous tales of life-changing decisions and character transformations while drinking excellent coffee and avoiding cookies.

Subscribe to her email newsletter for two free novellas at nina-jarrett.com/free

A DARING MISTLETOE KISS BY TANYA WILDE

Spice Level 🤍🤍🤍

CHAPTER 1

Dare.

—From the Diary of Lillian Wright

"*I*'ve decided to steal a kiss."

"What? Where? With whom?"

"At the Pearler charity ball next week."

Nancy choked on a sip of tea. "What?"

Pippa grinned at her best friend. "Who knew the gentlemen of the *ton* are so polite? Since they dare not venture into the wild state of their nature, I'm left with no choice but to take matters into my own hands."

Which was why, the moment Pippa had heard Lord Dare, a handsome rake, was attending the event, she knew the ball was the perfect place to seize the moment—and her first kiss.

Nancy's eyes widened. "You have someone in mind?"

"I do."

"I'm afraid to ask."

Pippa's smile rose a notch. "Lord Dare."

"As in the most shockingly infamous libertine in all of England. That Lord Dare?"

Pippa nodded. "Well, I can't kiss just any man. He needs to be daring. Who better than the man who carries the very word in his name?"

Nancy's eyes lit with a sparkle of mischief. "Sound reasoning."

"Besides," Pippa went on, "I'm already nineteen this year and nary a kiss in sight. This won't do. I refuse to enter the age of twenty without my first kiss."

Nancy placed her tea on the table. "Name aside, are you sure he is the best candidate? He's awfully scandalous. While I am not against you taking matters into your own hands, I don't wish for you to be ruined because of it."

"Lord Dare isn't *that* bad."

"It's rumored that he can rob you of your chastity with just one look."

Pippa laughed. "Nonsense. A man must do more than that to steal a woman's chastity."

"There is the innocence of the body and there is the innocence of the soul," Nancy pointed out. "You do not wish to lose your soul to a man like Dare, do you?"

"So, my soul's chastity is at stake, then?" Pippa pursed her lips thoughtfully. "I believe I shall take that chance."

A loud sigh interrupted their conversation, followed by the rustle of paper. Jeremy Locke, the third person who made up their friendship triangle, shot them a pained look. "You do realize I'm still present."

"And?" Nancy returned his look. "It's not the first time you've been present for one of our juicier conversations."

"Be that as it may, what man wants to listen to women talk about rumors and rakes? Or the wild natures of men, stealing kisses and innocence of the body." He shifted in his seat and muttered, "Sometimes I suspect you forget I'm a man. I've never been so uncomfortable in my life."

Nancy snorted.

Pippa ignored him. "I won't be caught. Besides, with the two of you at my side, what could go wrong?" They'd been friends for eons.

Jeremy arched his brow. "What if you do get caught? A man like Dare is not to be trifled with, much less taken advantage of. It is my duty, as a friend, to caution you against such things."

"Your only duty is to help me succeed in my dreams," Pippa countered.

"Your dream is to be kissed by Dare?" Jeremy asked.

"My dream is to be kissed. Given his reputation, Lord Dare is likely to be the most discreet. Plus, he is handsome."

Jeremy snorted. "The man's entire reputation is based on indiscretion."

"His known indiscretions. How many women do you believe he has kissed who never reached the gossip columns? A kiss is nothing to him," Pippa said.

"I thought you women placed sentimental value on your first kiss."

"On the kiss, yes," Nancy chimed in. "Not the man."

"Nevertheless, one kiss is oftentimes all it takes for a woman to get ideas."

Nancy shot him a curious look. "What ideas?"

"Marriage. Reform. True love."

Pippa laughed. "Well, since I'm the one stealing the kiss, I suppose I'll have to guard against Dare developing such flighty notions."

Nancy grinned.

"I can't believe we are even having this discussion," Jeremy groused.

"It's not a discussion. It's a plan in the making," Pippa said.

"A terrible plan." Jeremy let out a long-suffering sigh. "How can I be of service?"

Pippa chuckled.

Nancy, however, did not. "As long as you don't enliven the punch again this year. Last year, three drunken brawls broke out because of that, and Pippa fell into a bush filled with thorns. My brother scolded us for ages."

"Will he be attending this year?" Pippa's most treasured pastime was making sport of Nicholas Byrne, the Earl of Chatteris. The stuffiest noble in England.

"Of course," Nancy said with a note of frustration. "Haven't you noticed, ever since last year's antics, he's accompanied us to all of our events?"

True.

Not that Pippa minded.

"I won't enliven the punch," Jeremy promised.

"Just my glass," Nancy said with a smirk.

Pippa nodded. "And mine."

"As you wish." Jeremy directed his attention back to his paper. "Just don't send Chatteris to me when he discovers your shenanigans."

Pippa thought of the waistcoat she'd embroidered for the earl and smiled. She was anticipating his attendance just as she was looking forward to her first kiss. In fact, she had been dreaming of her first kiss since her sixteenth birthday. Quite literally, in fact. Although, in her dreams, she could never make out the face of the boy who had stolen the kiss. Be that as it may, she'd thought her first kiss would be captured by a gentleman in her first Season. She had thought wrong.

Her mother's diaries suddenly came to mind.

They were her most treasured possessions, filled with the audacious escapades and inner musings of her mother.

Pippa did not want to have any regrets in her life. And it just so happened that the Pearler ball announced the end of the Season. Last year, her first-ever attendance, she had marked it with her first taste of brandy punch.

This year, she would mark it with a kiss.

CHAPTER 2

Your first kiss should be sweet. It should be wild. It should be heaven.
—From the Diary of Lillian Wright

PEARLER CHARITY BALL

*P*ippa saw him the moment she stepped into the moonlit garden. Tall. Handsome. Puddings embroidered across his chest. Incredibly out of place.

The Earl of Chatteris.

A vivid picture worthy of a treasure chest filled with gold.

His was the type of chiseled features that were only depicted in those Roman picture books. A face that could snare a woman's attention and hold it. Yet an air of winter clung to his demeanor, keeping all the ladies at a fair distance.

Tonight, however, his cold aura was decked in a glorious waistcoat embroidered with one hundred tiny colorful puddings. A masterpiece that had taken her all year to fashion. All in all, a delightfully merry package. All positioned beneath an archway of vined greenery with patches of mistletoe entwined overhead.

Before she could slip away unnoticed, the earl's gaze locked onto her.

So frosty.

"Pippa?" A momentary flash of surprise sounded before he cleared his throat. "What are you doing out here alone? Where is Nancy?"

The familiar suspicion in his voice made her smile.

"Nicholas," Pippa greeted, purposefully ignoring the rest.

He stiffened at the use of his name. Like always. While he attempted to keep a distance with polite courtesy, Pippa thrived to shatter it with blatant impertinence. She smiled at the assortment of puddings. Of the waistcoat, he said nothing, as if he did not stand out like a Christmas treat.

"You did not answer my question."

"I must not have heard one," she said, the impulse to tease bubbling forth.

She could not help herself. Ever since she met Nancy in her childhood, she had spent the holidays with the Byrne family. In fact, she considered it her second home. Her father rarely came to London, and after he remarried five years ago, his main concern had become his new wife. That meant the time she spent at the Byrne house had become more permanent in nature. All her belongings had gradually made their way over to her chamber in the Byrne residence.

That, however, did not mean she had free rein. It only meant that the man before her considered her his ward. While that had never bothered Pippa, her relationship with Chatteris could be considered ordinary at best. They were not close. The man was just too solemn. And she ... the exact opposite.

That was probably why, over the years, Pippa had developed a habit of teasing him. No person should go through life *that* serious. Poking fun at the prickly earl was like skipping through a field of flowers with a fresh summer breeze tickling one's skin.

Extraordinarily delightful.

But most spectacular were his expressions. One would think such a cold, almost paralyzed face would not reveal much, but Pippa had found the intricacy of each subtle flinch early on. The hundred different lights that reflected in his dark gaze. The subtle clench of his jaw. The tick at the corner of his eye. The barely-there purse of his lips. Pippa could not help but hunt down these little treasures at each of their encounters.

Tonight was no different. Especially given the sight before her.

Pudding embroidery. Mistletoe. Gloriously rigid earl.

The urge to tease him sparked to life again, and instead of retreating, Pippa glanced at the mistletoe perched above the earl's head before her gaze dropped to a particularly wobbly pudding on his waistcoat.

A bubble of laughter rose in her chest. Such a cold, severe-looking man standing beneath a patch of mistletoe was a sight to be woven into the fabric of her memory.

This was not a chance to be passed up.

A mad desire prompted Pippa to take a step toward Chatteris. And another. And another. Until she had to crane her neck to meet his gaze.

Ah, there it is. The slight reaction that made her boldness worthwhile—befuddlement. It shimmered in the depth of his eyes like unrecovered treasure.

"What are you up to now?" Chatteris demanded. "Did you believe this atrocious waistcoat would have me dashing home, leaving you and Nancy free to stir up trouble?" He paused. "Why are you looking at me like that?" Another pause. "Are you going to answer any of my questions?"

Oh, I'll answer you, Nicholas Byrne.

But not with words.

Pippa stepped up onto her tiptoes, grabbed the collar of his coat, and kissed him.

* * *

THE FIRST RULE *of being an exemplary brother: Do not kiss your sister's best friend, no matter how alluring.*

. . .

Soft. This was the first thought that popped into Nicholas Byrne, the fourth Earl of Chatteris's head as Pippa Averly's lips connected with his.

Utter shock froze him in place.

He hadn't wanted to attend this charity ball in the first place. But Nancy had acquired tickets, so naturally, he dared not refuse. Not with how much his sister and her friends—especially one friend— loved to court mischief. Who knew what trouble they would stir up tonight if left to their own devices? They'd have England in a riot.

This moment served as the perfect example. He'd stepped out for a moment and already she was causing a riot.

With her lips.

Pippa, Pippa, Pippa. The most troublesome girl in all of England. Known for her outspoken ways and bold behavior. She had gotten into all sorts of scrapes and predicaments over the years. All in the name of *seizing the moment.*

And now she appeared to be seizing him.

A hand suddenly tangled in his hair, and Nicholas jolted awake from his daze. *Saints, preserve me.* Why the devil was he standing there like a half-wit, allowing this?

Common sense shot up his spine, and he began to push her away from him, but Pippa seemed to have grown tentacles that wrapped around him seamlessly, refusing to let go.

His grip on her waist tightened.

This wasn't just a riot. This was a rampage.

On his senses.

His self-control.

For a careless moment, years of restraint collapsed, and Nicholas surrendered to Pippa's eager embrace. The flavorsome punch tasted sweet on her lips. Not quite as sweet as the delicate notes of her scent —honey, if he were to guess—that teased prickles from his skin. Not even to mention the rounded flesh beneath his hands.

He shouldn't even be noticing Pippa's *curves.*

The last jolt, of common sense, shot upward.

Nothing about this scene was right. In fact, all of it was *wrong.*

Nicholas fought for control and ruthlessly pushed through the haze that had settled over him during Pippa's flavorsome kiss.

Wait a damn minute. Did he taste a subtle hint of brandy?

He broke away from her lips and very deliberately, very torturously took a sobering step back. "What the blazes are you doing? Are you foxed?"

"Must one be foxed to be making memories?"

Nicholas stared at her, dumbstruck. "You are most certainly foxed. I can taste the brandy on your lips." He ignored the wrongness of that sentence and simply narrowed his eyes at her.

Low voices murmured in the distance, and leaves shuffled nearby, reminding him of the consequences of being found alone in each other's company. Much less kissing.

"Perhaps I am a bit tipsy. You should lighten up, Sir Nicholas the Cold. The holidays are for seizing magical moments, don't you know?"

Nicholas the Cold? Was that what she thought of him? And did she plan on making more memories tonight? With whom? Him? Or someone else? In a more rational moment, it might have occurred to him that there was something off with his line of reasoning. But this was not a rational moment, and he was not dealing with a rational girl.

"How much did you have to drink?"

"Only a little." She motioned with her thumb and forefinger. "Well, I'm off to find Nancy! See you later!"

"Dammit, Pippa, wait." He grabbed her wrist. "You can't kiss me and just run off like that."

"Why not? It's only a kiss. Pretend it never happened."

Nicholas's jaw went slack. *Only a kiss? Pretend it never happened?* Impossible. It happened. It could not *unhappen.* The probability of him forgetting this incident was absolutely zero.

Nicholas scowled. "What if I demand you take responsibility?"

She chuckled. "What are you saying? I was just teasing you. Do not take it so personally. In any case, I didn't mean for it to be you. It's just when I saw you—"

Nicholas's heart nearly exploded in anger. "I beg your pardon. It wasn't *meant* to be me? Who the hell was your kiss meant for, then?"

Her eyes widened in her pretty heart-shaped face, as though she had carelessly revealed a crown secret. She froze, a little creature who'd caught the scent of a predator. And he was the predator, one that had been caged for too long and finally managed to break out.

Then her laughter rang out, catching him off guard. A familiar melody he had heard countless times before, yet somehow felt as if it were the first time he'd heard this particular laugh from Pippa. Mystical, almost.

His pulse leaped. Actually *leaped*.

Christ above.

Not to say anything about her, but what the devil was wrong with *him*? She was the last female on earth who should set his pulse leaping. The woman had spent years perfecting the art of trouncing on his boundary line. He ought to be used to her little tricks. Not to mention, there were some lines brothers should never cross.

As if her laughter hadn't already confused the hell out of him, she then did the most confounding thing—she lifted a finger to her lips and smiled. The most maddening smile Nicholas had ever had the misfortune of receiving. Not because it was smug. But because it made him rock hard. The kind of reaction he had spent years mastering to suppress whenever she gave him such a soft smile.

He watched her dart off to the ballroom.

What the hell had just happened?

CHAPTER 3

Never blame the wine.
—From the Diary of Lillian Wright

*P*ippa had lost her mind.

Yes, that was it. How else to explain her behavior? She had thought she'd have the last laugh; after all, she considered herself an expert when it came to teasing the Earl of Chatteris. However, something had gone devastatingly wrong. She ought to feel over the moon. Pleased as punch. Triumphant, even. After all, she'd known Chatteris for ten years, and never had she been able to shock him as she had done tonight.

However, she had startled herself into a befuddlement! In fact, she felt a bit perplexed. A touch beside herself.

That kiss ...

No, no, no. The kiss most certainly was not the reason she felt a touch beside herself. It should be the punch. Her hand must have slipped when she poured the brandy.

She let out a short breath and touched her lips.

They still tingled ...

Lord Almighty!

She had stolen a kiss from Nicholas Byrne. Never mind that. A first kiss was a first kiss. She had never meant to make much fanfare of it. She hadn't just stolen a kiss—she'd raised to the tips of her toes, grabbed the man by his lapels, for saint's sake, and pressed her lips against his. *And* he had kissed her back.

Where had the solemn and serious earl disappeared to? Oh dear, and what about Nancy? What would her friend say when she learned Pippa had kissed her brother! While she wished to seize every memorable moment of her life, kissing Chatteris bordered on dangerous.

Pippa's attention caught on two striking figures as she reentered the ballroom. Her sight landed on the tall man with prominent, foreign features before shifting to the beautiful woman beside him. They were bickering, but they still looked like they belonged together. A perfect match.

A pinch of envy squeezed her heart.

"Oh! There you are," Nancy exclaimed from a few feet away, Lord Dare at her side. "We've been looking for you."

Oh, right. She'd forgotten she'd promised Lord Dare a dance! He was her actual target for tonight, and she'd sought him out in the garden for that purpose. But now that she'd kissed Chatteris, she had no desire to steal a kiss from Lord Dare as well. She did, however, need a distraction.

"My lady." He offered her his arm and his most famous rakish smile. "Shall we?"

Pippa extended her hand to place in Dare's outstretched palm when a bigger hand intruded upon her field of vision. Her gaze flew up to … Chatteris?

"The lady is dancing with me."

Dare arched a brow. "Chatteris, good evening. You must be mistaken. Lady Pippa has promised this dance to me."

"No mistake."

"My name is clearly written on the dance card."

Chatteris gave a curt nod. "How remarkable that you would believe that."

"You've clearly lost your bloody head," Dare said.

Chatteris snorted. "That remains to be seen." With that, he all but swept Pippa to the dance floor.

"What are you doing?" she hissed before they were forced to part and circle around the other dancers.

"What are *you* doing?" Chatteris replied when they were once again drawn together. "Drinking. Kissing men. Dancing with rakes?"

"You just pawned your sister off to that rake," Pippa shot back.

The muscles beneath her palm stiffened, and she let out a small laugh when Chatteris snapped his head to Nancy and Dare, the tension only leaving his body when he spotted Jeremy.

"You did that on purpose," he ground out.

"You stole my dance."

"Can a dance be compared to a kiss?"

Probably not. It occurred to Pippa that in all her years of knowing the earl, they'd never once danced. Until tonight.

Was it because of the kiss?

For some reason, the idea unnerved her.

"Seeing as we've never danced before, it might not be that far off from a kiss."

"You meant to kiss Dare tonight." Before she could answer, he went on. "Don't bother to deny it. And before you tell me it's none of my concern, let me remind you that you are a guest under my roof. Everything you do is my business."

Pippa inhaled deeply, unable to escape the soft scent of pine. Even when she curtsied to another gentleman, allowing her a short reprieve from Chatteris's gloomy visage, escape proved impossible.

Pippa couldn't very well tell him about her mother's diary. They did not have the kind of relationship where they shared such intimate details. However, it seemed that she had awakened the beast within him with her actions tonight.

Seizing a moment with Nicholas Byrne had not been a wise thing. In fact, it might very well prove to be calamitous. It was the sort of moment, if left unguarded, one might regret in the future, and if there was anything in the world Pippa hated more, it was regret.

"So," he demanded when they reunited. "Are you going to tell me what has gotten into you?"

"I admit, my actions may appear impulsive, but I do have my reasons, which are quite sound."

"And what reasons might those be?"

"Why are you so riled, Chatteris?" Pippa countered. *Because I kissed you or because I didn't mean to kiss you?*

His jaw clenched. "Have you ever considered how *I* might feel about the kiss you so carelessly stole?"

She met the earl's deep, unfathomable gaze. Her heart began to pound. He left her no time to collect her thoughts. The moment the dance ended, he strode away.

* * *

THE SECOND RULE *of being an exemplary brother: Do not allow your sister's best friend under your skin.*

NICHOLAS SCOWLED at the wall separating their bedchambers.

He had never acted so rude in his life. Even after he'd cut their night short and dragged his sister and Pippa home, he could not settle down.

He had an alarming sense that all the principles that held up the pillar of his character were about to collapse.

Dammit.

He pressed against his heart with his palm. The beat had always been steady. Never this erratic. Now it was almost painful. Deuced uncomfortable.

He prided himself on his calm. Rules existed for a reason. They provided order. *Control.*

This fitful heartbeat … It hadn't steadied since the kiss. The sooner it settled, the better.

Why the hell did she have to kiss him?

For a mad moment, Nicholas wondered: Since it all started the moment she kissed him, would it end the moment he kissed her? The probability seemed small. But it did exist. It would certainly allow him to take back control.

It made perfect sense.

He did not care to dwell on the fact that he had returned her kiss. A mere slip in judgment ...

His eyes narrowed at the blue birds patterning the wall that separated him from that little troublemaker. Four inches of stone barrier. What was she doing on the other side? Was she curled up in her bed sleeping? He could not be the only one in such a wretched state, could he?

Too many doubts and questions circled his mind for him to shut his eyes. The moment he did, he would be transported back to the garden. Her taste ...

Unacceptable.

Before his brain caught up with his limbs, Nicholas strode to the bird-covered wall and placed his ear against the cold surface.

One moment.

Two.

Nothing.

Nicholas snapped straight and spat a curse at all the birds that seemed to be staring at him with beady little laughing eyes. What the devil had gotten into him? Eavesdropping like a child. Absolutely ludicrous. And probably spoke volumes of his sanity.

He turned on his heel and marched to the liquor cabinet beside a small crackling fire illuminating the chamber. He needed a drink. Several. He poured brandy into a glass and downed it in one gulp. The swirling liquid burned down his throat.

The taste reminded him of the spicy flavor of punch on Pippa's lips.

Nicholas almost groaned.

He raised his hand to touch his lips with the tip of his finger. He'd wanted to do that all night but refrained. He could not rid himself of the impact of the kiss; the sensation had engraved too deeply.

That Pippa Averly recklessly seized and savored moments was not news to him. That he had become a moment she had seized … That irked him beyond reason. He, Nicholas Byrne, Earl of Chatteris, was not just another moment to collect.

The mere notion sat wretchedly in his heart.

Seizing moments? The woman courted ruin.

His determination firmed.

Pippa needed to be taught a lesson, and he needed to take back the control she'd so carelessly stolen. Kissing her served this dual purpose. She would learn that a woman cannot kiss a man carelessly without consequences *and* they would be even. She kissed him. He kissed her. That would be the end of it.

A splendid plan.

Nicholas ignored that there might be something off with his line of reasoning. Nothing about this night and its sequence of events was rational. A man needed to be crafty when dealing with a crafty woman.

At the very least, a dark voice inside him argued, he would have a chance to taste her again.

Nicholas poured another brandy.

How many rules had he broken tonight alone? Rules he had set up exactly so that *this* would never happen. This spiral in his mental state. From the first moment he'd met Pippa, he'd known, deep in his bones, she would etch herself there if he did not put personal stipulations in place.

Rightfully so.

She hadn't seemed to be all that fond of him and found his character too stiff. Nicholas hadn't wanted to risk anything that might ruin Nancy's friendship. After all, desires were fleeting, but the value of family was worth more than its weight in treasure.

Now, with one kiss, Pippa had cast him into a void of confusion.

He swallowed the brandy in one go.

What good did those rules do in the end?

Pippa had already firmly lodged under his skin.

CHAPTER 4

If you cannot get over a gentleman's kiss, kiss a rogue.
—From the Diary of Lillian Wright

*P*ippa banged her head on one of the fluffy pillows scattered across her bed. Just how much punch had she drunk to steal a kiss from *him*!

Nicholas Byrne.

What had she been thinking?

Of course, that was the problem. She hadn't been thinking ... She'd been seizing!

In the past, Pippa had gotten into all sorts of scrapes with her unwavering philosophy. A grumpy cat had scratched her hand. She'd fallen into an ice-cold river after an attempt at fishing. Thorns had prickled her feet when she'd run barefoot across a country field.

But kissing Nicholas ...

This was beyond any moment she had ever seized.

The touch of Nicholas's lips against hers. The soft scent of pine that clung to his coat. Large hands encircling her waist. These were infinitely more dangerous than any previous consequences that had arisen from seizing a moment. Because they were so much more than that. They were gentle enticements. Little snares. And she had an alarming suspicion she'd been caught in their toils.

Pippa, Pippa, Pippa.

She'd gone and done it now.

She had always found Nicholas exceedingly handsome. And, once upon a time, she had some flirtatious fantasies. A natural occurrence since the man resembled a chiseled Adonis.

But this was *Nicholas.*

The man thought of her as his ward. Perhaps even as a second sister. So, the fact that her memory of him last night beamed as vivid as a blooming rose, triggered a sense of danger in her heart. The kiss. The dance. The stealthy glares.

All Nicholas.

Would acting as though nothing had transpired between them be enough? For him? For her? She certainly did not want to ruin their relationship because of her actions. That would most certainly affect her friendship with Nancy. Pippa would never forgive herself if her behavior last night estranged her from her best friend.

But then again, this *was* Nicholas.

Cold, yes, and serious to the extreme, but also a complete gentleman. Pippa had also gotten what she wanted—her first kiss. In all likelihood, the earl had already pushed the matter from his mind.

Her chest tightened at the thought.

A brief knock and Nancy entered the chamber with a skip in her step. "Awake? Why haven't you come down for breakfast? I am dying of curiosity! Did you kiss Dare?"

Pippa groaned and pressed her face into the pillow.

She'd run off to her room the moment they returned home, afraid that Nancy would just somehow *know* that she'd kissed her brother. Pippa didn't even want to think about what Nancy would have to say about that. The last thing she wanted was for Nancy to worry about their friendship or, heaven forbid, orchestrate a forced marriage. She could just imagine the earl's sour face!

Nancy yanked the pillow from beneath her. "Well? I've waited long enough for all the juicy details. Do tell."

"There's nothing to tell."

"Then it's as I thought." Nancy sighed. "Because of Nicholas, right? I don't understand how he so thoroughly abandoned his reason last night."

He wasn't the only one.

"He must have remembered our shenanigans of the previous year," Nancy said.

"Perhaps."

"Not to worry, we shall find another opportunity for you to kiss Dare. I've decided I shall steal my first kiss as well."

"You did? With whom?"

"I haven't quite decided yet. I'm still scouting the prospects."

"What about Jeremy? You've fancied him for years."

Nancy snorted. "The man is either as dense as a piece of wood or not attracted to me. Even if he is the former, he should have shown a hint of interest by now. A look of longing. A flirtatious remark. Anything. He's flirted with enough women for me to know he is capable, so I've decided to move on."

Pippa thought of Nicholas. He had never cast a longing look her way or made any flirtatious remark, either. And having borne witness to her friend's unrequited love for years, she understood no good would come from reminiscing on last night. Best to let it go.

Pippa sat up. "Well then, I shall help you scout. Or you can just kiss Dare, too." As for her, she might as well steal another one for good measure. At the very least, it ought to purge a certain earl from her memory.

Nancy yanked the covers from the bed. "It's already noon. Have you forgotten? We are to meet Jeremy at Hyde Park in an hour. I invited Dare, too. Let's see if he shows."

This caught Pippa's attention. "You invited Dare? When?"

"Yesterday at the ball when Nicholas plundered your dance. Surprised? Grateful?"

Pippa bit her lip.

She suddenly recalled one particular sentence in her mother's diary that had always amused her: *If you cannot get over a gentleman's kiss, kiss a rogue.*

Pippa had planned to kiss a rogue from the beginning. Rakes had no sense of commitment. An easy choice. Plus, according to her mother's diary, they were excellent kissers. Pippa decided to see for herself.

She would kiss Dare today.

* * *

THE THIRD RULE *of being an exemplary brother: Do not eavesdrop on your sister's conversation, especially if said conversation is with Pippa Averly.*

NICHOLAS COULD NOT QUITE EXPLAIN his current mood as he entered Hyde Park on the back of his horse. He hadn't meant to eavesdrop. Truly, he hadn't. A gentleman *never* eavesdropped. He'd only casually strolled by Pippa's chamber …

He hadn't slowed his steps.

Hadn't pressed his ear up against the door.

Hadn't overheard Pippa planning to kiss Dare. Nancy planned to kiss someone too. They were going riding at Hyde Park. Dare might be there.

Nicholas clenched his jaw.

What the devil was wrong with the women? Did they only have kissing on their brain? And Pippa … This, after she had already brazenly kissed him. After he had spent a sleepless night dwelling on her lips. Her scent. Was he a deuced rag to be tossed aside after being used?

Unacceptable.

The fire that had exploded in his chest earlier still raged on. He should have locked them in that chamber there and then. But he hadn't. Instead, he followed them like a scorned lover adamant about catching his partner in the act.

Bloody shameful.

He told himself to remain calm. Observe. Determine what those mischievous creatures were planning and nip it in the bud. Yet the moment he spotted Dare leading Pippa to his phaeton, all rational thought drained from his head.

Nicholas didn't bother with pleasantries as he halted his horse beside them. "It's too dangerous for a ride in a phaeton. The weather is turning."

"Nicholas?" Pippa's eyes widened.

Nancy frowned. "Weren't you heading to your club? Why are you here?"

"My plans changed."

Dare chuckled but said nothing.

Nicholas clenched the reins between his fingers.

Pippa shot him a meaningful glance. "There's not a cloud in the sky."

"Clouds have a way of following the depraved."

Dare's smile stiffened. "What are you implying, Chatteris?"

Nicholas ignored him. "The roads are also wet. Driving phaetons in these conditions is reckless." He held out his hand to Pippa, resolved to get her far away from Dare and any possible kiss between the two.

She glared at him.

Of course, Nicholas knew his behavior was rude, atrocious even. He just didn't care. The only thing that mattered was Pippa. The gawking onlookers melted away as Nicholas waited for her response.

In the end, she did not refuse him.

She placed her hand in his, gasping when he effortlessly lifted her up onto his horse in one fell swoop.

"If you will excuse us," Nicholas announced. "We have something to discuss."

"Pippa!" Nancy exclaimed in shock.

Nicholas caged her in his arms and flicked the reins before anyone could stop them, urging the horse into a gallop.

Her common sense returned before his, for she demanded, "Stop the horse and let me off."

"No."

"Everyone is staring at us!"

"Let them stare."

"This is highly unlike you, Nicholas." She was seated sideways and turned her head to glare at him. "Not even to say we can't hold a proper conversation in this position."

Nicholas leaned close. "Nothing about yesterday or today has been proper, why start now?"

"Have we not moved past the matter?"

"You don't tell a man to forget about a kiss if you want him to forget about a kiss. Now I can't forget about it even if I wanted to."

"So you interfere in my engagements?"

"Are you going to kiss Dare?" Nicholas countered, the mere thought driving him bloody mad. "He is the one you *meant* to kiss, no?"

Those beautiful eyes blinked. "My birthday is in a few days. I did not want to reach twenty without my first kiss."

"I see." Nicholas brought the horse to a halt, his gaze delving into hers. "Since you already shared your first kiss with me, why do you still plan on kissing another?"

"How do you ..." Her eyes widened. "You eavesdropped on our conversation?"

"A mere coincidence."

"Do you expect me to believe that?"

Nicholas cleared his throat, his mind still stuck on this first kiss business. He was the first man to ever kiss Pippa. An extremely satisfying thought.

"Be that as it may, forget about Dare."

"You have clearly lost all sense."

"*I* have lost all sense?"

"This is the second time you have left your sister unchaperoned with a group of men to whisk me away from a big, bad wolf."

"Jeremy is there."

"Is he a man?"

"All of England knows he is the equivalent of your hired help."

Pippa snorted. "For a man always in control, you don't seem to have a grip on matters. So, pray tell, what do you plan to do now that you have me?"

Excellent question. He'd nearly forgotten about his plan. Nicholas stared at her pretty face, filled with questions and so tantalizingly close to his, and felt his pulse leap. Damnation. His heart was experiencing another event. So much for his calm.

His gaze dropped to the soft arch of her lips.

Full.

Sweet.

Utter temptation.

He now knew how they would feel against his own lips. The soft sensation. The taste of sweetness that branded into his mind. His bones. His soul. He wanted to occupy her mind solely. Her lips. Everything.

He found her enchanting.

Always had.

"Well?" she urged.

Nicholas slowly came back to his senses and smiled. "I plan to take back control."

Her eyes rounded. "How?"

Nicholas's grin widened. Then he uttered words he never thought he would ever say to Pippa in his life. "If you want to kiss someone, kiss me."

CHAPTER 5

Dreams, love, and kisses ought never to be confused.
—From the Diary of Lillian Wright

*U*ntil the impulsive moment beneath the mistletoe, Pippa
had always tried her very best not to be swept away by the
force of feelings such as those that a single kiss had provoked at the
Pearler ball. And now the implication of what Nicholas had revealed
caused her world to tilt unexpectedly, plunging everything into
mayhem.

She made Nicholas lose control.

He wanted her to only kiss him.

Her whole body prickled with awareness.

Pippa stared at the man, not sure what to make of this side of him.
He'd always been cold and staid, not the sort of man to audaciously
flirt and give in to flights of fancy. She could not deny there was
something strangely endearing about this side of the earl.

Splendidly unexpected.

Pippa collected a deep breath into her lungs and exhaled the
tension that had gathered in her nerves. Hyde Park buzzed with liveliness, but at present, one could only faintly hear a hum of activity. She

had been spirited away to a secluded spot—and the entire park had borne witness.

"Have I left you bereft of speech?" a gruff whisper teased. "I've not seen you this speechless before. A riveting sight." He leaned nearer as he spoke, and she, too, seemed to edge closer, so that by the time he finished speaking, barely a hair's breadth separated them.

Her heart pounded. "I'm thinking."

His gaze lit with mock astonishment. "Another first."

Pippa glared at him. "I'm not a complete ninny. And if you want to speak of firsts, look no further than your own behavior."

He chuckled. "I'm only borrowing a page from your book, Pippa. I'm seizing moments. How about it? Have I mastered the art?"

Then his mouth claimed hers.

Pippa's brain melted the moment his tongue slid between her lips, demanding territory. The world spun about her as Nicholas did exactly what he said he'd do—recaptured the control he'd presumably lost, for surely hers scattered in the wind. His possession thundered through her brain like a thousand galloping horses. She went hot all over. It didn't seem possible. Nicholas was kissing her. This time, *he* had taken the initiative. Not in a thousand dreams would she ever have imagined he could behave so delightfully out of character.

Pippa wanted to taste all his secrets.

She wanted more.

But dare she embrace the risk …

Her train of thought evaporated when a large hand clutched her waist. Everything disappeared. The park. The people. The consequences. Nothing mattered except to do what Pippa did best—*seize*.

She poured all the dreams and doubts that cradled her heart into the fire that entangled their tongues. She held nothing back. Focused only on the intoxicating flames their kiss created.

A forever kind of moment.

"Pippa …" He breathed against her lips as he pulled back slowly. His voice sounded different. Dangerous. "Promise me you won't kiss Dare."

Her pulse thundered in her ears. Her gaze met his, sharp and piercing. She could not look away. "I promise."

The hand still clasping her waist tightened when the steed made a restless step to the left. She loved his strength.

Wait, that's not the point.

Pippa surveyed their surroundings before she let out a breath of relief. "Thank heavens, no one saw us."

"Is that not the point of seizing moments?" Nicholas asked. "The thrill?"

"Certainly not," Pippa said. "It's about not missing a moment one might regret if missed."

"Are you implying if you had not kissed me at the Pearler ball you would have regretted it?"

Pippa thought back to the breathless impulse that had urged her to kiss him that night. Without having to dwell on it much, she knew within her soul, she would have regretted missing the moment had she not seized it then.

"Perhaps, perhaps not," she teased. "All I know is that I haven't begun to regret the kiss. Yet."

"Oh? What about the one we just shared?"

"Is that not your moment?"

"I don't regret it," he said with certainty. "And since you don't regret yours, the matter is settled."

Pippa froze. Did that mean this was the end of it, then? Were they even now? A touch of disappointment accompanied his reassurance. Until his next words ...

"From now on, I'm yours to seize."

* * *

THE FOURTH RULE of being an exemplary brother: *Do not kiss your sister's best friend in public. Also, do not leave your sister in the presence of a rake. Again.*

. . .

FACED WITH HER WIDE-EYED STARE, Nicholas was seized by another unpardonable, duty-defying urge to kiss her. She sat enclosed in his arms, all but taunting him with those glittering eyes and red, moist lips.

Beautiful.

He hadn't meant to blurt out the first thing that came to mind. For the first time in his life, Nicholas's actions, thoughts, and mouth were led by pure instinct. Kissing Pippa Averly was damn near perilous.

And her warmth imprisoned him.

He hadn't understood what the events of his heart meant. His pulse thundered. *Seize me*, every unsettled beat seemed to roar. He tipped her chin up as he lowered his lips to hers again for a quick peck.

Peril aside, kissing Pippa had also become a necessity.

Her eyes searched his in a daze, incredulity glinting in their depth. And something else. Something that made his chest constrict with emotion.

Awe.

Had he truly kissed Pippa Averly senseless? The look suited her. Wildly seductive.

Then, she blinked. "Seize you? I can't believe you just said that. In fact, this past hour is a dream. It's a dream, right? I haven't woken up yet." Her eyes narrowed on him. "Pinch me."

"This is not a dream."

She gestured to her arm. "Pinch me."

"I'm not pinching you."

"You kissed me but won't pinch me?"

"Are kissing and pinching the same?"

"What about biting?"

"I don't bite." Nicholas dropped his gaze to her lips. "Unless you want me to take a bi—?"

"No! No biting!" She shook her head. "You'd *bite* but not pinch?"

"Old men pinch, young men—" He stopped. "This is ridiculous. You are not dreaming." Nicholas paused. "Do I kiss you in your dreams?"

"This is exactly my point. You'd never ask me such things in the waking world. Never abduct me in the park. Kiss me on the back of a horse. Say such things to me. What else, if not a dream?"

"None of that matters."

She directed a pair of suspicious eyes at him. "How can you say that? The real Nicholas would *never* say that."

"Because you kissed me at the ball. Because now I want to kiss you again and again. Of course, life would be much more convenient if this were a dream. I wouldn't need to hold back every instinct to make you mine."

Her eyes widened. "Surely you jest?"

"I never joke about matters of great importance, Pippa. Believe me when I say this matter is vital to me. More important than air. You started this at the Pearler ball. How we end is entirely up to you."

"What exactly do you mean by that, Nicholas?"

The horse restlessly shifted beneath them, as if suddenly sensing the rising tension. Before Nicholas could explain, the horse unexpectedly reared, sending a chill down his spine. Caught off guard, the reins slipped from his fingers. Without further thought, he circled both arms around Pippa as they toppled from the horse, hitting the dirt with an audible thump.

Nicholas's head spun as pain shot through his body.

"What on earth ..." Pippa squirmed on top of him. "Nicholas? Are you all right?"

I'm fine ... Truly.

"Nicholas!"

He caught the note of panic in the urgent call, but his reassurance came out in a grunt. The next moment, the world turned black.

CHAPTER 6

Your heart has its reasons. They ought not to be dismissed.
—From the Diary of Lillian Wright

*P*ippa's heart nearly left her body. She scrambled from Nicholas's body as the horse took off, afraid her weight would add to his injuries.

"Pippa! Nicholas!"

Pippa hardly registered the call of voices and the approaching hooves. Her entire being focused on the man lying unconscious on the ground.

"What happened?" Nancy asked, falling onto her knees beside them.

"Snake." Dare pointed to where a snake coiled nearby. "Must have startled the horse." He flicked it away with his cane.

"Help me lift him into the carriage," Dare instructed Jeremy. The two of them managed to deposit Nicholas onto the phaeton with little effort.

"I'll drive him back. Locke, you retrieve Chatteris's horse."

Pippa found her voice. "There is not enough space in the phaeton."

"There's a small seat reserved for the groom behind the body," Dare said.

Pippa and Nancy glanced at each other.

"You go," Pippa said to her friend. "I'll return with Jeremy."

Nancy nodded.

No matter how much Pippa's heart pained, Nancy was surely just as terrified, if not more. And Pippa needed a moment to collect her wits.

"He broke my fall. A doctor …" Pippa trailed off numbly as emotion clogged her throat.

Dare seemed to understand. "Already sent my man for one."

They delayed no more. Dare and Nancy set off with Nicholas, and Pippa and Jeremy went to find the skittish horse. It took one torturous hour before they returned home. They met Dare in the entrance hall.

"How is Nicholas?" Pippa asked urgently.

"He suffered a small blow to the head and an injury to the waist. Don't fret, my lady. Chatteris has thick skin and an impenetrable skull. He started grousing the moment he woke up."

"He's awake?" Relief flooded her.

Dare nodded. "His sister is threatening all sorts of ways to keep him in bed." Dare looked to Pippa. "Might I have a word?"

"Of course, my lord."

"I'll go report our return to Nancy," Jeremy said. "She must be worried about you as well."

"Thank you," she said and led Dare into the nearby drawing room.

He pulled a parchment from his pocket and handed it to her.

"What's this?"

"You dropped it when Chatteris abducted you."

Pippa's eyes widened as she unfolded the paper and stared at a familiar face. Usually, this drawing was tucked safely in her mother's diary. Today, however, for some unfathomable reason, she'd removed the sketch and tucked it into her bodice. In fact, she had drawn many pictures of Nicholas over the years. But this one … this one was her favorite.

"The likeness is quite good," Dare said, the corner of his mouth twitching. "He looks so *carefree*."

Pippa trailed her finger over the soft lines she'd penciled. The very first one she ever drew of him. "The first time we met was when I caught him sniffing flowers in the garden." She had always loved this memory of Nicholas.

Love.

Pippa loved him.

And this picture was the start of that love. Or to be more exact, the start of her obsession. The enthusiasm to tease. Fascination to taunt. Fixation to poke through that thick armor that clung to him.

Pippa met Dare's gaze. "Thank you for returning this to me."

He inclined his head. "I am just relieved you are unharmed."

"I appreciate your concern."

Dare waved a casual hand. Then he laughed. "It's a peculiar feeling, this feeling of being used."

"I'm not sure I understand, my lord."

"The reason I find myself in your and Lady Nancy's company the past two days. However, it has been quite interesting."

What else could Pippa say but, "We didn't actually get to the using part."

Dare laughed again. "I'm not sure whether that's a blessing or a tragedy."

"A blessing for us both, I assure you, my lord."

Excitement thrummed through her veins. The only thing left to do … Seize the man she loved.

* * *

THE FIFTH RULE *of being an exemplary brother: Do not leave your sister alone in a bedchamber with another man, even if the man is the equivalent of a nursemaid.*

"WHY HASN'T SHE RETURNED YET?"

"She is fine, Nicholas. They should be here any moment. Jeremy won't let any harm come to her."

Nicholas clenched his fist. He hadn't sensed the unease of his own animal. Now he was confined to his bed while Pippa was off, Lord knows where, retrieving his horse. Nancy said she hadn't been injured, but he wouldn't be at ease until he could see that with his own eyes. There was no containing the feelings that threatened to erupt.

He loved her.

He loved Pippa Averly.

Hopelessly.

He couldn't even say when it happened. There had always been something different about Pippa. He sensed it from the very first moment they met. She represented the sun while he, the vast cold night. But he never thought a woman such as her, so warm and spirited, would ever spare a glance his way—a man who could never match her vibrancy.

Cold.

Even Pippa had called him that. He could not do much about his personality. He just wanted to be close to her warmth. Her mere proximity could thaw the frost he exuded with his temperament.

Only her.

Nicholas met his sister's reproachful look. She smacked his shoulder. "What has gotten into you? Do you know how the tongues are wagging? You are sure to be in the gossip pages tomorrow."

"Let them wag."

Astonishment flashed across her gaze. "Who are you and what did you do with my brother?" Her eyes narrowed. "What happened between you and Pippa? She is my best friend, Nicholas. If you two are at odds, I will choose her side!"

"Disloyal brat."

She smacked him again. "What are the two of you fighting about? Something happened at the charity ball, right? Is it because of that waistcoat?"

Nicholas's lips twitched when he thought of that ugly thing.

Anything Pippa made him, he would happily wear. "We are not fighting."

Nancy shot him a disbelieving look. "You're not?"

Nicholas ignored her, his calm returning when Jeremy walked through the door. His gaze darted past him.

"Where's Pippa?" Nicholas demanded, sitting up when he realized she hadn't come with Jeremy.

Nancy pushed him back down. "What are you doing? The doctor said you should rest."

"Devil take it! I'm fine! It's just a bruise."

"Your skin is black and blue!"

He twisted his torso. "See, it doesn't hurt at all." It hurt like hell, but he wasn't about to admit that out loud.

"I'm sure your future wife shall be ecstatic," Jeremy mocked.

Nicholas turned a deaf ear to those loaded words. "As if such a small mishap can foul me."

Nancy looked at Jeremy. "Where's Pippa? Weren't you together?"

"Yes, why isn't she here mocking my misfortune?"

Jeremy rolled his eyes. "We encountered Dare downstairs. She is receiving him instead of fawning over you."

Nicholas bolted upright. A nasty curse formed on his tongue. "That libertine hasn't left yet?"

Nancy and Jeremy shared a brief glance before she said, "Dare helped us today, should he not receive some gratitude?"

Gratitude, my ass.

Nicholas ripped the covers off himself and maneuvered to his feet. This damn heart of his. Going off again. Only Pippa could settle its tortuous rhythm. He needed her. Her scent. Her presence. Her teasing.

"What are you doing?" Nancy demanded.

"To settle a matter."

"What matter?" Nancy snapped. "Don't be absurd."

"Who is absurd? Are you and Pippa not the ones bent on kissing that rake?"

Nancy's mouth dropped open.

Jeremy frowned.

Nicholas didn't explain further, done with them. He pushed past the pain and limped from the room with a renewed sense of purpose. She had promised she wouldn't kiss Dare. But what if Dare kissed her? Under *his* roof? Not while he still had the strength to kick the man out on his ass.

CHAPTER 7

Love is the ultimate stage. Seize all its hours.
—From the Diary of Lillian Wright

"You should go to him," Dare said. "Chatteris won't rest until you're in his sight."

Pippa slowly nodded, but in her heart, she hesitated. How to face the man who had boldly declared he wanted to claim her? Now that her thoughts had cleared, doubt and uncertainty once again made their way into her reasoning.

"He's right," a low voice drawled. A large silhouette filled the doorway of the drawing room.

"Nicholas?" Pippa couldn't quite hide her surprise. She examined him from top to toe. "Why are you not in bed?"

Nicholas's gaze swept over her. "You didn't come to me, so I came to you. You weren't hurt in the fall?"

Gooseflesh broke out over her skin. "I'm unharmed."

Dare chuckled. "Since you are here, I shall take my leave." He winked at Pippa. "Take care, my lady."

"You too," Pippa said. The moment he left, Pippa scolded, "You should return to bed. Why are you so stubborn? Does your head not hurt?"

"No."

"Liar."

"When I think about you, it doesn't hurt."

"Impossible."

The corners of his mouth quirked. "Dare seems quite taken with you."

"No," Pippa denied. "I dropped a drawing at the park. He returned it to me."

Dark eyes burned into her. "Do you still want to kiss him?"

Pippa nearly choked on air. "Of course not! Why would you think that?"

"I merely wish to clarify your intention."

"*My* intention?"

Nicholas nodded. "Mine is clear. I wish to marry you."

"You do not!" She blurted the first thing that came to mind. Marrying Nicholas would be a dream come true. But she was selfish. She didn't want him to marry her out of duty.

"Yes, I do."

"You're always scowling at me."

"Because you're always getting into some scrap or other. Like the time that mangy cat scratched you after you attempted to pet the thing."

"I saved the cat, and it wasn't mangy. As I recall, you growled at me that day. *Growled.* Like an animal!"

"You had scratch marks all over your hand." His eyes narrowed. "That is all you remember? I also dressed your wound."

Pippa thought back. He really had. "A gentleman's act of kindness."

"Does that kindness extend to dressing your wound every day for a week?" He scoffed. "And what about the time you stumbled into the Thames, who was the one who pulled you from the freezing waters?"

"Well"—Pippa gave a small cough—"the water wasn't *that* cold."

"And when you fell ill after that, who nursed you back to health?"

"The doctor."

"On my orders. Nancy might have stayed by your side, but I didn't leave the house until you were well again."

Pippa could barely contain her excitement. Her mind raced. She recalled all these incidents but hadn't thought much about them. Nicholas had worn a look of displeasure in each of these moments, which, incidentally, only fueled her desire to tease him. Then again, if she thought about it, Nicholas had never been a man of many words. A grunt here, a growl there. His actions spoke clearer than his words.

She never even imagined …

Her heart suddenly settled, and she smiled at Nicholas. "Did you know that my mother's last words to me were to live my life without regret. She said to gather as many moments as stars in the sky."

"I remember her to be a remarkable woman." His voice lowered. "Just like her daughter."

Pippa blushed. "She made a lot of mistakes. Wrote about all of them, yet she never regretted her choices because they were hers. Just like I will never regret that I stole a kiss from you."

His gaze sharpened. "Does that mean … Will you marry me?"

"Are you being sincere?" Pippa had to be sure. "If we are to be united in marriage, we must be sure. Nancy is your sister and my dearest friend. If you are not being sincere … If you wish to marry me out of duty …"

Her mother had never won the love of her father. Yet she never regretted her marriage, but Pippa doubted she could do the same. She wanted to love. More so, she wanted to be loved in return.

"Pippa, I'm beyond all hope." He took a limping step toward her and clasped her hands in his. "The Pearler ball left me no room for denial. I am utterly obsessed with you. I cannot say when the obsession started, I can only say that you hold my heart, Pippa Averly. Undeniably. I love you."

Pippa could no longer contain her joy. "You love me?"

"I love you."

She laughed happily. "Then I must admit, from the moment I kissed you, I never wanted to kiss another man." Her smile widened when he merely arched a brow. "Well, except for this morning when I thought to forget about your kiss."

"No forgetting," he commanded before claiming her lips in a hot kiss, as if to remove the notion completely from her mind. "Only me," he breathed.

Pippa flashed her teeth. "Where is the legendary control you wrestled back from me?"

A soft huff. "You've whole-heartedly ensnared me, love. My heart. My soul. My sanity. Where you are concerned, the word holds no meaning."

Inside, Pippa brimmed with delight.

She handed him the sketch, finally understanding that, in the end, the only thing worth seizing was happiness. Nicholas had always been that. She wanted him to know she saw all of him.

"What's this?" he asked, then froze. His gaze lifted to hers. "You sketched this?"

Pippa nodded. "It's the day we met. I've wanted to tease you about it so many times, but I never had the heart. So, I poked fun at other things, hoping to catch a glimpse of this Nicholas—the earl who sniffs flowers in the garden."

"Pippa ..." He brought his ungloved hand up and slowly stroked the back of his fingers along her cheek.

Her pulse quickened, and Pippa finally said, "I love you too. Yes, I will seize you. Marry you. Kiss only you."

* * *

THE SIXTH RULE *of being an exemplary brother: Lead by example.*

NICHOLAS'S LIPS followed Pippa's confession, and he only pulled away when both of them ran out of breath. This was not the place to ignite their desires. What he needed was a bed. And time.

Lots and lots of time.

"Your injuries ..." she whispered.

"Don't hurt," Nicholas denied. "Not when you're here."

She laughed. "Do you think I believe that? If it hurts, it hurts, whether I'm present or not."

"Have a heart, love." He trailed a thumb over her lower lip. "You're finally in my arms. A small injury is nothing. Tell me you love me again. No, wait. Don't. I won't be able to hold myself back. Let's get married. I can get a special license within the hour. Three at most."

"We haven't yet told—"

He caught her answer on his lips. He couldn't help himself. She was just too damn irresistible, and he refused to listen to anything but *yes*. Unfortunately, or perhaps very fortunately, Nancy's bright voice sliced through the spell that had almost woven them together.

"Am I interrupting *something*?"

Pippa gasped, and Nicholas encircled her waist when she attempted to scramble from his embrace.

"Yes," he outright declared.

Nancy put her hands on her hips, eyes narrowed on them. "My brother and best friend have thrown dust into my eyes. I shall not let this pass!"

Jeremy appeared behind her, a grin displayed on his face. "Don't mind me, I'm just here for the theatrics."

Nicholas remained nonchalant. Now that his sister discovered the truth all by herself, they could get married sooner rather than later.

"When did this start?" Nancy demanded. "*How* did this start? Neither of you told me anything!" She held up her hand when Nicholas opened his mouth. "Wait ... It should be the Pearler ball, right?"

"I kissed Nicholas instead of Dare," Pippa admitted. "You were there for the rest."

"*What?*" Nancy exclaimed, eyes turning to Nicholas. "The same night you pawned me off to the most notorious rake in England?"

"The very same."

Nancy's mouth opened and shut. "You won't even deny it! Am I not your loving sister? Aren't you supposed to protect me from libertines on the prowl?"

"It was unavoidable." Nicholas paused, then added, "Jeremy was there."

"Jeremy? Is he not a man as well?"

Jeremy snorted.

"Nevermind that," Nancy said before she rubbed her forehead. "I need a minute to process this."

The room fell into silence—for all but one second—before Nicholas made a grunting sound. It had the desired effect.

"Are you in pain?" Pippa grabbed his arm. "You should rest. Let me help you back to your chamber."

Nancy scoffed. "Do not even try to hoodwink me. I want answers."

"Pippa has agreed to become my wife," Nicholas simply said. "Do you have any objections?"

She pursed her lips. "What if I do?"

Pippa stiffened in his arms, and Nicholas gave her a reassuring squeeze. He knew his sister too well. She might not look it, but Nancy was practically beaming imperceptible happiness.

"I suppose," he said thoughtfully, "we shall then have to elope."

"Don't you dare!" Nancy exclaimed. "I shall never forgive you if I'm not included in your wedding!"

"You're not disappointed?" Pippa asked.

"Of course not." Nancy's pout transformed into a wide grin. "You've always been my sister in heart, now you shall truly be family."

Nicholas lowered his head to inhale the delicate scent of honey wafting from the arch of Pippa's neck while Nancy nagged about their improper behavior and keeping her in the dark. Proper. Improper. He couldn't care less about impropriety at this moment.

He had found his love.

He was never letting go.

AFTERWORD

Thank you for supporting this anthology! Did you enjoy Pippa and Chatteris? Can't wait for Nancy's story? Keep up with news by joining my newsletter. You also get some free books. 😊

OTHER BOOKS YOU MIGHT LIKE BY TANYA WILDE:

LADIES WHO DARE

- Not Quite A Rogue

MIDDLETONS

- An Invitation to Marriage
- The Perks of Being a Duchess
- A Promise of Scandal

ABOUT THE AUTHOR

Tanya Wilde developed a passion for reading when she had nothing better to do than lurk in the library during her lunch breaks. Her love affair with pen and paper soon followed after she devoured all of their historical romance books! In 2020, she won the Romance Writers Organization of South Africa (ROSA) Imbali Award for Excellence in Romance Writing for Not Quite a Rogue.

When she's not meddling in the lives of her characters or drinking copious amounts of coffee, she's off on adventures with her partner in crime.

Wilde lives in a town at the foot of the Outeniqua Mountains, South Africa.

Join her newsletter for a free book, Under The Highland Sky: https://bit.ly/Under_The_Highland_Sky

LILY'S SCANDALOUS SECRET BY PAMELA GIBSON

Spice Level 🤍🤍🤍

CHAPTER 1

She remembered the snow—tiny crystalline flakes that tickled the skin and created a wonderland when they settled on the ground. Soot, litter, even drops of blood, magically disappeared as if one needed to be reminded that nature could erase ugliness.

Lily Whittington gazed through the frosted panes and chose her memories carefully, avoiding thoughts of another snowy day long ago, a day when her life changed.

She shuddered and dropped the curtain back in place. London was a foul place, and she hated it. She'd been back only once in fifteen years, when her brother was ailing. Now she was here again, in the home of her niece, staring out the window in the hope that a calm would settle over her, much like the delicate, drifting flakes covered the landscape with a soft, white blanket.

"Aunt Lily?"

Lily jumped. She turned to see her niece near the door of the drawing room, leaning against the frame. "Have your pains started? Shall I summon the physician?"

Emily, Lady Cardmore, was *enceinte* and her time was near. Lily had only agreed to come to London because Emily's mother was ill, and her husband was away.

"No. Please. I didn't mean to alarm you." Emily waddled over and eased into a chair. "I keep telling anyone who will listen it will be another month. I wanted to see if the ballroom had enough light for your painting. I appreciate your willingness to leave your home to keep me company while Andrew is away. I feel terrible that I cannot convey you to Bullock's Museum or the art gallery at Somerset House or to see other new sights since you were here last. Then I remembered you don't care for London."

Lily dropped into the chair next to Emily and took her hand. "You're my favorite niece. You needed me, so I came, and you know I'm a recluse. I need no entertainment."

Emily withdrew her hand and rested it on her stomach. "I miss my husband, and I miss my children. I wish Andrew hadn't talked me into leaving them with their nanny at Cardmore Hall."

"In the country, they'll have much to do to prepare for the approaching holidays. George is old enough to help entertain his sister, and it won't be long now before they have another sibling. Here they'd be restless, and you'd let them talk you into activities you should avoid."

"I suppose you're right. Andrew promised to bring them here if I haven't delivered by Christmas."

"A perfect solution."

Emily tilted her head. "You've never told me why you dislike London. Is it the crowds? Although I daresay you love the village fairs near Langston Grange, and they are well-attended."

Lily studied her hands. A paint stain marred her thumb. She must remember to scrub it more thoroughly. "It's not that. I adore a crowded village fair. Here there's … perpetual smoke from coal fires, beggars on the streets, and ragged children sweeping street crossings hoping for coins from charitable passersby. 'Tis depressing, and it hurts my heart."

"There's poverty in villages, too, Aunt."

"I know. Perhaps it's also due to memories I don't care to relive."

There. That was the truth.

"I'm so sorry, Aunt Lily. I keep forgetting this is where your husband died. I know you must have loved him dearly to have stayed away from the city for so many years. Forgive me?"

"Of course." Lily forced a smile. "Now, if you'll indulge me, I want to finish the watercolor I started yesterday." How awful to keep secrets from someone who only wanted one to be happy. Lily had lived the grieving widow lie for so long she could almost believe it was the truth.

She rose, straightened her skirt, and patted her niece's hand. "Why don't you play the pianoforte? I know it soothes and challenges you."

"Perhaps I shall. Talking about poor street children makes me think of all the babes in foundling homes."

"It's sad, is it not? Charitable institutions do what they can, but they have room for only a small number even though the need is much greater."

Emily grinned and looked away.

Why was she smiling? It wasn't a topic to cause merriment.

"I'm glad you share my concern, Aunt Lily. There's going to be a charitable event at the end of the week to raise funds for a foundling home."

"How wonderful. There is such a need. How will the funds be raised? Are they selling tickets?"

"It's called the Grand Mistletoe Assembly, and there will be dancing, a dinner, and a silent auction. I'm planning to donate a reticule I'm sewing, since I can't attend in my state."

"You and Cardmore received an invitation?"

"We did, and we bought tickets even though it distressed us to have to decline. I adore dancing, as you know."

Lily turned toward the door. "I once loved to dance. The last time I did was when you lived with me and insisted we practice the waltz."

"Oh, that was fun, wasn't it? I trod on your toe, and you hopped around the room, squealing. I nearly had apoplexy."

"Until you discovered I was teasing."

They both laughed at the memory.

"I'll be in the ballroom," Lily said. "The light is good, and I want to work on that still life with those beautiful hothouse flowers from your papa. I've arranged them in that crystal vase your husband brought you from the Waterford factory in Ireland."

"I'll send word when the tea arrives. You know I have to nibble and drink tea in the afternoons these days."

"You loved your afternoon biscuits even when you lived with me. Should you be indulging so often?"

"No scolding. You know I'm close to tears at the tiniest criticism."

Lily nodded. "Which is probably why Cardmore decided now was a good time to purchase that mare from his friend, Lord Ralston, who is conveniently at his seaside cottage."

She loved Emily, but the girl was up to some mischief and had a difficult time hiding it. The glint in her eyes gave her away. What could it be?

Lily hurried to the ballroom, where her easel and watercolors sat near tall windows. She couldn't possibly capture the facets of the crystal vase. The flowers were different. She'd painted them before and had studied them carefully by fingering the petals and sliding her fingers along the leaves and stem. Flower markets didn't sell daffodils this time of year. Wherever did her brother find them?

She dipped her brush in the bright yellow paint and dabbed it on the canvas. Painting had soothed her for years, helping her to forget that awful time when she'd been accused of murder and had to go before the coroner's jury at an inquest in a tavern, of all places. Jack Whittington's death had been ruled an accident, despite the accusations of an emboldened maid, who swore she had heard raised voices before Lily shrieked and ran out of the room, covered in blood. The presence of Lily's brother Harry Sinclair, the Earl of Langston, at the inquest had probably helped influence the coroner's verdict of accidental death.

Jack's sister Hannah, whose sizable dowry had allowed her to contract a marriage far above her station, was incensed at the verdict and vowed to ruin Lily if she ever set foot in London. So, she'd hidden at her family's country estate, to avoid reliving any part of the nightmare.

A maid entered the ballroom and stood at Lily's shoulder. "Coo, that's right beautiful."

"Thank you."

"Lady Cardmore said to fetch you. The tea is served in the drawing room."

"I'll clean my brush and join her as soon as I can."

The maid curtsied and left. Another smudge appeared on the apron Lily wore when painting. Lily shook her head as she removed the garment, leaving it on a chair. Tea would be nice, but she wanted to finish this before she returned home to Langston Grange.

She made her way along the corridor and stopped at the open door of the small family sitting room. No Emily. Perhaps she was in the formal drawing room, closer to the front hall.

As she came to the head of the stairs, she heard voices. Who was with Emily? She didn't usually entertain guests, not in her condition.

Lily cautiously descended and stopped at the door. Two pairs of eyes focused on her, and a gentleman stood and walked toward her, a broad grin on his face.

Her heart stopped. No, it was merely beating so rapidly she could barely take a breath.

"Alastair?"

He took her cold hand in his warm one and raised it to his lips. "In the flesh."

CHAPTER 2

"Instead of staring at each other, why don't you sit down and have tea?" Emily sounded amused.

Lily gathered her wits and complied. She'd forgotten how tall he was, and how devastatingly handsome. His eyes were still that special blue of mature violets, and his straight, aristocratic nose had a thin scar on the bridge. Threads of gray scattered through his tawny hair like sun streaks, reminding her of summer days when they would shed their hats and race to the lake near Langston Grange.

He was no longer the awkward, chivalrous, nineteen-year-old boy she'd last seen, a boy full of swagger, eager to go off to war, while reluctant to leave his first love. He was a man of dignity now, one who held himself like the soldier he'd been for years, even though his smile still set butterflies to wing in her stomach.

Emily handed her a cup of tea fixed exactly as Lily liked it, with two sugars and no milk. Sipping it gave her time to compose herself and to wonder what on earth Major Alastair Kinkade was doing here.

"Your niece has told me you've become quite an accomplished artist." His deep, dulcet tones washed over her, spreading warmth through her body. Lily adored compliments, and one from Alastair was special.

"I dabble. But thank you for your kind words." She searched Emily's face, then Alastair's. "How did you know I was here?"

He averted his eyes and a blush appeared on his cheeks, an endearing habit he'd had since boyhood and apparently hadn't outgrown. When he raised his head, his gaze was on Emily. "You didn't tell her, Lady Cardmore?"

"Tell me what?" A trickle of fear slid down Lily's spine.

Emily's eyes sparkled with glee. "Remember our discussion about the Grand Mistletoe Assembly? I mentioned there was to be an auction of items to support the foundling home."

"Yes."

She took a deep breath and placed her hand on her stomach. "I submitted one of your paintings for the auction, and it was accepted. Isn't that wonderful? Everyone will know what a fine artist you've become."

Lily swallowed as her shoulders tightened. Setting her teacup down carefully, she wanted to jump up and shout, "No." That would be churlish, and she'd embarrass her niece as well as herself.

Alastair added, "I was on the screening committee to judge the items under consideration, and I must tell you, I haven't seen a more detailed, evocative piece than your painting of the two swans on the lake at sunset. When I realized I *knew* that lake and those swans, I sent a note to your niece asking if I might call here, to discover the name of the artist. It is unusual for a piece to be unsigned."

Lily swallowed. "Surely there are more accomplished pieces. As much as I care about young children, I don't think my picture would receive the kind of bids you need." She stood, nearly upsetting her cup. "I must withdraw it."

She'd gone too far, created a scene. Emily's lip trembled as if she'd burst into tears any moment, and Alastair sat frozen in his chair, most likely not knowing what to say. How could she do such a thing to her poor niece? And now, she appeared foolish and dramatic to Alastair, who probably had an aristocratic wife with perfect manners.

The watercolor was not signed. No one need know who had painted it. Without a signature, it was unlikely anyone would purchase it. She'd overreacted once again. Trying hard to calm her racing heart, she swallowed and turned to her old friend. "I apologize. I tend to disparage my work because I know what real art looks like. If you want the painting in the auction, keep it. I hope you won't be disappointed if there are no bidders."

Emily rose, the quiver in her voice making Lily feel even more guilty. "I must excuse myself for a moment. Can you preside at the tea table, Aunt?"

"Of course." Lily reseated herself and offered their guest a plate of biscuits. "She is near her time and tends to be very emotional. I am totally at fault if she's upset, but she'll be fine."

He accepted a biscuit and chewed slowly. Lily forced herself not to sigh. They had once been totally, passionately, sinfully in love, and here they were, both nine and thirty, calmly eating lemon biscuits and drinking tea from dainty Sevres cups.

"Are you still in the army?"

"No, I sold out right after the defeat of Napoleon. I'd been gone so long I was sure my daughter wouldn't recognize me."

"Do you also have sons?" There, she was capable of polite conversation.

"Just one daughter. Constance is my delight, the one who begged me to accept the task of selecting the paintings for the silent auction when I was asked. She thinks I have a discerning eye."

"I had forgotten your interest in art. Are you living in London now?" Damn. She was chatting like a fool, but she feared *he* might begin asking questions she didn't want to answer, and she needed time to devise satisfactory responses.

"I'm staying in the family townhouse while in London. I'll be retiring to my country estate when Parliament ends its session. I am the Earl of Selwick now. Did you not know? My brother died in a carriage accident three years ago."

Lily gasped. "I'm so sorry. I never get to London and am totally ignorant of what happens in society. I hadn't heard."

"I idolized my brother. I always believed I'd be the one to die first, having spent half my life in the service of the king." He smiled ruefully. "What about you? I know you married. I admit I was surprised. I always thought ..."

Yes, she knew what he was about to say because she had thought the same. They would wed as soon as they were of age.

Alastair took out his timepiece and shook his head. "I fear I must depart. Please tell Lady Cardmore it was a pleasure taking tea with her and with you."

"I shall. I'll call a footman to retrieve your coat, hat, and gloves."

She rose and followed him into the corridor, where Gerald, a young footman, already held out Alastair's garments. Eavesdropping, was he? She'd have a word with Emily when she returned.

"It's been a pleasure renewing our acquaintance, Lily." Alastair paused. "May I call you that? As close as we were, it seems silly to use surnames when not in company. Please call me Alastair, but not Pokey, that ridiculous nickname you had for me."

"It's because you always lagged behind when we were riding."

"Perhaps I enjoyed watching your backside."

"You are a devil, Alastair."

"Am I?"

Were they flirting? Oh yes, they were.

She laughed. She couldn't help it. They'd been so young and carefree. The world had been theirs for the taking. Until he, an earl's second son, left for the war, and Lily's father perceived a way to repair the family finances by selling her to a wealthy cit.

Alastair stopped at the door. "Would you be willing to accompany me to the theatre tomorrow evening? I believe they're doing *The Merchant of Venice* at the Theatre Royal on Drury Lane."

"Do you and your wife have room in your box?"

"My wife died years ago. I'm a widower," he said, without emotion, merely stating a fact.

"How heartbreaking for you and your daughter." She searched his face for sadness, but there was none.

"Do you still like the theatre? I'd be honored to use the opportunity to become reacquainted with an old friend."

Theatres were dark, and if they were late, no one would see them.

Most gentlemen of the *ton* had a box, and she could sit back in the shadows. She adored theatrical performances, and he remembered. What would be the harm? She was a widow nearing her fortieth year. She could do as she pleased. Emily was always scolding her for being such a recluse.

Plus, it was Alastair.

"I'd like that."

"Wonderful." He took her hand in his warm one and raised it to his lips. A tingle of heat traveled all the way to her core. Oh my, where did that come from? She'd forgotten how a simple touch could make her hyper-aware of her own body.

Lily remained at the window as Alastair climbed into a phaeton and left.

"Did Lord Selwick leave?" Emily asked from behind her.

"Yes."

"Quite dashing, isn't he?" Emily sat back down to her tea, rang for the footman, and asked for a fresh pot.

"Did he tell you we knew each other years ago?"

"He did, and was quite surprised that you are once again living in your ancestral home. He said he'd lost track of you."

Lily stared at the carpet of snow outside. Tiny crystals hung from tree branches in the square across the street, making it look like a fairy's forest. "I must paint this scene before the snow melts."

"Come, sit. I want to hear about your visit with our guest."

"He's a widower."

"Yes. I've met his daughter. Lovely girl, about to become betrothed."

Lily sat and accepted a fresh cup from the teapot brought by the footman. Emily frowned as she chewed her third biscuit. "I hope you're not upset with me, Aunt. I'm sad I can't attend the assembly and wanted to contribute. I loved that painting of the lake and the mated swans. But I was sure I could persuade you to give me one of your other pieces for my sitting room."

"Of course I'm not angry. Charitable giving is good for one's soul. I hope the painting doesn't languish without a single bid."

"You're too modest. If it makes you feel any better, Papa will recognize the setting and bid on it if no one else does, but I suspect a certain gentleman will be the winner." Emily's sparkle was back. "Shall we invite him to dinner? Cardmore will be returning in a few days."

"Trying to play matchmaker? No need. We're merely old friends, and to that end, I've accepted an invitation to the theatre tomorrow."

Emily squealed. "Tomorrow. What will you wear?"

"My black bombazine will do."

"Absolutely not. I have the perfect gown. You and I are the same height and build, or at least we were before I became a cow. Come. You should try it on in case I need to alter it for you."

"Your sewing is superb, but haven't you a competent lady's maid to do that?"

"You sound like my mother." She swished her skirts. "Come. Let's see if we can transform you from fade-into-the-woodwork Lily Whittington into the vibrant, exotic Lady Lily, sister of the Earl of Langston."

Lily laughed and followed her niece up the stairs. She certainly hoped she wouldn't regret this. Wasn't it long past time to emerge from her chrysalis? She'd be in a theatre, and with luck, no one would see or recognize her. How many people remained who would remember that old gossip about her? Probably none.

They entered Emily's suite, and Lily followed her into the dressing room, telling herself this adventure was taking Emily's mind off her coming ordeal in the birthing chair.

Tomorrow was only hours away and Lily would be out in London society with Alastair.

Be brave.

Easy to say. Not so easy to do.

CHAPTER 3

"*Y*ou look amazing, Aunt Lily." Emily stood back and set her finger alongside her mouth. "Let's see, shall we thread a few pearls through your hair? It would be a lovely touch."

Lily studied her reflection in the glass. Her niece was a talented seamstress, who had made this green velvet dress and a matching pelisse for herself a few years ago. It had only needed a few alterations, which she'd made early this morning. Perfect for the theatre, as Emily had only worn it once at Langston Grange.

"It's been so long since I've been out in Town, I'm not sure how to act," Lily admitted.

"You'll do fine. Remember the plays you enjoyed when the traveling theatrical troupes performed in the village?"

Indeed, but no one from London was ever present. Her biggest concern now was encountering someone who might remember the old scandal, the inquest, the accusations, the whispered words behind fans, and on two occasions, the cut direct by well-known matrons. Only Hannah, Whittington's sister, could be so rude as to raise the subject after more than a decade. Lily did not know what had become of her former sister-in-law. Surely, she was no longer in London.

"I suppose a few pearls wouldn't be too ostentatious."

Emily opened a box where such hair ornaments were kept. Her maid, Alice, made a selection and began threading the pearl-studded combs through the elaborate coiffure she'd created for her employer's aunt.

When Alice finished, Emily handed Lily her scent bottle. "I know you've always loved this fragrance. Papa said you used it sparingly, not wanting to smell like a … hmm … let me see if I can remember his exact words."

Lily nearly choked with laughter, gasping to catch her breath. "I know exactly what they were, and they're not fit for company."

They shared a chuckle, and Lily appraised her reflection in the looking glass once more. She barely recognized herself. Was this Lady Lily, daughter of the late Earl of Langston and sister to the current one? It certainly wasn't Mrs. Whittington, widow of a cit, who had lived in London, but mostly in Oxford, and had kept her sanity by giving free art lessons to village children.

"Are you ready? I believe Lord Selwick arrived twenty minutes ago."

"What? And you allowed me to dawdle?"

"Spencer, our astute butler, gave him a tot of brandy and escorted him to the drawing room, where I'm sure he amused himself by admiring the paintings that adorn the walls."

Lily rose and allowed Alice to help her slip on the pelisse. She picked up her reticule, adjusted her gloves, and followed Emily down the staircase. Lily stopped at the door of the drawing room. Alastair stood in front of one of her watercolors, a still life of fruit in a bowl. Not her best, but her niece loved it.

He turned, and for a moment, time melted and they were both nineteen, terribly in love and anxious for the years to pass so they could wed. As his eyes softened and his gaze held hers, she was conscious of the rapid galloping of her heart and her lungs nearly bursting with air. Then he grinned and sauntered forward, and she almost forgot to breathe again. The boy had always caused a flutter in her stomach. The man made her want to do delicious things she hadn't thought about in years.

"You're still a beauty, Lily." His rich baritone voice stroked her insides like a velvet glove. She trembled and held out her hand. Taking it, he kissed the air above, as was proper. "Shall we depart?"

Making herself concentrate, Lily spoke to her beaming niece. "Send a message if you need me."

"I promise."

Alastair helped her into the carriage and sat beside her, placing his hat and cane on the seat across. He took her hand and held it, all the while peering into her eyes. "Have you been to the Theatre Royal?"

"Sadly, no. I hear it is magnificent."

"Remember when we attended a village production of *A Comedy of Errors*? You laughed so hard I thought you might swoon."

"I adore Shakespeare's comedies. I think I liked that one best because I saw it with you."

"Ah, now you've ensured I shall have a wonderful evening."

They shouldn't be holding hands. No, they should not. Wasn't it lovely that they were? No one would know because they were in the interior of a well-sprung carriage, and when they alighted, they would not do anything to call attention to themselves.

A jolt of fear threatened her peace of mind. She would not allow it. She needed this, a morsel of happiness after so many years of loneliness. When they arrived, she would swallow her trepidation and force herself to look people in the eye. Who would know her? Not one person, she was sure. They'd merely nod and smile because she was on the arm of a well-known peer. They'd probably think she was his mistress.

Let them. I will not deprive myself of this one pleasure.

They were late, and the queue was short. They entered the theatre barely in time to be seated in Alastair's box before the play began. She chose the second row of chairs, not the first, which allowed more privacy. A warm hand grasped her own, sending tiny frissons of heat into her nether parts. The play was familiar. The actors were not, but they were wonderful, and Lily chastised herself for hiding in the country and missing so much of what she once enjoyed. During an intermission, she sat back in the shadows while Alastair left to secure refreshments. If anyone wondered who she was, her handsome companion could tell them. She no longer cared.

How absolutely blasé you've become.

The rest of the play was equally good, and when they wound their way through the crowd on their way out to the street, she stopped as if an icy talon slid down her spine. She'd caught a glimpse of the one woman who could not be here. Or had she? Nerves, that's all this was. Surely it wasn't Hannah.

Alastair acknowledged several friends and seemed unaware of her reaction as he called for their carriage. They didn't speak until they were both inside.

"Are you glad you came?" he asked.

"I am. The play was wonderful." She was in control again.

He took her hand and gently stroked her covered wrist. She closed her eyes and let herself feel the erotic strokes, imagining those fingers elsewhere. When the carriage stopped, Alastair leaned closer.

"I know we've just recently become reacquainted, but it seems like the years have fallen away. May I escort you to the charity assembly at the end of the week? Your niece told me you are reclusive, although I've yet to understand why, but I shall honor your decision if you choose not to go."

She wanted to say yes. She wanted to spend as much time in Alastair's company as she could before returning to Langston Grange. She wanted to savor his expressions, his seductive voice, and his turns of phrase. She wanted memories of him to cleanse the horrors in her past.

Others would be at the assembly, people he knew and who had known his wife. His daughter would be there. No. She couldn't risk being recognized by a dowager who might remember the old scandal.

The evening had been perfect, and here she was, contemplating ruining it by refusing to give him the answer he sought. She shouldn't be churlish. Nothing happened at the theatre. She was being a ninny. She should say yes, say she was looking forward to the assembly.

They entered the quiet house and slipped into the drawing room, away from the prying eyes of the night footman. "Can I offer you a brandy? My nephew's late father put down an impressive cellar both here and at Cardmore Hall."

"I have a better idea." He looked into her eyes as he slowly tugged her glove completely free. He lowered his mouth to her hand, and when his lips touched the inside of her wrist, tingles went straight to her center. His tongue traced a pattern there that nearly melted her knees, then he drew her gently toward him and kissed her.

She'd forgotten what a delicious kisser he was, eliciting murmurs and sighs as the kiss deepened and their tongues entwined. His mouth brushed her ear. "Say yes, Lily. Say you'll attend."

When his lips caressed her neck and feathered kisses behind her ear, she knew what her answer would be.

"Yes. Yes. I'll go." She stepped back and held both his hands. A candle in a wall sconce gave her a clear view of his expression. "I have a caveat."

"And what is that?"

His voice was low and seductive, so she leaned forward until she reached his ear. "You must promise to find a way to kiss me again, exactly like this."

He stood back, his mouth curved in a half smile, his lids half-closed.

"You are still a wild minx, Lily Sinclair. It must be all that glorious red hair."

Only she wasn't Lily Sinclair. She was Lily Whittington, a woman some thought had murdered her husband.

CHAPTER 4

*S*he should have said no. She was too old to be seduced into saying yes with delicious kisses that made her feel young again. Emily would not be attending, and Lily should not arrive on Alastair's arm. So, she would think of an excuse to stay home and remember their kiss as a tender interlude, one of those special moments caught in time that crept into one's mind when least expected, putting a smile on one's face and an arrow in one's heart.

She sighed and ascended the stairs to her bedchamber. She had no maid, but Emily's Alice, doing double duty, had thoughtfully laid out her nightclothes and sat snoring in a chair.

Lily shook her shoulder. "Go to bed, my dear. I can manage."

Alice opened her eyes and stood abruptly. "I'm here to help you undress, madam."

"If you insist. Work on the buttons and unlace me, and I'll do the rest."

When Lily finally got into bed and closed her eyes, she found herself reliving every minute of the past evening. She was smitten all over again, and the wonder of it took her breath away.

In the morning when she awoke, she could still feel the smile on her lips. Dressing in her shift and an old, loose gown that buttoned in the front, Lily made her way to the breakfast room where her niece sat with a full plate in front of her.

Emily set down her fork. "You're awake early. I expected you to sleep longer."

"You know I can't. I'm anxious to finish the still life I'm working on. I'm sure your husband will be home any day now, then I'll be off to the Grange."

Emily frowned. "Did you enjoy the theatre and Lord Selwick's company?"

Lily couldn't keep the smug smile from her lips. "Both were wonderful, if you must know."

"Why would you leave?"

Yes, why would she? This obsessive aversion to London had kept her from many entertainments over the years.

"Lord Selwick asked if I would attend the ball with him. I told him I would. Now I realize I can't. If I accept his escort, there will be gossip—rude gossip on the lips of some, especially after being seen with him at the theatre."

Emily grinned. "I was hoping he'd persuade you. If you're sure you can't allow his escort, you can use one of our tickets, and Papa can take you. Mama still can't leave her sickbed. She'll be happy Papa won't be alone."

"Your mother and I ..."

"Tolerate one another, I know. She's aware you and Papa have a special bond. I insist. You have a painting in the auction. You must see how much it brings. A great deal, I predict."

Emily had always found ways to persuade her to do what seemed impossible. Going with her brother would be perfectly respectable, but then people would realize who she was. Lily loved her older brother, a man who had stood by her in her darkest hour, who had accompanied her to that awful inquest after her husband died and stared at the coroner and the jurors so hard they surely must have been intimidated into bringing a hasty conclusion to the formality.

Her brother believed he owed her a debt, one he could never repay, because it was she who filled the family coffers when Papa gave her in marriage to Whittington in exchange for repayment of debts. What a nightmare that had been. She'd bravely done her father's bidding because her kind, competent, jovial brother didn't deserve to inherit an estate mired in debt. She'd left her home and her friends to become the wife of a drunken fool, shutting out thoughts of Alastair, whom she loved with all her heart and had hoped to marry. That had been the part that hurt the most.

"Perhaps I'll reconsider, as long as your mother doesn't object."

"She won't." Emily finished her toast and rose from the table. "Aren't you eating?"

"I'm not hungry. I'm going to the ballroom to paint."

Lily worked for an hour and finally set aside her paint box. Standing back, she viewed the work from several angles and lifted her brush once again. Were the leaves quite the right color? It was a spring bouquet. At least a few should be lighter.

"I love watching you work." Alastair leaned against the door, one booted leg crossed over the other. His seductive voice carried across the room and wrapped around her like a warm cloak.

"I didn't hear you come in."

"You didn't because I wanted to surprise you." He sauntered in and stood behind her. "This is exquisite work. The detail in the flowers is extraordinary for a watercolor."

Lily set her brush in a pot of water and turned to him. He stood close enough that she caught the scent of a spice. Bergamot? It had a citrus note. She was not familiar with male shaving soap anymore.

He laughed and took out his handkerchief. "You have a dab of yellow paint on your cheek."

He dipped the cloth in a fresh bowl of water that hadn't seen a paintbrush yet and dabbed at the spot near her left eye. She stood still and allowed the gentle strokes to soothe her as Alastair bit his lower lip and tilted his head as if trying to see if he'd missed any spots. "Your gown is spattered. A good scrubbing will be necessary for this frock."

She frowned. "I believe this gown may find itself in the rag bin."

A soft, dreamy expression in his eyes, Alastair slowly moved forward. His lips touched the spot he'd wiped clean. "This isn't an alcove, but I couldn't resist. I always loved kissing you in daylight."

She reached up, held his face between her palms, and pressed her mouth to his, sighing as their tongues twined, and he pulled her against him. His body was hard, as she expected a former soldier's to be, and she tingled everywhere their bodies touched. Breathless, she shifted back, pressed her hand to her lips, and hoped he didn't see too much mischief in her eyes. "I believe you now have need of the hand-kerchief, milord."

"Is the spot the color of the daffodils?"

"No, it's the green of the leaves. It was on my fingertips."

"Perhaps you should do the honors this time."

They giggled like children, and when Lily finished, she emulated his previous actions, planting tiny kisses where the streaks had been. "Would you care to join me in a cup of tea?"

"And forgo all these delicious kisses?"

She sashayed toward the door, winking as she turned her head. "We do have another occasion coming up, do we not? Surely there will be an alcove or an unused room available for perhaps one more kiss?"

"I shall gladly have that tea while we discuss with whom you will be sitting in that alcove."

Oh, she was indeed a minx. Her family had always deemed her wild. They blamed her red hair and her artist's temperament. Even Emily had glimpsed Lily's natural affinity for mischief and pleasure when she had lived briefly with her aunt at the Grange. Alastair said that was what had attracted him to Lily all those years ago—her free spirit in a time when ladies were supposed to be straitlaced and meek.

She stopped at the door of the study to invite Emily to join them. She was not within. They'd take tea alone in the drawing room.

When they were seated, Lily poured.

Alastair leaned forward. "What time should I collect you for the charity event?"

Lily sighed and warmed her hands around her teacup. "I've

decided to attend with my brother. His wife is ill, and Emily said he has been looking forward to the occasion."

Alastair studied the biscuit in his hand and transferred it to his other hand. "I'm disappointed. I won't be if you'll sit with me at dinner and dance the opening set with me."

"I promise."

"We can steal away and find that alcove when we view the silent auction items."

"You are a hard bargainer, Pokey."

"Uh, uh, uh." He shook his finger. "You promised not to use that old ... What was it?"

"An endearment." She grasped his bare hand, and an immediate feeling of warmth engulfed her.

Had it always been like this when they were young and in love? Because now they were old and, dare she say it, on their way to becoming what they once were. His eyes and his kisses told her how he felt. Was he ready to love again? She didn't know when his wife had died.

Oh Lord, she could not bear being heartbroken again. What they'd had years ago seemed to be blossoming. Would it wither and die as soon as he heard the rumors of her old scandal? Would he be disgusted and angry that she risked his reputation and his daughter's by being in his company? Society was cruel to those who broke its rules. A man could survive being seen in the company of the scandalous Mrs. Whittington, especially when she retreated to Langston Grange never to be seen in London again. A marriageable daughter might not. She couldn't risk tainting them. She must put a stop to this budding romance—for Alastair and for Constance—as much as her heart did not wish it.

"There you are, Aunt." Emily walked slowly into the drawing room, her hand at her back. "And Lord Selwick. Are you paying a morning call ... in the morning?"

They all laughed. Everyone knew morning calls were paid in the afternoon. Emily, bless her heart, had saved her from making a fool of herself and stumbling through an awkward excuse as to why the

Grand Mistletoe Assembly might be the last time she'd be seen with Alastair. If he mentioned future engagements, she'd have time to formulate believable excuses.

When had she begun to tell lies?

The night her husband died.

CHAPTER 5

"Say I'm indisposed," Lily insisted. She steepled her fingers as last-minute nerves plagued her.

Emily stood with her hands on her hips, her mouth in a thin line. "Absolutely not. Papa will be here to collect you in two hours, and you are going."

"You don't understand." Lord, she sounded like a servant who'd been caught pilfering the family silver.

"Help me to understand." Emily's voice was softer now, her eyes compassionate. "I know you and Lord Selwick have a history—a romantic one, according to Papa. It looks like the old romance is rekindling. If you remain at home, feigning illness, the spark won't be able to ignite." She rushed over and put her warm hands on Lily's shoulders. "You've been alone far too long, Aunt. This is a chance at real happiness. Please go. I can't force you, but for some reason I can't explain, it feels like this is an important moment."

Lily could only counter that argument by telling her the real reason for her reluctance, and she would risk condemnation and worse. Emily had been a child when the scandal erupted. She'd never been told.

Lily sighed. She would have to attend, despite the fact she'd decided it would be best, after all, to remain at home. "Very well. I shall go, but don't be surprised if I return early."

She hurried upstairs and ordered a bath. Alice placed a dark-red silk gown she'd never seen before on the bed.

"Where did that come from?"

"Milady designed it for herself before she became *enceinte*. She finished it yesterday, making a few alterations, so it would fit you. 'Tis the latest style, with a slightly dropped waist and fitted sleeves. This color will be perfect with your hair."

"I don't know what to say. She just finished it?"

"She also sent her fur-lined cloak with a hood. There's snow on the streets."

Lily's heart was so full she wanted to cry. No wonder Emily had been disappointed when she'd tried to back out. Oh, she was an ungrateful wretch.

She bathed in record time, dressed with Alice's expert help, and was downstairs before her brother arrived. Emily puttered, straightening a fold, adjusting an errant curl in Lily's coiffure, and wringing her hands because Lily had declined the use of many of her offered jewels.

"This isn't a low bodice. The neckline is delicate. I'm wearing your diamond earbobs. Enough is enough."

Lily was enclosed in the floor-length hooded cloak when her brother entered the house to collect her.

When they arrived and were announced at the event, Alastair came forward to greet them and promptly placed her arm on his sleeve. "Shall we promenade? The Pearlers' house is magnificent, and I'm guessing you've never been here."

"I thought you were already seeking an alcove," she teased.

He grinned and leaned down to whisper, "I don't think that will be necessary. I've already spied several clusters of mistletoe placed in strategic locations. I'm confident one will suit our needs."

They wandered away from the ballroom into a corridor where items for the silent auction were displayed. Lily's painting already had a few bids, although an evocative oil painting by an artist whose work she admired had more interest. "I'm pleased to see a work by Adam Buck. His painting should bring a great deal."

"Yours will too."

"You're kind, Alastair."

"And you're modest, Lily."

They examined several offerings, including an exquisite necklace designed by Gustav Pearler himself. Pearler had royal patronage as a jeweler, and his designs were sought after.

Alastair seemed thrilled with the crush. As one of the foundling home's patrons, he said they were hoping to raise enough funds to enlarge the facility, and he'd agreed to oversee it. Lily remembered Alastair had wanted to become an architect before his father purchased a commission for him. Perhaps he could pursue his dream now that he was Selwick.

"I hear the orchestra tuning. You promised me the first dance, and it's always a quadrille."

"Then let's make our way back to the ballroom."

They took their places in line and began the steps. Lily was sure she'd forgotten them, but apparently her feet had not, although one of her partners was clumsy and tromped on her toe. When it ended, Alastair led her to a vivacious young woman who had several ladies around her. When Alastair approached, she grasped his hand. "Papa. Just the person I wanted to see."

"Constance, may I present Lady Lily Whittington. Lily, this is my daughter."

"I'm happy to meet you."

"As am I to meet you." Constance peered into her face. "Papa said you were a dear friend. I daresay he should have said a beautiful, talented, dear friend."

"Thank you for your kind words."

Alastair whispered in his daughter's ear, making her eyes sparkle in merriment. He excused himself and led Lily back to where the Earl of Langston had been sitting. The chair was empty.

"Are you hungry?" he asked.

"No, but I am thirsty." The quadrille was one of the livelier dances in the musicians' repertoire.

"Then let's find a glass of champagne."

They made their way to the dining room, where a lavish buffet had been set out. Stuffed mushrooms, vegetables soaked in butter sauce, trifle, a pyramid of marzipan—Lily nearly drooled in anticipation. If she ate her fill, she'd never fit into this lovely dress again. Not that it mattered. She'd leave it behind when she left. At Langston Grange, she would have no place to wear it.

When Alastair grabbed two glasses of champagne from a passing waiter, he and Lily toasted the success of the event and sipped the cold beverage. "If you don't mind, I'll find the ladies' retiring room."

"While you do that, I shall peek into the chambers beyond the dining room to find that perfect space we promised each other."

She winked. "I'll be right here when you've finished your perusal."

Lily followed two women who were ascending to the next floor. When they entered a bedroom set out for use by ladies with various needs, she withdrew behind a screen and examined the dark blemish on her left evening slipper left by her foot-stomping partner in the quadrille. Not too bad. Alice should be able to remove the spot.

She put the slipper back on and reentered the main room. Two ladies stood before a looking glass.

One turned and gasped. "You!"

Lily froze, afraid to move or speak.

The chatter fell silent as Hannah, her late husband's younger sister, bared her teeth. "How dare you show your face in polite company. You're nothing but a whore who enticed my brother into marriage and murdered him in his own bedchamber. How did you get an invitation? Did you bribe someone? You've hidden yourself away so long I was sure God had punished you by now, and yet here you are, all decked out like a real lady. You belong in a brothel with the other trollops."

Bile rose in Lily's throat as she turned toward the door, brushed past shocked faces, and ran into the corridor.

The strident voice followed her. "And where's your high-and-mighty brother? Here to protect your arse like he did during the inquest?"

Lily stopped. She needed to find her backbone. She couldn't let Hannah win.

She straightened, turned, and marched back into the room full of shocked faces. "Think whatever you like, but don't you dare voice your foul complaints in a public setting. Your brother was drunk. He stumbled and fell, hitting his head against the stone hearth, exactly as I said at the inquest. He was not murdered, and I was found not guilty. Take care whom you tarnish with lies in the future." Despite her brave words, her hands trembled.

She stomped out and rushed to the ballroom. Her brother was nowhere to be seen, nor was Alastair.

Air left her lungs, and she swayed on her feet. She had to leave. Now. She couldn't stay here another minute.

She hurried toward the front door. Eyebrows arched, a footman in full livery quickly opened the door as she rushed past. The icy cold slapped her in the face. She surveyed the snowy walk and the carriages lining the street. How would she get home? She couldn't walk in Emily's dancing slippers.

"Milady, do you wish for your cloak? I am happy to fetch it for you."

She took deep, steadying breaths, and nodded, giving the footman a description. He left her there on the steps leading to St. James's Place. When the door opened again, it was Alastair with her cloak.

"What's happened? I saw you hurrying toward the door."

"I need to go home. Now. Please find a hackney for me. No need for you and Constance to go."

"Constance came with her best friend and her friend's parents and is staying with them tonight."

He called for his carriage, and when it arrived, he bundled her inside and climbed in beside her. Lily shook, not with cold, but with remorse. She'd ruined everything. She shouldn't have come to London. She should have stayed at the Grange.

Sobs she could no longer hold back escaped, and Alastair placed his arm around her and drew her close. He said nothing, which she greatly appreciated, and when the carriage stopped, he helped her inside.

"Where ... where are we?" Lily spoke through gulps of air as he led her upstairs and into a sitting room with a blazing fire.

"This is my home." He removed her cloak and sat her in front of the fire, then he knelt and took off her wet slippers.

Lily curled into the settee and thrust her fist in her mouth.

"I'm going to get you a brandy." He left and returned with a bottle and two crystal glasses. He splashed brandy in each and put one in her shaking hand. "Sip it slowly. If you're not accustomed to it, it will burn your throat."

He sat next to her as she sipped and drew her head to his shoulder. "As soon as you feel better, tell me what happened. You're safe here, and there will be no interruptions. My staff is extremely discreet."

She nodded, took another sip of her brandy, and set the glass on a nearby table. It was long past time to face her past. Alastair deserved to hear the entire story, even though afterward he might never want to see her again. She looked into his eyes and let the horror flow through her, the memory as real as if it were happening in the moment.

CHAPTER 6

FIFTEEN YEARS EARLIER ...

*J*ack Whittington stumbled into the bedroom, slammed the door, and ripped off his coat, cravat, and waistcoat, dropping them on the floor.

"Cowering under the covers, are ye girl? You think hiding in your room will save you from my attentions? Ha! I paid well for you, my dove, and I expect a vigorous romp tonight."

"You're drunk again, Jack. Get out."

"Now, now. Don't get all high in the instep with me, wife. You may be a well-born lady, but 'twas my blunt that saved your precious home, what's it called? Ah yes, Langston Grange."

He shed his boots, shirt, and his trousers and spread the bed curtains wide. "There you are, but what's this? A cotton night rail? You know I want you bare as a new babe. Take it off or I'll rip it off."

Lily climbed out of the bed, clenching her jaw, and stood in front of her husband. She would fight him tonight. When he was thoroughly foxed, he usually had trouble in his nether parts and blamed her. He was rough and rude, having grown up on the docks before making his fortune as a shipping merchant, but he'd never struck her. But there was always a first time.

She sniffed the air, recognizing brandy and something else unfamiliar, something sickly and sweet. "Where have you been, Jack? 'Tis almost sunup."

"None of your business. Just shed that gown, so I can get to work."

She slid by him and ran to the fireplace, warming her cold hands in front of the grate. He came up behind her and pulled her into his body. She felt no telltale sign of his lust, shuddered, and took a deep breath.

"Why don't you lie down, Jack, while I warm myself in front of the fire. There's a draft in this room." If he complied, he'd be snoring in a trice, and she could slip away to a guest chamber.

Instead, he grabbed her long braid and loosened the end, spreading her hair over her shoulders. "I love all these red locks. A fiery, passionate redhead. That's what I wanted. Not the cold fish you turned out to be."

She turned then and faced him. "You stink of rum and whatever else you took. Go to bed and leave me be."

He lashed out with his fist, and she ducked to avoid the blow. Instead of connecting with her face, his fist swept through air. He lunged back toward her, and she pushed him, throwing him off-balance. His head hit the stone fireplace with a thud, and as Lily staggered to her feet, he fell to the floor, a loud crack disturbing the silence of the night.

"Jack?" She knelt beside him.

His eyes were wide open and his mouth in a scowl, as if cursing her for all eternity. Blood seeped from behind his head, staining the floor and the hem of her gown. She leaned down to listen to his chest, her hands in his blood. No heartbeat.

She screamed then and ran out the door, calling for the servants. Breathing in gasps, the room spun and a white haze descended. When she woke, she was in a guest bedchamber, her blood-stained nightgown still on her body, her ears attuned to the maids whispering nearby.

"She killed him all right. Ain't nobody gonna believe it, 'cause she's the sister of a toff. But she did it. Blood all over her and him naked as the day he was born."

* * *

As LILY RECOUNTED HER STORY, she remained as still as a statue, afraid to breathe.

Alastair rose and topped off her brandy glass, handing it to her. "There was an inquest?"

"Yes. Jack's sister accused me of murder. She'd spoken to the maids, who said they'd heard harsh words and shouting. My brother attended. The twelve men called to be jurists found me innocent, and the coroner made the pronouncement. Hannah's never let me forget it. She told everyone in the ladies' retiring room tonight that I was a murderer and my brother had somehow bribed the coroner and jurists into letting me go free."

Alastair took her face in his warm palms and gazed into her eyes. "Why did you marry him, Lily? Why didn't you refuse?"

"I wanted to, but the estate was in shambles. Father had gambled away all of his funds and was in declining health. He'd sold or wagered away the hunting lodge and the unentailed farms. I love my brother. He didn't deserve to inherit a disaster, nor did the staff at the Grange deserve to lose their homes and their livings."

She placed her own hands over Alastair's warm ones. "And you hadn't returned for me on my twenty-first birthday, as we'd planned."

He wrapped his arms around her waist and lifted her onto his lap. "I tried to get leave. It was denied."

She rested her head against his heart.

"I sent a letter, explaining," he said into her hair.

"I received no letter, unless Father destroyed it. I ... I thought you were dead until my brother's wife informed me of your marriage."

His arms tightened. "I never really understood what Shakespeare meant by star-crossed lovers until now."

They sat entwined, not speaking. A clock somewhere in the house chimed twelve times.

"I'm feeling better now. You can send me home and return to the assembly."

"Must I?"

She raised her head and looked into his face. Amusement turned solemn as heat filled his deep blue eyes, and his mouth lowered to hers. Lily shuddered at the touch of his lips, afraid to unleash the passion that had been building between them. When he opened his mouth over hers, she was lost.

Blinding heat consumed her as clothing fell in heaps around them and his hard body met her soft one. Whispered murmurs of endearment fueled gentle kisses in places she'd never imagined, and she strained for more, her breath coming in gasps as strokes of velvet made her heart beat faster. And when the delicious pressure built to a searing crescendo, peace filled her senses and mingled with the lingering scent of bergamot, the taste of brandy, and a feeling of sensual joy that at last they had come together and become one.

The reality was so much more than what she'd imagined years ago when they'd playfully explored their sensuality, mindful of becoming too carried away, knowing they skirted propriety and dared fate with the risks they took. They'd even talked about an elopement, angry because their parents had forbidden their marriage until they were of age.

Now they were adults engaging in what they should have had if fate had been kinder, and oh, it was worth the wait. Boneless and content after an hour of mindless pleasure, Lily closed her eyes and drifted into a dreamless sleep.

When she awakened a short time later, she found herself in a large bed, her beloved beside her, his breathing deep. She rose and tiptoed to the window, noting the darkness outside. If she was careful, and quiet, she could slip away. Events as lavish as the Grand Mistletoe Assembly did not end until almost dawn. No one would find it strange when she let herself into her niece's townhouse. The trick would be to find a hackney at this hour. She had no idea where Alastair's house was located.

Leaving her corset and various petticoats behind, Lily fastened her gown the best she could and wrapped herself in the hooded cloak. She clutched her reticule and made her way to the front door. A night porter was on duty, and she stiffened her backbone and confronted him, as if a woman leaving the premises in the wee hours of the morning was a common event. "Would you be so kind as to find me a hackney, young man?"

If he was flustered, he gave no indication as he bowed and went outside. He returned a short time later and graciously assisted her into the coach. She gave the coachman her direction and prepared a story in case Emily was awake. Oh Lord. She hoped Emily hadn't needed the physician. If she had, she would have sent a note to her father.

No one was about when she arrived at Cardmore House, with the exception of Emily's night footman, who knew she'd been out.

"Good evening, or should I say good morning?" She greeted Miles and climbed the stairs to her chamber. She'd been told to awaken Alice, but she would do no such thing.

After removing the gown, which was half-unbuttoned in the back, she took the rest of the pins out of her hair, put on her wool night-gown, and crawled into bed. Sleep would not come soon. When it did, she was sure it would bring absolute contentment and a sense of peace.

Alastair had given her a gift beyond measure—a new, delicious memory to take out and relive again and again in the coming years of loneliness. He had made love to her despite her confession. Most likely, he would not want her to leave, and yet she must. Hannah was still in Town and appeared to now move in the best circles. She still told anyone who would listen about Lily's scandalous secret. Alastair had a daughter who was about to become betrothed. Society was cruel. Association with a scandalous woman could jeopardize the girl's engagement. As much as she loved Alastair, she could not do that to him and his daughter.

She would leave, and she would remind herself each day that she had done the right thing.

She did not deserve happiness, because Hannah was right. She *had* killed her husband, and the guilt would be her penance for the rest of her life.

CHAPTER 7

*L*ily wandered into the breakfast room early and found Emily already seated. Her plate was piled high with kippers, eggs, and toast.

"How can you eat all of that?"

Emily swallowed. "I'm eating for two, remember. Did you enjoy the assembly? I wanted to stay up and hear all about it, but I fell asleep in front of the fire. Spencer awakened me and called Alice to put me to bed." She leaned closer. "You can tell me now."

Lily sat at her place and asked the footman for coffee. "It was quite a crush, and Pearler House was magnificent. I daresay the organizers of the event were pleased. I have to guess the proceeds from ticket sales and the auction raised a good deal of money for the foundling home."

Emily sat forward in her chair. "Whose bid won your painting?"

"I'm not sure. There was so much going on I didn't follow all of the proceedings."

Her niece made a face. "I'm truly disappointed. Perhaps Papa will know. He sent a note saying he's calling here sometime this morning."

Lily squirmed. "I see." She gulped down her coffee, nibbled her toast, and excused herself.

"You've hardly eaten, and I wanted to ask you about Selwick. Did you dance with him? Can I hope you two became closer?"

"Indeed we did. Dance, that is. And yes, we became much closer." Too close, but her niece must never know.

Emily clapped her hands. "I knew it. Your old romance has been reawakened."

Lily forced a smile and dashed upstairs. She must pack and be ready to depart when Cardmore arrived. The weather had not worsened. He should arrive today, and once horses were changed, she could be on her way home.

What of Alastair?

If she was lucky, Alastair would realize the folly of their coupling and be happy she'd left without a fuss.

A brisk knock on her door startled her. She opened it to find Spencer.

"I do beg your pardon, madam. There is a gentleman to see you. Lady Cardmore is not available. Shall I put him in the drawing room?"

"Who is it?"

"Lord Selwick."

Of course it was. She'd left without a note or message. He'd be making sure she got home safely. If only she could remain in her chamber and plead a headache. *Coward.*

"I shall be right there."

If she explained carefully, Alastair would understand why she had to leave. Their chance at happiness died twenty years ago. He must think of Constance.

Lily glanced in the mirror as she passed it, tidied her hair, and smoothed a wrinkle in her gown. She wanted to appear settled, confident, and strong. Taking a deep breath, she stood up straight, and went down the stairs.

Alastair stood with his back to the door, his boots shined and not a hair out of place. Just hours ago, she'd run her hands through that hair while he pleasured her. Her knees nearly buckled at the memory. Best to finish this before Emily appeared.

"I should have left a note."

He turned, his gaze holding hers, daring her to look away. "Why did you leave? I told you to awaken me. I wanted to see you home."

"You seemed so peaceful. I didn't want to disturb you. Your night footman was quite helpful. I do hope he is discreet."

"All my servants are discreet. I pay them well. Now why don't you sit so I can as well. I'm sensing we're going to have a row."

"Why would you say that?"

"The butler said you are packing."

Lily sat in a chair off to the side. Alastair pulled his chair in front of hers, close enough that their knees were practically touching, as Emily breezed into the room.

"Lord Selwick. I am delighted to see you."

Alastair stood. "If you wouldn't mind, Lady Cardmore, I need to have a private conversation with your aunt. Would you be so kind as to leave us and close the door?"

She frowned and stared at Lily as if waiting for some kind of signal.

Lily nodded. "It's quite all right. This won't take long."

"Very well."

Alastair sat and took Lily's hands. "I'm here for a purpose. I love you, and I want to marry you. This has nothing to do with last night. If that had never happened, I would feel the same."

She swallowed past the tightness in her throat. "This isn't only about us. Society can be malicious and unfair to anyone who breaks its rules. I have to go, not for you or for me, but for Constance, your kind, beautiful daughter, who will suffer if you marry me. My scandal will tarnish her. I can't let that happen."

"You did nothing wrong."

"I killed him. I pushed him, and he fell. If I had not, he might be alive today."

"You pushed him away to protect yourself. No one can blame you for that. You're not at fault, Lily. Stop feeling guilty."

"That's easy to say. I've lived with this for so long I'm not sure I can dispel it. Guilt feeds on the soul, consuming it bit by bit until nothing is left. I don't know if I have a soul left to give, even to you, someone I love."

He stood and paced, hands behind his back, stopping in front of her.

"Don't assume I don't know what you mean, because I do. I decided to propose to my wife three days after I learned of your marriage. She was my parents' choice. When she died, I felt the same kind of guilt you experienced. I should have been a better husband. Instead, I devoted myself to my regiment. My wife was fragile, and I neglected her. If you think your actions killed your spouse, then I killed mine, too."

He dropped back into the chair and grasped her hands. "Marry me and give our love a chance. If Hannah or anyone else confronts you again, I shall shout the truth about Whittington. I shall not let him hurt you or anyone else from the grave."

"And Constance?"

"Constance will be fine. She's strong—stronger than we were at her age. She's had an offer she wants me to accept, and unlike our parents, I won't make her wait to wed. The young man is a second son, as I was, and is in the foreign service. He's being posted to Lower Canada, so they will live there. Even if the old scandal was revived, it won't touch her there."

"And you? The worst tongues would say you married a murderess. Your colleagues would look at you askance. You'd be a laughingstock. Especially now as there were at least four women present in the ladies' retiring room who heard Hannah's accusations."

Alastair rose and crossed his arms. "You're making excuses now. If you don't want to marry me, say so, and I'll end this and leave."

She filled her lungs with air and willed her throat to let enough air through to speak. Raising her eyes to Alastair's beloved face, she swallowed twice. "I cannot marry you."

"Fine. Enjoy the rest of your life in the country." He turned and strode from the room. He didn't even slam the door.

Lily put her hands on her face and let silent tears seep through her fingers. She would not wait for Cardmore to return. She would hire a coach and leave immediately.

The door quietly opened and closed. Emily, no doubt, coming to comfort her aunt. When she raised her head, it was not Emily. It was her brother.

He handed her a clean handkerchief and led her to a sofa. "I met Selwick on his way out. I gather you refused him."

She sniffed and stared at her brother. "How did you know?"

"He arrived on my doorstep early this morning. I was barely awake when he demanded an audience. I greeted him in my private sitting room in my robe. He said he'd come to secure my blessing, even though both of you were long past the age for such a requirement." He placed his warm hand over her shaking one. "He loves you, sister. Quite madly. He says he always has. I remember your relationship of years ago. I never knew you'd discussed running off to Gretna Green when Father refused his offer."

"Too much time has passed. We missed our chance. It's too late now, given what happened to Jack."

"I know now what you gave up for me—yes, me—was a great deal more than I realized at the time. What Father did to you was monstrous, only to assuage his guilt so I wouldn't be left with nothing when he was about to die."

"We've been through this."

"We have, and it's my turn to urge you to accept Selwick's offer. You deserve to be happy. It's long past time."

"I want to. Believe me, but I prefer not to contaminate him by association. I'd never forgive myself if anyone treated Constance unkindly because of me. Remember what happened to your wife. She, too, suffered because her husband's sister had been accused of murder. That's why I cannot accept. My broken heart will eventually heal."

"I heard about what happened at the ball last night. I also know a few things have changed since you last encountered that horrid creature, Hannah."

Lily blew her nose. "What have you heard?"

"Her husband—the one Jack found for her—has a mistress he's kept for years and several offspring from that union. Which is probably the reason our malicious madam has taken to drink. Oh yes. She's as bad as her brother was, and while she married a title and still has enough wealth to be invited everywhere, she's not liked, merely tolerated. A few facts placed in well-connected ears would ruin her, and she knows it. There's also talk about a certain necklace that went missing from a house party, one which she hosted. I can't prove she was at fault, but I'm as ruthless as she is if it saves my sister from a lifetime of loneliness."

"No, do nothing on my behalf. I can't be responsible for creating any more unpleasantness. Promise me."

Her brother nodded. "I have conditions. You won't leave until Cardmore returns, and you will reconsider. If you still choose to hide in the country, I'll support your decision."

CHAPTER 8

The snow had stopped by mid-afternoon, and only a light dusting remained on the ground. Wind howled through the trees outside, thrashing tree branches and denuding them of their few remaining leaves. Lily gazed out the drawing room window, the turmoil outdoors echoing the restless unease plaguing her peace.

Stay. Go. Spend her days pouring her soul into her art. Or make a home for the man she'd always loved.

She'd given herself endless reasons for remaining in the country. All seemed reasonable and well thought out at the time. Avoid the place where a horrific experience had occurred. Stay away so the old scandal would die and her brother's family wouldn't suffer at the hands of mean-spirited people with long memories.

These had been excuses, she now realized. It was shame that consumed her spirit and left her without hope. And cowardice had kept her away.

How did she let that happen? She'd been rebellious as a young girl to hide the pain of parental neglect. Alastair had been the stable, tempering element of their relationship. When he left, she'd tried to be more orderly, more settled. When he didn't return as expected, she'd been devastated and depleted. She'd meekly complied with her father's demands.

Five years of abject misery. Five years of conforming to her husband's idea of how she should behave or else be forbidden to see her brother's family. When Jack died, she'd waited for some kind of divine retribution, a punishment for pushing him away. It had come in the form of loneliness.

Did it have to go on for another two decades? Both her brother and Alastair believed Hannah's outburst at the assembly was an isolated event created by the shock of seeing her, that it would not be repeated.

Was it time to forgive herself and move on with her life?

Another gust of wind rattled the panes and blew a tree branch against the window. Something green seemed to be caught in the barren twigs. Was that mistletoe? She and Alastair hadn't kissed under the many mistletoe sprigs at the charity ball. Not that they needed them.

Making a quick decision, she called for her heaviest cloak, penned a quick note to Emily, and flew out the door. Buffeted by wind, she loosened the sprig and huffed back into the house. "I need a hackney, Spencer. I regret having to send a footman out in this cold, but I have an urgent appointment."

"There will be one just two streets over, madam. I'll send Gerald."

When the hackney arrived, she had no idea what street to tell him, so she ordered it to Pearler House, which was not far from Alastair's. She remembered passing that residence when she'd returned to Emily's from Alastair's home. The gaslights had been ablaze, and stragglers had been coming out. When the coach reached the next street crossing, she got out and walked until she found Alastair's house.

A surprised butler announced her and led her into the drawing room. She removed her cloak and clutched the mistletoe sprig as she halted in front of a painting—the one of the two swans, mated for life, on the lake near Langston Grange. Alastair had been the successful bidder.

"It's us, you know."

She turned, and there was her beloved, smiling, as if he knew why she was there. When he opened his arms, she ran into them, the feeling of peace she'd been searching for all day finally sweeping over her.

This was right. This was where she wanted to be. Now, and forever, safe in the arms of the man she loved. When his lips touched hers, she let the mistletoe drop from her hands.

Time healed, hearts mended, and love endured. She should stitch that on a sampler, because it was true. Held tightly in Alastair's arms, she was finally free, and she and her beloved would spend the rest of their lives being grateful for the Grand Mistletoe Assembly where they'd found each other once again.

AFTERWORD

If you enjoyed this story, you might like others in this series:

My award-winning novel, Scandal's Promise, featuring Lily's niece, Emily Sinclair, and Andrew Quigley, the Earl of Cardmore, as they learn to love again after years apart.

Emily also appears in Scandal's Child, another award-winner, where former lovers, victims of a cruel hoax, find their way back to each other.

SCANDAL SERIES

- Scandal's Prequel
- Scandal's Child
- Scandal's Bride
- Scandal's Promise
- Scandal's Deception
- Scandal's Redemption

MISSION BELLES SERIES

- Shadow of the Fox
- Return of the Fox

CONTEMPORARY SERIES

Check out my Love in Wine Country Series by clicking books on my website. Six novels and five novellas.

Books that make you fall in love, over and over again.

www.pamelagibsonwrites.com

ABOUT THE AUTHOR

Author of eight books on California history and twenty romance novels, Pamela Gibson is a former City Manager who now lives in the Nevada desert. She has a bachelor's degree in history and a master's degree in public administration, but her passion is and always has been writing.

Having spent three years messing about in boats, a hobby that included a five-thousand-mile trip in a 32-foot Nordic Tug, she now spends most of her time indoors happily reading, writing, cooking, and keeping up with the antics of Ralph, her Siamese rescue cat.

If you want to learn more about her activities go to Pamela Gibson - Author of Romance Novels and Historical Fiction (pamelagibson-writes.com) and sign up for her blog and quarterly newsletter.

SURPRISING CAPTAIN DAVIES BY JEMMA FROST

Spice Level 🩶🩶🩶

CHAPTER 1

NOVEMBER 18, 1820, LONDON, ENGLAND

he stranger desired her.

Bryony Chapman knew it to be true from the odd intuition that came with dreams. Reaching out a hand, she tried to touch his shoulder, to make him face her so she could identify him, but the air became molasses, slowing her movements.

"Sir?" The word refused to be spoken—had she lost her voice?

But the man must have felt her presence behind him because he turned around, revealing himself to be none other than Captain Nathaniel Davies, her brother's best friend. The man who'd occupied all of her girlhood fantasies.

"Nathaniel ..." Again, no sound filled the space between them, but he smiled anyway as if happy to see her.

He desired her.

As she did him.

But then his visage transformed into a far less welcome sight. Oscar. Her dead husband.

Except it wasn't truly him. Garish fangs filled his mouth. A menacing gleam shone in his sunken black eyes. Hideous laughter erupted as his clawed fingers lunged forward, scratching at her hair and skin.

No! No!

She tried to run away but her feet were frozen, the molasses turned to ice with no escape in sight.

No! No!

"No!" Bryony shot awake from the nightmare with a yelp, sweaty tendrils of hair sticking to her forehead while her blankets lay tangled between her legs. The morning sun peeped through her closed bedroom curtains, and she flopped back to her pillow with a groan, leftover fear slowly abating to be replaced by frustration.

Another restless night.

Another dream turned nightmare.

All because of those cursed paintings.

One would think all vestiges of her late husband's affairs had been eradicated years ago after his death. Once the appropriate amount of mourning time had passed, Bryony had ordered his possessions to be locked away in the attic, forever out of sight and unable to plague her with painful memories.

Until last week.

An industrious maid had found the key to an old, locked closet and found five miniature paintings Oscar had commissioned for his mistress. How the man could still taunt Bryony from beyond the grave truly astounded her. But she would have the last word this time. Tonight, in fact.

Her evening plans, the Grand Mistletoe Assembly, provided the perfect solution for ridding her home of the paintings once and for all. They would be auctioned off for charity, and the proceeds would help the foundling home.

Bryony could return home free of the cursed things. She couldn't wait.

Her lady's maid, Nancy, knocked on the bedroom door before peeking inside. "My lady, are you all right? I heard a shout."

Flushing—this was the second time this week Nancy had caught her shouting after a nightmare—Bryony dragged forth an expression of calm. "A spider ran across my slippers," she fibbed. "Or so I thought. Turns out it was just a trick of the light. Shall we prepare for breakfast?"

The girl nodded, apparently accepting the explanation, and retrieved a morning gown from the armoire as Bryony stretched her arms high overhead before easing out of bed. "Mrs. Healy said everything's set for this evening. She removed the wax stain with a hot coal wrapped in a rag. I'd never heard of such a thing, but it looks good as new!"

"Excellent! Please thank her for me."

Since the charity ball centered around the holiday season, Bryony thought it fitting to wear her favorite gown for the evening—an emerald masterpiece made of velvet. Thank goodness her housekeeper's knowledge of stain removals knew no bounds. The imperfection she'd found on the back hem yesterday had almost been enough to convince Bryony that attending the ball would be foolish.

Who knew what gossip would arise when the paintings were unveiled? She'd weathered the lowered voices and curious stares when her mourning period ended and society events were open to her again. Navigating another round of censure didn't rank highly on Bryony's list of Town activities.

Her brother Carter was attending. He could be her proxy. No, she was done letting Oscar—or his ghost—control her actions. She'd attend the charity auction, head held high.

Bryony's emotions might range from disappointed to furious during the auction, but at least she'd outwardly appear put-together. A fashionable benefactress. A cool-headed widow, whose only concern was raising funds for orphan children, not fretting over nosy busybodies or exorcising another demon from her marriage.

But how many more must she slay to be free? However many it took as penance for her ill-fated choice in a husband, she supposed.

"There. Do you need anything else, my lady?"

Interrupted from her maudlin thoughts, Bryony shook her head and followed Nancy downstairs, cursing her foolish decision to marry Oscar all those years ago.

She'd fancied herself in love with the man. Handsome and close to her in age, he'd brightened every society event and made her feel seen, beautiful. Something sorely lacking in her life. Too chubby to be fashionable. Too mousy to be claimed a Diamond of the First Water. Those were her attributes. Those were *not* what potential suitors wanted.

Except for Oscar.

She knew better than to hope Nathaniel would suddenly declare his undying affection for her, so Oscar seemed like a reasonable substitute. They liked each other, which was more than could be said for most married couples of the *ton*. Her parents excluded.

Of course, she'd be the product of a rare love match. Seeing the affection between her mother and father had given her unrealistic expectations. Well, unrealistic once she fell in love with Nathaniel—a man out of her reach due to his friendship with her brother. A dashing captain who could have any woman he wanted, instead of the infatuated younger sister of his best friend.

So Bryony married Oscar.

Unfortunately, the affection between them had lasted as long as their honeymoon in Italy before Oscar began dallying about Town with other women. Her husband preferred variety in his life, propriety and marriage vows be damned.

The breakfast room welcomed Bryony with its golden sunlight filtering through the curtains. It encouraged happy thoughts and positive emotions, items she struggled to find at the moment, stuck as she was in the past. She'd spend the morning pitying herself, but tonight …

Oh, tonight!

She'd rejoice in ridding herself of the evidence of Oscar's infidelity. Perhaps she'd even take advantage of her widow status and flirt with the bevy of attractive men sure to be in attendance at the ball.

Too plump?

Too mousy?

That was the old Bryony.

Now she was Mrs. Bryony Chapman, an experienced young woman, determined to finally live life out of the shadows.

CHAPTER 2

"*T*ell me again why my attendance is required tonight?" Captain Nathaniel Davies's gaze traveled over the heads of the charity ball's patrons much like he used to observe the officers under his command aboard the HMS *Silver*. Towering over most men of his acquaintance, his extreme height proved useful at times like these—when he desperately sought escape from the crush of London society.

"Bryony will be here." Lord Carter Matthews searched the crowd for his aforementioned sister. The Matthews family had accepted Nathaniel into their fold years ago after he rescued their only daughter, Miss Bryony Matthews, from drowning in a neighboring lake. Now it felt like they were more his kin than his own flesh and blood.

Except for her. Lady Bryony Chapman née Miss Bryony Matthews. Unfortunately, he'd never been able to view her as a sister. A mere year younger than him, Bryony had blossomed into a beautiful young woman around the time he began noticing such things—a damn inconvenience when her brother, his best friend, had decided they needed to chase every skirt in London. Nathaniel's interest lay solely with one particular skirt.

"She attends multiple events, I'm sure. What makes this one so special?" He finally caught sight of her sensuous curves as she lingered near a columned doorway, and he pointed her out to Matthews.

Clearly, Nathaniel wasn't the only one itching to flee the crowded ballroom. Bryony didn't look like she was especially enjoying the party. Tension tightened the skin around her mouth and eyes. An aura of indecision hung about her—perhaps debating should she stay or should she go?

"You've been away at sea so long, you missed her entire mourning period. This is her first Season out since Lord Chapman's demise, and while she's kept busy attending balls and musicals, this one's different because of the auction. There's talk about the paintings she put up for sale. Apparently, they're domestic scenes by Adam Buck ..."

Nathaniel's expression remained blank. "And suddenly, we're all agog about watercolors? Buck's talented but not worth an evening of suffering through matchmaking mamas' effusive efforts to introduce their daughters to me."

Matthews chuckled, well aware of his esteemed friend's reputation. Dashing and blessedly unmarried, Captain Davies's exploits at sea filled the society pages. His daring pursuit of Spanish galleons. His monumental capture of a French ship hauling barrels of the rarest wines. Everyone loved to whisper about the prize ships Nathaniel had ensnared during his time with the Royal Navy, and the wealth it entailed. Mamas and papas alike wanted to snag the bachelor for their family coffers, along with the prestige he would bring to their bloodlines.

"Buck's not the center of gossip. The subject of the paintings is ... Lord Chapman's mistress, Mrs. Alicia Lott, not my sister, *his wife.*" Matthews spared a telling glance Nathaniel's way before greeting Bryony as they finally reached her position at the edge of the ballroom.

"How's my favorite sister faring this eve?"

"I'm your only sister, dear brother." The ringlets framing her face shook with a jerk of her chin, though a teasing smile hovered on Bryony's lips. Sweet, kissable lips. Acutely aware of his thoughts spiraling into indecent territory—would their pretty pink deepen to cherry red from his mouth?—Nathaniel directed his attention else-where, spying a messy altercation between a young lady and a male servant.

Decorated in food remains, the poor woman resembled the carrots strewn at her feet, the orange of her dress fitting rather nicely with the ruined vegetables. Yes, this was a much better distraction than ogling Matthews's sister.

"I was just telling Davies about the items you put up for auction. Have you perused the bidding since your arrival?"

A melancholic shadow darkened Bryony's eyes, deepening the brown to the color of roasted chestnuts. "No, I haven't, and I don't intend to. The funds raised—however crass it may sound—don't matter to me. The paintings' departure from my life isn't hinged on any monetary value. I just want them gone."

"I understand." Matthews patted his sister's shoulder.

Nathaniel must have missed more than Bryony's mourning period if Matthews was speaking so calmly about the late Lord Chapman's infidelity. If Nathaniel had known ... Well, even now, his fists clenched in anger, itching for a chance to beat some sense into the idiot lord.

Matthews stepped forward. "I'm going to complete my social duty before checking on the items for auction. If no one's bid on yours yet, then I will, and they'll be transported directly to the garbage heap. You won't have to deal with them again. Davies, would you stay with Bryony while I'm gone?"

"I hardly require chaperonage."

"Nevertheless, you shouldn't be alone in your emotional state. Davies?"

Nathaniel nodded, observing the stubbornness in his friend's stance—he wouldn't leave them be until they agreed to his edict. Not that it was a hardship being bound to Bryony's side, but it did require a certain amount of willpower to keep his desire in check ... along with curbing the temptation in his fingers to trace the column of her neck so deliciously on display to him.

"It's been ages since we've spoken, Lady Chapman," he said,

uncomfortable with the silence left between them after Matthews's departure. "Aside from the loss of your husband, which appears to be not much of a loss at all considering tonight's drama, how have you been? Widowhood treating you kindly?"

A flush imbued her cheeks with a red glow as she huffed in annoyance. "We're at a holiday ball where I'm auctioning off the paintings my dead husband commissioned for his mistress. Does it sound like I've been treated kindly thus far?"

The Bryony he'd known prior to her marriage had been polite and a tad stiff in his presence—a genteel lady careful with her manners. This show of frustration intrigued him. But he couldn't afford to be intrigued.

Buxom with rich auburn tresses, Bryony's attractions were never in doubt, but the barrier of her innocence and propriety had kept Nathaniel at bay. As did her familial relationship with his best friend. However, a luscious widow with experience of the world, who scored him with her sharp tongue ... Well, he wasn't quite certain his loyalty to Matthews was enough to chain his desires.

And what sort of fair-weather friend did that make him?

"At the moment, no," he admitted. "But once you're relieved of the paintings, the night may take a turn for the better." A terrible idea entered his mind. A terrible yet wonderful idea. "In fact, I know exactly what you need. A place we can go where you'll be able to act as you please with no social recourse. Where you can exercise your widow's freedom without reprisal. If you dare ..."

He must be absolutely mad to suggest such a thing. Especially as her escort.

Bryony's head tilted as she studied his carefully composed expression. Her gloved arms crossed beneath her chest, hoisting the generous mounds of her breasts higher. "Are you proposing we leave the ball together? To go where?"

"This isn't the only holiday event occurring tonight. There's another less ... *restricted* party being hosted by a friend of mine at Berkshire House." Only a ten-minute walk away.

Logic warred with his instincts. Nathaniel knew he shouldn't press, knew he should tell Bryony to forget he'd mentioned anything. He should find other acquaintances to act as a buffer between the two of them. But something in his gut goaded him into continuing, and Nathaniel never ignored his gut. It had saved his and his men's lives countless times at sea.

"We could stroll down the street, and if you don't find the party to your liking, we'll return here to Pearler House with no one the wiser."

"Including my brother."

"Precisely."

She nibbled her bottom lip. Jovial music began playing, and couples gathered for another dance. Nathaniel prepared himself for her refusal and almost suggested they join the men and women on the dance floor instead.

But then her hands bunched in her skirt, her slippers shuffling backward through the doorway behind them. "Excuse me for a moment." And like a shot from one of his ship's cannons, she abandoned him in the ballroom to fly down the hall.

He was a damned imbecile. What did he expect from a lady of class? He prayed she didn't cry to her brother over his inappropriate advance.

Nathaniel tugged at the bottom of his jacket in frustration and darted out of the ballroom as well, searching for respite. And a drink. Perhaps something to calm the nagging sense of disappointment pricking his skin. Pricking his heart.

CHAPTER 3

*D*id that really just happen? Had Captain Davies—the long-held man of her dreams—proposed a scandalous jaunt about Town together?

And Bryony ran off like a complete ninny in response.

She groaned in embarrassment as she entered the women's retiring room and headed straight toward the privacy screens set up in the rear, avoiding the floor-length mirror, where a couple of ladies stood examining their gowns and coiffures for the slightest aberration. Once hidden away from prying eyes, she collapsed into a feather-tufted chair, and shock gave way to burgeoning excitement.

Nathaniel's challenge spun in her mind like ice skaters on the Serpentine River. Years ago, it'd frozen over, and she recalled the multitude of people converging together, slipping and sliding over the ice. Her knees had wobbled with every push forward, while Carter skated circles around her. The same feeling of dizzying delight shot through her veins again, more intense than anything she'd experienced before.

Could she accept Nathaniel's proposition? Should she?

Society allowed widows certain freedoms, a fact he'd happily pointed out, and Bryony desperately wanted to explore her newfound independence. But was it wise to do so with a man of Nathaniel's caliber? A former naval captain renowned for his risky exploits at sea as well as whispers of sensual prowess among the women of the *ton*?

Of course, she didn't possess an excellent record when it came to choosing men. She'd loved Oscar once upon a time—believed they'd live happily ever after—only for that dream to disintegrate into a million little pieces after discovering her husband's propensity for affairs.

But Nathaniel wasn't Oscar. He didn't propose marriage. Just an opportunity to venture into another side of society. A glimpse into the kind of woman she could be if she dared take the risk.

"It's not as if following the rules has done me any good," Bryony muttered to herself. Why shouldn't she leap at Nathaniel's offer?

Her dream from earlier played in her mind, and she wondered if perhaps it was a sign—her subconscious encouraging her into Nathaniel's arms. Those brawny arms were still imprinted on her memory from when he'd rescued her from the lake all those years ago. When he'd held her tightly to his chest. When her infatuation with the man had cemented itself in her heart.

"How dare you show your face in polite company. You're nothing but a whore who enticed my brother into marriage and murdered him in his own bedchamber. How did you get an invitation? Did you bribe someone? You've hidden yourself away so long I was sure God had punished you by now, and yet here you are, all decked out like a real lady. You belong in a brothel with the other trollops."

The vitriolic words tore Bryony's attention away from Nathaniel as she peeked around the privacy screen. What in the heavens? Never in her life had she witnessed such a dramatic scene, and Oscar had provided quite some competition.

Two women faced off in the center of the room before the accused raced out the door, only to return a moment later when her attacker lobbed another insult.

"Think whatever you like, but don't you dare voice your foul complaints in a public setting. Your brother was drunk. He stumbled and fell, hitting his head against the stone hearth, exactly as I said at the inquest. He was not murdered, and I was found not guilty. Take care whom you tarnish with lies in the future." Standing tall, the woman exited the retiring room with the grace of a queen who'd sternly put her subject in place.

Gossip erupted as ladies rushed to the red-faced woman, who glared daggers after her adversary.

Bryony had been sequestered in the country mourning for too long. She didn't recognize either woman and couldn't recall a murder trial with a lady as its main defendant. She didn't think she'd ever be grateful to Oscar for anything, but she supposed him breaking his neck while haphazardly riding his horse was a boon, after all. No one could accuse Bryony of murdering him—no matter how often she'd angrily entertained the idea. Thank goodness for small favors.

Somewhere in the manor, a clock chimed the time. It was now or never.

Determination invigorating her muscles, Bryony exited the retiring room, hurrying past the furious woman who'd cast murder accusations, and searched for Nathaniel in the crowd of guests. She caught a glimpse of Carter's ginger head bent toward a laughing debutante and headed his way.

"Pardon me, may I steal my brother for a second? I promise to return him soon." Not waiting for a response, Bryony dragged Carter to a secluded corner of the room. "Have you seen Captain Davies?"

"Isn't he supposed to be with you?" Carter retorted. "I expressly remember telling you two to stay together."

"And I recall you were supposed to come back after checking the bids for Oscar's paintings. Yet I find you flirting instead."

A reluctant chuckle conceded her point as Carter scratched the back of his neck. "Sorry, sis. Miss Portia required assistance, and one thing led to another and—"

"It's all right. You're free to do as you wish." As was she. Which was why she needed to find Nathaniel. "But I must speak with Captain Davies. Do you think he's gone off to smoke or drink in the card room? Could you check?"

Perhaps she'd waited too long. Perhaps he'd found another woman to accompany him this evening. Her belly twisted in nerves as she cursed her impulsive flight of fear. If only she'd stayed—like a mature widow rather than a prudish young chit—and accepted Nathaniel's offer forthwith.

"My, you're quite frantic, aren't you? Decided to finally confess your girlhood infatuation in the spirit of the holiday?"

Saint Nicholas himself could have appeared at the ball toting gifts for everyone, and Bryony wouldn't have been more aghast. "What did you say?"

Carter smirked, tweaking one of her curls. "It's no secret, Bry. You go all calf-eyed over Davies whenever he's near, even if you do try to act unaffected. You're both lucky I know the sort of gentleman he is, or else I would've warned you away from him long ago."

"Does Captain Davies know?" Bryony's poor heart might expire on the spot if he'd been aware of her tendre for him all these years.

"I don't think so. He's not a very good actor either, and I doubt he would've kept silent if he knew your true feelings. Although you were married during part of this time ..." Carter had a speculative look in his eyes, so she pinched her brother's forearm to get him back on track.

Lord, save her from annoying older brothers.

"No need to get violent!" He rubbed the sore spot with a grimace.

"I apologize, but you can't reveal life-changing information without sharing the whole story. Are you implying Captain Davies reciprocates my feelings?" Discussing men with her brother should have been awkward—before Oscar, it would have been. But Bryony was done tiptoeing around subjects.

What if Nathaniel had desired her since that day at the lake, too? She certainly never would have fallen for Oscar. Even back then, she recognized the emotions she held for her betrothed weren't the same as the kind she held for Nathaniel. But a relationship between them had seemed impossible. He was her brother's best friend! A handsome naval captain sailing the high seas! Why would he want her—an unremarkable daughter of the *ton*?

"Why don't you ask him yourself? He's over there." Carter gently turned her to face the windows looking out over Green Park. A man of considerable height leaned against the wall, one arm braced above his head as he observed the view below.

Nathaniel.

"Thank you, dear brother." Bryony started in the captain's direction before pausing. "As a courtesy, I'm letting you know that we'll be attending another party tonight. *Together.* I'm trusting you won't suddenly turn into an overbearing parental figure with this knowledge."

Carter glanced at his friend then back to her and stroked his chin. "I'm trusting you to be careful. You're a widow and finally unencumbered by that wastrel of a husband, so I don't begrudge you an evening of frivolity. But don't make any decisions you'll regret."

"I'll keep your words in mind." Bryony continued toward Nathaniel, sending an impromptu prayer of gratitude heavenward. Carter really was a good brother, even if he wore on her nerves at times. Thanks to him pushing her and Nathaniel together earlier, she would experience an evening spent with her first love, an evening that could herald the beginning of a new chapter for both of them.

With determination quickening her step, Bryony practically ran toward Nathaniel and this new future, unable to hide her enthusiasm for where the night would take them.

CHAPTER 4

*G*usts of white drifted past the glass pane as Nathaniel
contemplated how abysmal this Grand Mistletoe Assembly
was becoming. More like a Grand Miserable Assembly. He'd
downed a tumbler of brandy earlier but failed to find a quieter spot
than the one he currently occupied.

He should leave. Forget attending the soirée at Berkshire House.
Forget Lady Bryony Chapman.

Easier said than done.

"There you are. If you're finished brooding by the window, I
believe you promised me a night of freedom and exploration." As if
he'd conjured her with his thoughts, Bryony's cinnamon scent teased
his nose, her full curves brushing his side.

Straightening from his bent position, Nathaniel noted the tapping
of her toes, the gleam of anticipation in her gaze. Energy radiated
from her pores. "You've decided, then. You'll accompany me to Berkshire House." He had to be sure. Feared he misunderstood her
meaning.

"Yes."

The swipe of pink across her bottom lip left a shining dampness
that Nathaniel greatly wished to taste, but years of discipline kept him

composed. Instead, he proffered an arm to Bryony and guided her toward the vestibule to gather their outer garments in preparation for the winter weather they'd encounter once leaving Pearler House.

"We should find your brother before departing." Though how he'd explain the situation to Matthews, Nathaniel hadn't a clue.

Oh, by the by, old chap, I'm escorting your delectable sister to a scandalous soirée at Lucille Hanover's. Please don't concern yourself as she will be perfectly safe in my arms ... or bent over a chaise ... or pressed into a secluded corner.

A snort of amusement almost burst forth as he imagined the furious shock sure to paint Matthews's face.

Damn, he was a horrible friend.

But Bryony's allure was too strong to resist anymore. His resistance—his resolve to admire her from afar—had unraveled the moment she agreed to his proposition.

"No need. I told him we were leaving before I found you. He's probably returned to flirting with some other young society miss by now."

The attendant retrieved Bryony's redingote, an identical match to her emerald green dress, and she shrugged into the thick wool garment.

"Your brother knows we're departing together? How did he react?"

Auburn brows rose in bemusement. "We're leaving, aren't we?"

Indeed. Perhaps Matthews knew something of Nathaniel's attraction toward his sister, after all.

"So, what should I expect at Berkshire House?" Bryony asked as they stepped outside and passed the carriages lining the street.

Her arm wound through his, and for the first time, Nathaniel allowed himself to imagine what life would be like if she belonged to him. If they were like other couples strolling the pavement. If he were free to warm Bryony from the November chill with the touch of his lips to hers.

"Expect a loosening of societal strictures. Mrs. Hanover is renowned for hosting events where guests are unfettered by rules."

A gasp of delight transformed into a frosty puff in the air. "Mrs.

Hanover! I've heard stories, of course, but to actually attend one of her infamous fetes ... You were right to suggest this outing. It's high time I take advantage of my widowhood by frequenting wicked parties previously closed to me."

"Temper yourself, love. I won't let you run too wild." Unless she ran to him.

"I'll do as I please, Captain Davies." She emphasized his title as if he were a wayward child in need of scolding.

Minutes later, their footsteps—his measured to match her shorter strides—carried them up the stone steps of Berkshire House, and he knocked on the grand entry door before issuing one last warning. "Noted, but know I'm not afraid to dole out discipline when necessary." His palm twitched just thinking about it.

Stubbornness outlined Bryony's features until the door swung open with a sweep of the butler's arm.

"Welcome! Welcome!" Lucille Hanover motioned them into the sparkling entrance hall decked in green foliage to mimic a rustic Christmas, despite it being weeks too early for such decor. But Lucille never followed etiquette; she broke it with nary a thought. "Before you enter my little soirée, the toll must be paid."

She pointed upward where a ball of mistletoe hung above the doorway. Laughter and music emanated from the room beyond, but nothing could be seen until they paid their dues.

Damn and blast! Nathaniel's focus bounced between the mistletoe and Bryony. He'd wanted to show her the freedom afforded a widow, to erase the air of melancholy that surrounded her at the charity assembly, but this wasn't in his plan. Foolish, really. He knew the types of parties Lucille threw, yet somehow, he'd conveniently ignored the price they might need to pay for entry.

"Come now, Lucille. I'm a wounded captain." He rubbed a hand down the arm he'd injured while chasing down a Spanish ship full of armaments, the reason he'd been honorably discharged from the Royal Navy. "Surely, I deserve a reprieve from your silly games. Lady Chapman is new to this world. We mustn't frighten her away yet by forcing kisses."

"I'm not frightened," Bryony piped up from beside him. The hand wrapped around his forearm squeezed harder as he felt the lush curve of her bosom press into his side.

Lucille smirked, and glee sparkled in her eyes. "See? The only one with an issue, it seems, is you, Captain Davies. You're no novice when it comes to my parties. You knew what you were getting yourself and your lady into. Now will you pay the price of admission, or shall I refuse you entry?"

"We'll pay it." Bryony—a previously proper Englishwoman suddenly transformed into a hot-blooded siren—swept forward with determination swishing her skirts before turning to look at him expectantly.

He couldn't kiss her. She was his best friend's little sister.

A best friend who apparently had approved of this little jaunt.

Besides, she was a grown woman who'd been wed and widowed—no virginal miss here.

Her full mouth beckoned Nathaniel. Tempted him beyond restraint. To hell with it. He'd take what she offered him—savor what was being forced on them—and damn the consequences.

CHAPTER 5

*H*appy Christmas. The holiday might officially be weeks away, but Bryony's gift had arrived early. Because Nathaniel's firm mouth was pressed to hers in a real-life kiss. A kiss previously only ever enjoyed in her dreams. Reality was a great improvement.

She dug her nails into the front of his jacket, afraid he'd pull away too soon, retreat before she had enough time to imprint this moment on her heart, her soul—into the very essence of her being. It wasn't salacious. It wasn't fiery with passion.

Instead, it captured her entirely with its simple sweetness.

The beginning of a night beard shadowed Nathaniel's chin and cheeks, grazing her sensitive skin in a delectable slide. Warm remnants of brandy lingered on his breath, and Bryony yearned for more.

Nathaniel eased away with a gentle push to her hips and confronted Mrs. Hanover. "Will that suffice?"

Bryony struggled to regain her composure.

A rigidity hardened his muscles—the cords of his neck lengthening, his shoulders bunching—did he dislike their kiss? Or the fact they'd been compelled to, not out of desire but for a silly parlor game?

"Don't look so stern, Captain. Your lady enjoyed herself as well as you did." Mrs. Hanover's attention dropped lower to below Nathaniel's waist, where Bryony saw a sizable bulge stretched the fabric of his trousers. Elated by the sight, feminine satisfaction bloomed in her belly.

He didn't dislike kissing her at all ...

Another knock sounded on the door as Nathaniel ushered Bryony forward past a smug Mrs. Hanover. Boughs of holly and mistletoe hung from the walls and ceiling while a string quartet played a merry holiday tune. The entire decor centered around the holiday season.

"Mrs. Hanover holds quite a fascination for Christmas, doesn't she? It's not even December yet."

Nathaniel nodded. "With the Season ending later this year due to Parliament, she wanted to take advantage of having everyone in London for an early Yuletide celebration."

"Here we come a-wassailing ..." A trio of young men stumbled by them while caroling to no one in particular, and Bryony covered a laugh at the ridiculous scene.

This party was nothing like she'd ever experienced before. Men and women conversed freely, touching each other in open flirtation. The rules of society didn't apply here among the married or widowed, the bachelors or spinsters who'd reached an age where propriety mattered less than it did as a young miss of eighteen.

"Wise decision, I suppose. It almost inspires me to order the staff at the country estate to begin holiday preparations. Returning to a cozy home of fresh greenery and bowed ribbons sounds delightful."

"You'll start a new tradition," he teased, guiding her around a group of raucous revelers laughing at a companion covered in flour.

"Why, that's bullet pudding! I haven't played in years." Bryony turned to watch another game begin with a bullet placed on top of a mound of flour, which was cut away in slices by each player until the bullet fell.

"Captain Davies! I thought I recognized you! Come join us in a game of Snapdragon." A lithe man in chartreuse waved them over, but

Nathaniel raised a brow in Bryony's direction, silently waiting for her decision.

"Let's go ... I haven't played Snapdragon in ages either." Not since before her marriage to Oscar.

Their marriage had drained her of all fun and spontaneity. Her husband began gallivanting about Town without her, slipping into the house in the early hours of the morning with women's perfume emanating from his clothes. Breaking Bryony's heart each time he ignored her in favor of his mistress. A woman she'd naively been unaware of during their courtship.

"I can't remember the last time I played either. We try not to play with fire on board ships," Nathaniel teased as he guided her through the crowd to a second room.

She wondered if he kept a mistress, too. Wondered if he brought her to galas such as this.

Don't.

Nathaniel wasn't Oscar, she reminded herself for the thousandth time. Truth be told, she trusted Nathaniel far more than she had ever trusted her husband, yet niggling doubt, a consequence of her dreadful marriage, refused to release its clutches on her heart.

"Why, of course. One wayward flame could bring down an entire fleet. Shall we choose our places?" Several bowls of raisins and brandy were set up around the room, and players jostled for a spot around the games. Suddenly, the candles were snuffed, casting everything in darkness.

Mrs. Hanover's clear voice rang above the gasps of delight. "As a reminder, Snapdragon is a game of risk." On cue, each bowl of brandy was lit by a servant, effervescent fires casting dancing shadows on the walls. "Snatch a flaming raisin but don't get burned. I wish you all good fortune."

Nathaniel stood beside Bryony in front of a glowing bowl, while another couple joined them on the other side. She'd never played the game in complete darkness. It added an element of intrigue. Of wickedness.

Heat rose from the flames, but it was the man at her side who warmed her so fully. His level breathing brushed her ear as he crowded nearer. His cologne mingled with the burning brandy to create an intoxicating aroma of man and spice—a heady combination Bryony dearly wished to bottle for herself, for those lonely days when she longed for companionship.

Longed for Nathaniel.

"Your turn," the woman across from her prompted, and a flush of guilt spread over Bryony's cheeks and chest.

Thank goodness for the lack of light. She'd spent too long daydreaming about the handsome captain warming her side rather than focusing on the game at hand. Anxious to shift attention to someone else, Bryony recklessly thrust her hand into the liquid for a raisin and jerked back with a squeal. Pain radiated over her fingertips.

Their compatriots chuckled good-naturedly before continuing to fish for raisins, but Nathaniel immediately pulled her aside, his rough palm cupping her abused hand.

"Foolish woman. Has it been so long you've forgotten how to properly play the game? Are you all right?" He inspected her fingertips under the minimal light cast by the flames of neighboring bowls.

"I'm fine. It only burns a little."

Then it burned a lot—for an entirely different reason. Nathaniel's lips tenderly sucked at the tips of her fingers, licking away the sting of remaining brandy, and she gasped at the blaze of desire brightening his eyes.

"You taste sweeter than I imagined, love," he rasped as his tongue lapped at her skin. "Like sin. Like absolution. Your brother would gut me like a fish if he knew the filthy dreams I've had of you."

"Then I'd deserve the same retribution," she admitted. Her lashes fluttered closed when his mouth traveled to her palm, her wrist, suckling the delicate patch of skin. Breathless with desire, Bryony finally voiced the secret she'd kept locked away in her heart. "Nathaniel ... it's always been you. In my dreams. In my heart. Even when I believed myself to be in love with Oscar, a hidden well of adoration for you remained deep in my soul. Is that shameful? Am I as immoral as Oscar?"

"Never." His fierce denial soothed some of the shame she'd harbored all these years. While she'd been a devoted wife—never once considering breaking her vows with Nathaniel or any other man—Bryony sometimes wondered if she'd been the cause of her husband's unfaithfulness. Wondered if Oscar somehow knew he didn't possess every ounce of her devotion and punished her by giving her none of his.

"Your husband treated you abominably, and if you found a measure of comfort in thinking of me, then no one could fault you. Certainly not me."

Tears threatened to fall, and Bryony glanced upward, blinking rapidly to dispel them. This was a happy moment. A momentous occasion. She didn't want to ruin it by turning into a watering pot.

Uncertainty flashed in Nathaniel's eyes before disappearing behind tender hope. "I may be damned for suggesting this, but ... shall we find somewhere more private to chat?"

Mouth trembling in an encouraging smile, she dipped her chin in acquiescence, eager to explore the mutual attraction they'd finally admitted to.

Their Snapdragon opponents continued playing between flirtation, and it was clear they couldn't care less if Nathaniel and Bryony abandoned them.

Wandering through the dark room to find an equally shadowy hall, one of the door handles finally gave way to Nathaniel's hand. Within moments, they tumbled into an empty study. Bryony held back giggles at the absurd pair they made—two grown adults sneaking around a party like wayward children—but for the first time in years, she was truly enjoying herself.

"What if we're caught?" she asked breathlessly, not caring one way or the other as long as Nathaniel kissed her again. His mouth had driven her to distraction for years, and their brief peck under the mistletoe wasn't nearly enough to satisfy her yearning. Nor were the kisses to her burned fingers.

"What if we are?" His mouth skimmed down her cheek and lowered to her neck. "You forget these aren't your high society prudes. No one here will judge us or spread gossip because it could very well be them who's discovered next."

"Fair point." Tonight's party was leagues apart from the ball they'd attended earlier. Whereas the charity auction remained sedate and full of social decorum, Mrs. Hanover's soirée resembled one of those bawdy paintings of Greek orgies—not that the guests were quite as scandalous, or so she assumed, but they were certainly freer with their favors than the attendees of the Grand Mistletoe Assembly.

"Now if you're done worrying about your reputation ..." He whipped her around to face the desk at the center of the study, and a large hand at her back urged her forward until she was bent over, palms down on the mahogany. Nathaniel leaned down to whisper in her ear, causing wisps of curls to tickle her skin. "... I believe I promised a thoroughly debauching evening."

"Did you?" Surely she would've recalled such a promise.

A devilish rumble of amusement vibrated from his chest at her back. "Perhaps only in my mind. This evening's been a war between what I should do as a gentleman, and what I crave to do as a man. I'm afraid the wicked side of me won out."

Thank goodness.

Anticipation darted through Bryony's veins, her heart beating as fast as a runaway carriage, as she awaited his next move.

The warmth from his robust form at her back disappeared before the featherlight touch of his fingers traced the delicate bones of her ankle.

What was he doing down there?

"I've always admired you, Bryony. Did you ever guess at my secret attraction?" A hand settled on the calf of her other leg. The chill of the room breached the layers of her gown to glide across her skin as Nathaniel steadily pushed the fabric higher. "You were always so prim and proper. And exceedingly beautiful. It frustrated and panged me at the same time, wondering if you ever cared for me—even a little."

"I cared for you too much. That's why I clung to the rules of etiquette. Why I took pains to be unerringly polite," she admitted. Best to lay all her cards on the table now that they were traveling down this path of honesty.

CHAPTER 6

*B*ryony cared for him. *Too much.*

Nathaniel felt like he'd captured the greatest prize of his career, and it wasn't Spanish or French—it was a perfect English rose, his Bryony.

Skimming his lips over the ticklish spot behind her knee, he hummed low in satisfaction. "And now? You've thrown off the manacles of etiquette and politesse in favor of ... What? What do you desire, love? Just a kiss beneath the mistletoe? Or more? So much more ..."

Bryony shivered, whether from the cool room or the heat of his mouth, he wasn't sure, though he knew which he preferred.

"I want everything, Nathaniel. Everything you'll give me."

"Do you understand what you're asking for?" He ghosted a breath over the inside of her thighs, gently spreading her legs farther apart as she draped lower on the desk to accommodate him. "If I taste you ... If I give you what you want, what we both need ... Our friendship will irrevocably change."

"It already has," she whispered through heavy breaths. Something rolled across the desk and bounced off his shoulders, evidence of Bryony's restlessness as she fidgeted under his hands. "Now we know about each other's attraction. Have learned the exact shape and pressure of the other's lips. How can we possibly go back to friendship? Back to both of us living with this hunger buried in our hearts? The answer is we can't. We must see it through to the end."

Nathaniel didn't like that. Didn't care for the idea of anything ending between them.

"If that's the case, then I suppose I must proceed as planned. Tell me, love, have you ever been kissed ... here?" His long fingers slid between her damp folds to rest against the pulsing bud of her sex. The sweet smell of her arousal twined around his senses to settle deep in his gut, then lower to draw a drop of seed from his own throbbing member.

It had been years since he'd bedded a woman. For some reason, the ladies of his acquaintance had stopped appealing to him, his lust reserved for one woman alone. Even if it had seemed hopeless at the time.

It wasn't hopeless now.

A stuttering "no" almost made him shout with joy. It was barbaric. Ungentlemanly. Yet Nathaniel couldn't help the swell of male pride ballooning in his chest. He'd be the first man to drink from her honey, and he intended to be the last.

"Then hold tight, love," he warned, leaning forward to begin the seduction of his sweet Bryony.

A teasing nip here.

A hard suck there.

He kept Bryony on edge, building the tension with each lap of his tongue. He wanted to erase memories of her horrid marriage. Needed to replace every thought of her dead husband.

Until Nathaniel was the only man in her mind.

Until a high-pitched cry of her release echoed in the room. Easing her through the waves of shuddering pleasure, he dropped soft kisses along her center and inner thighs before standing to his feet, tenderly drawing Bryony up and into his chest.

"That ... that was ..." Words failed to materialize in the aftermath of their lovemaking, so he urged her nearer, clutching her curvy form tightly to eradicate any empty space between them.

"Shh ... I know. It's the same for me."

"But you didn't ..." She gestured toward his obvious erection as curiosity sprouted in her gaze. "I could ..."

Chuckling, Nathaniel shook his head. "No, you couldn't. Not right now. This evening's for you, and I don't need anything more than what you've already given me."

They stood together in contented silence, exulting in their new bond, until raucous laughter nearby, followed by the crash of breaking glass, disturbed their intimate moment.

"As much as I love holding you in my arms after all these years apart, perhaps we should return to the party?"

"If we must ..." Bryony reluctantly retreated, though a cheeky grin tipped the corners of her mouth as she grabbed his hand. "The night's still young, after all. Carter's probably still at the auction to ensure I never have to see those cursed paintings again, which means we have nothing but time to enjoy the rest of Mrs. Hanover's unique soirée."

The casual mention of her brother immediately raised Nathaniel's hackles. Somehow, he'd separated Bryony from Matthews, conveniently forgotten their connection, forgotten about his best friend.

Bloody hell. What had he done?

Withdrawing his hand from hers, his fingers flexed, sweat coating the palm. Lust had overpowered his good sense. Years of mounting desire had clouded his good judgment.

He knew Bryony wanted him, too, but how could they be together with Matthews between them? Nathaniel didn't want to ruin his friendship, nor did he want to lose Bryony. Would Matthews truly accept their relationship despite knowing the violent acts he committed while in service to the navy? Despite witnessing Nathaniel's escapades in brothels across the Continent as a young man?

He wasn't so sure.

"What's wrong?" Bryony asked, studying his suddenly stern

expression. She reached for his hand again, but he deftly avoided her touch.

"This was a mistake."

"Pardon?"

"Us." He motioned between them. "We shouldn't have done this. Out of respect for your brother, I should have controlled myself."

"My brother? Carter has nothing to do with us."

Nathaniel gave a harsh bark of laughter. "Nothing to do with us? He's your brother. My best friend. He deserves some consideration."

"Have you forgotten how he practically shoved us together at the charity auction? He basically gave his consent to our relationship when he revealed he was aware of our mutual attraction."

"You may be right, but until I speak with him, we shouldn't be alone together."

He needed to get them out of here.

"What happened to a widow's freedom? Don't I have a say in this?" Disbelief coated her tone, an angry blush suffusing her cheeks.

"I'm doing what's best for you. I want to protect your relationship with Matthews as well as my friendship with him."

"I don't need protecting. Especially from my own brother." She whirled toward the door with a huff.

Bang! The hardwood slammed into the wall as she stomped out of the room. Thankfully, the merry revelers around them were either incapacitated by drink or too focused on their own romantic liaisons to notice the argument brewing between him and Bryony.

He followed her through the hall out to the vestibule, where she requested her redingote before exiting Berkshire House.

Struggling to don his coat while chasing her down the pavement, Nathaniel growled in frustration. "Bryony, stop this madness. There's no need to throw a temper tantrum."

"So, now I'm a child." She thrust her hands up in the air, the snow falling heavier now to cover their tracks toward Pearler House. "I experienced pleasure with you that I never had with my husband, and instead of whisking me to your home for more or declaring yourself hopelessly in love with me, you choose to use my brother as a barrier to our intimacy. Yet *my* actions are under scrutiny."

"Can you please be reasonable?" They were getting nowhere with this line of conversation. The only obvious fact was that they both felt they were in the right and refused to be swayed.

"Fine. Let's be reasonable." Bryony stopped at a carriage he presumed to be hers. "I'm going home. Alone, like a good Christian widow. You can find Carter, since he seems to be your only concern. Good night, Captain Davies."

And with that, she hopped into the carriage and called for the driver to take her home.

"Bryony! Lady Chapman!" Like a fool, he shouted after her to no avail.

How did everything go so wrong so quickly?

CHAPTER 7

Snow splattered across Bryony's chest—a direct hit. Preparing for retaliation, her mittened hands shaped another mound of snow into a firm ball.

"Who threw that?" she shouted into the laughter of her brother and cousins, everyone running merrily about, lost in their own icy battles.

Her broad-shouldered attacker emerged from a copse of trees at the edge of the snow-covered lawn, and Bryony scoffed at the audacity Nathaniel possessed to come here on Christmas morn as if their evening together after the Grand Mistletoe Assembly had never happened.

It had been weeks. Perhaps he'd forgotten.

Unlike her.

Rather than nightmares every night, Bryony dealt with explicit dreams of pleasure, featuring the current bane of her existence— Captain Nathaniel Davies.

"Are you mad?" She launched her snowball at his entirely too handsome face. A volley he easily ducked, to her dismay.

"Your brother invited me, as did your mother. Am I forbidden from celebrating the holiday with a family I've known for years?"

"You are now. A gentleman should know better than to traipse into my family's Christmas festivities after ... Well, you know why you shouldn't be here." Tingling awareness chased the chill from her cheeks as Nathaniel neared. No one else seemed to notice or care about his arrival—too focused on triumphing over their chosen opponents in the snowball fight.

Chaos swirled around them. Snowflakes fell overhead like the softest of kisses while heftier snowballs arced across the sky.

Yet their attention remained on each other.

Crouching to gather more ammunition, Bryony warned, "Leave now or else."

"Or else you'll pelt me to death with snow? I'll take my chances." Nathaniel continued to pace forward, so she tossed the ball in her hand at full force. This time he allowed himself to be hit, though it hardly slowed his footsteps. "I suppose I deserved that ... I've come to apologize. To beg your forgiveness."

"For what, exactly? Because I don't regret what we did. And I swear if you spout more nonsense about Carter and the imaginary barriers between us, I'll pummel you with snowballs until frostbite threatens your extremities." She'd never have described herself as particularly bloodthirsty, but he brought about the fiery side of her— the passionate desire and frustrated rage.

"I don't regret anything except for my behavior after ... our kiss." The polite way of referring to the cataclysmic delight she'd experienced under his hand—or, rather, *mouth*. "Doubt invaded my mind. Fear over losing Matthews as a friend, and more importantly, you losing a brother if he decided to exact his displeasure with our relationship on you, too. There's no logical explanation for my worries. Your brother's always been a good and understanding friend, yet the mind has a way of twisting reality to confirm one's worst fears."

Bryony understood this to be true. Her own thoughts often spiraled into a quagmire of concerns that never came to fruition.

But she wasn't quite ready to forgive him yet. "So you're sorry for how the night ended, but what happens now? Shall we go on our jolly way, pretending platonic friendship as we did before?"

She urged him to say no. Couldn't bear moving backward, retreating behind polite facades.

"Never." He clasped her hands in his, holding them aloft. "I spoke to Matthews this morning, and he agreed to my suit. Bryony, I want you as my wife. Of course, considering your past with matrimony, I understand if you don't wish to marry again. You've been betrayed, and I don't wish to force anything on you that you don't want. However, if you find it within yourself to try again—to trust me with your person —I guarantee you won't regret it. After all, I love you. Have loved you from the moment I rescued you from the lake all those years ago."

It was the declaration she'd dreamed of hearing since childhood.

Nathaniel loved her.

Her. Not particularly special, overly plump Bryony Chapman.

"So, because you love me, I'm expected to just forgive your actions that night?" She stepped backward without a glance—a step he followed to close the space between them. The sounds around them faded to a dull roar as she held Nathaniel's determined gaze.

"No, because you love me, Bryony, you're going to forgive me for acting like an ass. Then you're going to let me make it up to you." Mischief twinkled in his eyes, and she fought hard to maintain a strict expression, though her lips twitched with the urge to grin.

Raising a lone eyebrow, playful contemplation stole into her voice. "*Am* I in love with you?" Another step back. A wintry dance in the snow, the movements known only to them. "You sound sure of yourself, Captain. Arrogance isn't an admirable trait in a man."

Bryony tried to retreat again, but this time, Nathaniel wrapped an arm around her waist and tugged her close, her hands colliding with his solid chest.

"It's not arrogance when it's the truth." He bent his head to her ear and whispered, the hot breath shooting a shiver of heat down to her very core, "You love me, or else you never would have allowed me the liberty of your favors—the spice of your kiss, the sweetness of your honey on my tongue. Some women may gallivant about Town giving their bodies without a thought toward love, but not *you*. Not my sweet Bryony. You forget I know you too well."

"Oi! Are you going to kiss her or not? We're all tired of this game of pretend the two of you've played the past decade. Claim your betrothed and be done with it, man!" Carter's jibe dampened some of her ardor, and she vowed to exact retribution on her brother for interrupting this momentous occasion.

Nathaniel laughed at his friend's teasing, eyeing her in challenge. "Well, what will it be? A kiss to seal our engagement, or do I need to use more ... wicked tactics to earn your consent?"

Bryony promised herself they'd circle back to those 'wicked tactics', but for now, she'd settle for a kiss. By now, her entire family had focused on them rather than playing in the snow. She caught her mother dabbing a handkerchief under her eyes and knew it was only a matter of time before the woman would drag them inside to discuss wedding plans.

"It's fortunate we're not alone. I was prepared to make you suffer longer." The taunt was muffled as Nathaniel finally took her mouth with his, whooping and hollering igniting behind them.

He tasted the same as before—had he downed a nip of brandy to buoy his courage?—and Bryony reveled in the familiarity.

Soon, she would become familiar with more than just his mouth, his hands. She would have the privilege of exploring his sturdy form at leisure after they wed ... or before, if she felt daring enough to sneak away with him once again.

But it was more than just his body that Bryony would learn. For as long as she'd known Nathaniel, a chasm of propriety separated them, one that forbade intimate conversations. Now, they were free to discuss whatever captured their fancy.

He could share about his time with the Royal Navy. Elaborate on the short articles she'd read in the papers. And she could finally feel safe enough to talk about the truth of her marriage. Share what wasn't public knowledge.

"Congratulations! An engagement on Christmas. How romantic!" As predicted, Bryony's mother converged upon them along with everyone else, a large group hug of sorts forming.

Good tidings echoed from her cousins, and a smile of relief loosened the last bit of tension in her body as Carter embraced Nathaniel, grinning like a fool. It was obvious how heartily he approved of a match between his dear sister and best friend.

Nathaniel had worried about nothing. Just as she'd told him. And she'd happily remind him again, when he was making up for his previous blunder.

She couldn't wait.

EPILOGUE

he papers loved the story of a widow falling for the acclaimed naval captain. News articles seemed to print every day, and Bryony found it amusing how much of her life was suddenly on display for the entire world to see. She was used to sticking to the shadows, not drawing attention to herself for fear of prying questions about her marriage to Oscar. But no one cared about her former husband in light of her new dashing one.

They were dubbed the Merry Match of the Season, a moniker Nathaniel liked to make fun of for its lack of originality, but she thought it quite fitting. They were merry, and they were a match. If unoriginal, the name still proved true.

"Reading another gossip column about us, love?" Her husband brushed a kiss over her forehead before settling on the chaise next to her, his strong arm wrapping around her shoulders.

They'd decided to reside in his London home after their hasty wedding, allowing Oscar's heir—a distant cousin—to take over her previous residence. There was no love lost leaving that house behind, for it had never truly felt like her home. Breaking the last tie to that part of her life had been a relief because she didn't want any vestiges of her previous marriage darkening her fresh start with Nathaniel.

"I want to save every piece written, so our children will know what a wonderful love story we had." Besides, if the paper still found them newsworthy after all these months, the least she could do was save each mention.

"The wonderful love story we *have*. And they'll know it's wonderful because they'll witness it every day of their lives." He gently removed the newspaper from her hands and set it on the mahogany table before them. Expertly, Nathaniel drew her legs over his and positioned her body close to his chest. "Why don't we start practicing, hmm?"

"Practicing what, exactly?"

Warm breath bathed her neck in heat before his lips brushed her heart, which beat delicately. "Showcasing our love story with an exhibition of our ... feelings. This will be a private viewing, of course."

"Naturally," she agreed, enamored by the idea.

Nathaniel had changed after their wedding, not in a terrible way like Oscar, but in a sense that he became more himself. He gave his laughter more freely, and a youthful exuberance emanated from him whenever they made love, which was shockingly often. Like now, as his lips trailed over her skin, his fingers dipping beneath her bodice.

He liked to say she surprised him by agreeing to accompany him to Mrs. Hanover's that fateful night, but she wondered if they both hadn't been waiting their entire lives for the moment they could truly be themselves. Waiting for their one true love. To feel safe in evolving into better people—together.

Perhaps she'd ask him later during one of their intimate post-coital discussions, but in the meantime, Bryony would enjoy her husband's kisses. And express her keen gratitude to the Lord for granting her one prayer—to love and be loved by Captain Nathaniel Davies, to call him *hers*.

AFTERWORD

WANT TO SEE BRYONY AND NATHANIEL AGAIN?

Don't miss their appearance in *Earls Prize Curves*, a steamy age-gap romance featuring a curvy heroine and an earl, who also happens to be her friend's father!

THE GARDEN GIRLS SERIES

- Charming Dr. Forrester
- All Rogues Lead To Ruin
- An Earl Like Any Other
- The Scoundrel Seeks A Wife
- A Gentleman Never Surrenders

LORDS LOVE CURVES SERIES

- Earls Prize Curves
- Barons Adore Curves

ABOUT THE AUTHOR

Jemma Frost grew up in the Midwest where she visited the library every day and read romance novels voraciously! Now, she lives in North Carolina with her cat, Spencer, and dreams of stories to be written!

Don't miss exclusive sneak peeks, behind the scenes info, and more by joining Jemma's VIPs here!

THE FOOTMAN'S MISTAKE BY EDIE CAY

Spice Level 🤍

CHAPTER 1

*R*uby Jackson bit back a laugh. This place was flat ridiculous. The Drury Lane crowd had nothing on these people. Even their *clothes* were shiny—satins and silks, not to mention the bits and bobs hanging from ears and necks and fingers. She might have called herself after something precious and sparkly, but she'd never seen anything like the sea of finery in front of her. The *Grand* Mistletoe Assembly, indeed.

Corinthian John put his hand on her lower back and pushed her forward. To all the world, it seemed like a gentlemanly gesture, but Ruby knew when she was being told to hustle her arse. She couldn't stand in the doorway forever, she supposed. Corinthian John's wife had taken ill—probably another babe on the way was Ruby's guess—and Bess Abbott told her to take this invitation and keep her mouth shut. It weren't anything Ruby'd ever done before, nor heard of any of the other girls doing, but if her trainer told her it would be good for her career to go to a party where rich toffs ate good food and drank good wine and called it charity, then so be it.

Lady Andrepont, eyes forward, leaned past her husband, who flanked Ruby's left side, and said, "If you were a male fighter, no one would bat an eyelash at your attendance here tonight. Remember that."

Ruby squared her shoulders. That's right. She wasn't here as a young lady; she was here as a boxer with her sponsors. Corinthian John and Lady Andrepont were siblings, sharing a love of the Sweet Science. Ruby had watched Corinthian John fight all her life, had even hoped he was her father at one point. But there was no way they were kin—Ruby's squarer face and darker coloring were in direct contrast to their narrow features, strawberry hair, and almost translucent blue eyes. People had told her she was pretty, and that boxing was a terrible idea as it would ruin her natural luck. But she was good with her fists, and it was hard to put the sport aside because a handful of people paid her a compliment.

Ruby didn't have a formal education, though she could read. Her accent, Bess Abbott told her, was like broken glass, and it would do her no favors to speak. So, Ruby took it all in. Beauty was every which way, with glittering crystals and glass, a hall filled with candlelight and paintings. Lady Andrepont told her there would be an art auction, dancing, and most importantly, food. She trained so hard these days that her appetite was more akin to the tides—food coming in, but her hunger always surging out for more.

Following her sponsors, they entered a smaller room, full of toffs but not bursting like a newly-stuffed heavy bag as the main entrance hall had been. Two tall, liveried footmen placed trays of food on tables and removed empty ones. One gave her a look of recognition as he retreated. But Ruby didn't care if the servants knew who she was. She could smell the mushrooms stuffed with cheese and breadcrumbs, and her mouth watered. While training, she wasn't supposed to eat cheese, but oh, it was *cheese*. And tonight was a party, so it weren't as if her training regime was that important.

She'd have to wait until she could politely maneuver herself to the food. If there was anything Ruby knew, it was patience. Waiting for an opening in her opponent's guard.

In the meantime, her sponsors promised to introduce her to more members of the Fancy, backers of other bare-knuckled boxers, who might show up for her set-tos, wager on her, and help get her name in papers. But Ruby had another angle at this party—something she dared not share even with Lady Andrepont, kind and understanding though she was—for rumor held that Ruby's father might be here, another fighter held aloft in the esteem of these fine folk. That is, if Ruby was correct about her father's identity.

* * *

"THAT'S HER, I'm telling you." Max stupidly glanced over his shoulder on the servants' stair, as if he could see through the walls and watch Ruby Jackson float through the anteroom.

Roger put his hands up in surrender. "I believe you. But we've a bunch more platters to bring up, and you know Mr. Hastings won't take kindly if we drag our feet."

Max rolled his shoulders and sighed. "Mr. Hastings always thinks I'm dragging my feet. Not my fault I've got these sleepy-looking eyes."

Roger laughed. "Ain't your eyes, mate. You're slower than me grandmother. And she's been dead three years."

Max punched Roger in the shoulder as they reached the landing. The housekeeper, Mrs. Frances, tsked at them. Her tsks were as loud as a goose honking at St. James's Park, but no matter. They knew what it meant—get to it, there's a party on. What else did a footman do but haul things from the bottom of the house to the top and then back again?

They grabbed their next silver platters and headed back up the steps.

"I'm going to try to talk to her," Max said.

"Are you mad?" Roger stopped short on the stairs, almost causing Max to spill his tray.

Thankfully he reacted quickly, and while the food slipped to the side, nothing slid off. "You think she won't like me?"

"I think Mr. Hastings will have your hide for speaking to a guest." Roger shook his head. "Daft bugger."

"She's a guest, yeah, but she ain't a proper, proper guest. She ain't a duchess or nothing. If I seen her in her shift, I can speak to her without an introduction."

"And if she don't like you, she'll knock your domino box down your throat. Don't you remember last week's mill?"

Max and Roger were a pair, and Baron Gregory Stone—a friend of the Pearlers, a member of Parliament, and an unapologetic gambler—took them both to mills. It gave Stone protection and status to have the pair of them at his side, and it gave Max and Roger a chance to watch the fights. Ruby Jackson was currently the undefeated women's fighter, though she didn't have as many opponents as she would if she were a man. Some might say she wasn't respectable, but Max didn't care about that sort of thing. How was that any different from a girl who became a housemaid, or a seamstress? Why did it matter what kind of work you did, so long as you were good at it?

And Ruby Jackson was a stunner. Not just her rabbity-jabs, but she had what the Fancy called *bottom*. That limitless reserve to take abuse and come back to dish it out. Something Max felt they had in common. The last time he'd seen her, she had a fat lip and a bloody nose. Her hair had been braided back, and in the low light of the basement, smelling of sweat and tallow, she'd smiled her triumph right at him. He'd felt her victory, like she had stared right into his very heart and shared it with him.

Roger was the daft one. Max would find a way to speak to Ruby Jackson tonight, no matter what Mr. Hastings would say.

* * *

"So might we ask you how the foundling home is run, since you began your life there?" A pompous, jowly old man peered at Ruby through his spectacles. Lord Andrepont rolled his eyes.

She fought the urge to spit.

Lady Andrepont cut in before Ruby could embarrass herself or her sponsors. "Lord Frederick, have you seen the paintings up for auction? I know your lady wife had discussed refreshing your morning room. Might I suggest we promenade in that direction? I think you'll find the watercolors particularly pleasing." She took the old fart's arm and dragged both him and the scowling Lord Andrepont through a doorway.

"My sister has a knack for managing difficult personalities," Corinthian John told Ruby. "Try not to take it personally."

Ruby shrugged. Her stays were new, firmer than her old ones, and they didn't move with her body. The beautiful deep orange dress—for it weren't red, according to Lady Andrepont—required Ruby to get new undergarments. Her normal stuff was all woolen and lumpy, and this dress was sleek like an otter. The sensation felt completely foreign, and Ruby couldn't figure out if she liked it or hated it. Instead, she blew out a sigh. "I don't fit in here."

The prizefighter gave her a smile, making his face crinkle. Graying at the temples, just muting some of the vibrancy of his red-blond hair, he was still handsome, despite being old. "No one does. Just remember that everyone is pretending."

Ruby fought the urge to pull at her undergarments. Her satin stockings were still tied in place, but damn, they felt as if they'd fall any moment. "Someone fits here. It just ain't us."

"You think I don't fit?" The old fighter huffed, but she could tell he was only teasing.

"You could prolly kill half these blokes with one good jab. The other half, I could."

Corinthian John surveyed the room and the soft bodies it contained. "Ain't saying yer wrong, Ruby."

Ruby barked a laugh. Fighters knew fighters. They knew that strange world full of sweat and concentration. People thought prize-fighters were stupid—being hit about the head and whatnot. But it wasn't true. A fighter had good instincts, saw movements before anyone else, and could read their opponents' bodies and know how they'd fight.

Ruby should keep her mouth shut, but she trusted Corinthian John, despite herself. "I think my father might be here." She leaned away from him, already regretting she'd mentioned it.

The man blinked at her in surprise. "And who is your father?"

Ruby opened her mouth. Then closed it.

"Out with it."

"Daniel Miller."

"Are you certain?" Corinthian John scanned the crowd, then took a few steps to see through the doorway into the main hall.

Ruby shook her head. "Just a hope."

Corinthian John looked at her, not with pity but with recognition. She knew he and his sister were orphans, but they hadn't gone through the foundling home. They'd had family and friends—the Irish were like that, sticking together when they could. But Ruby wasn't Irish—not as far as she knew, anyway. In Ruby's fuzzy memory, her mother had been sick when she'd left her at the foundling home. Ruby was perhaps three or four, and she'd been clutching newspapers that described organized set-tos. Daniel Miller was the common thread in the articles, which made Ruby believe he was her father.

She'd seen him at a distance a number of times, and they shared the same peach-ruddy skin, brown hair, and hazel eyes. Of course, many a person in England could boast the same.

"Have you ever been introduced?" While Corinthian John seemed all business, she could tell he was searching her features for the other man's likeness.

"No, never spoke to the man." Ruby felt all the smaller and stupider for her admission. Should have stuffed one of those cheese-filled mushrooms in her mouth instead of speaking.

Corinthian John turned to her with a smile that lit up his face and made him seem just as impish as his sister, Lady Andrepont. "Then let's rectify that." He grabbed her by the arm and hauled her from room to room, using his height to see over the crowd.

Ruby tried to keep her mouth closed as she inwardly gaped at all the finery. Bloody hell, those were actual rubies dangling from that woman's ears. And the gold! So much gold. Ruby tucked her free hand in close to her waist as they dodged around a couple staring into one another's eyes like love-sick bumpkins.

"You're in luck," Corinthian John tossed back over his shoulder. "There he is."

Ruby followed Corinthian John's gaze to where Daniel Miller was speaking with two men in military uniforms. He had thick features, a square jaw, and a nearly shaved head. His shoulders were broad, making him almost as wide as both of his companions. Could this be her father?

Her mouth went dry, and suddenly, she couldn't manage another step.

"C'mon now," the prizefighter encouraged.

She'd paid attention to her heart while she trained—how fast it pounded when she jumped rope, when she practiced with the sawdust dummy. She calmed it during fights to last longer. But here, in this wondrous house full of beeswax tapers and jewels, her father standing close enough to reach out and touch, it felt like her heart stopped completely, and she couldn't breathe.

She felt the sharp touch of metal on her side, and then a gentle impact on her skirts, like a troop of friendly mice had leapt on her all at once. But surely, there were no animals at this party.

"You fool!" someone yelled.

Ruby's dress clung to her legs, and she felt wet? Drenched in … butter? She tore her eyes from her father to look down at her beautiful, orange satin skirt, now stained dark red, pooled with vegetables in a butter and wine sauce. Instead of the furry mice of her mind, there were limp asparagus and carrots scattered about her.

She raised her eyes to a bewigged footman, his face blanched white. He held an empty tray. Empty because its contents were all over her.

"I'm so sorry, miss. I can't, I mean, I'm terribly, terribly, terribly sorry," the footman stammered.

Another footman wearing identical livery appeared at his side, his expression just as horrified.

Ruby examined her skirts. She smelled like … a very good dinner. But not even the most skilled servant could save either the dress or the food. She brushed off a pea that had found its way into the folds of fabric.

She felt the weight of the whole crowd staring at her. She'd rather peel down the top of her dress for a fight than stand here fully clothed, covered in the dinner menu.

Next to her, Corinthian John murmured, "I'll go find my sister."

Ruby nodded dumbly, and then felt even more ridiculous standing there alone.

The footman began to babble again.

Ruby held up her hand. "The only way to fix this, sir, is to dump the roast beef on next. That way, my meal will be complete."

The shocked crowd laughed, and Ruby glanced over to see her could-be father guffawing.

The footman relaxed his shoulders. "May I show you to the ladies' lounge while you await your …?"

"Sponsors," Ruby supplied, giving a big smile. She picked a few lucky guests—the rich-looking ones—to eyeball as she announced her need of patrons. "I'm a practitioner of the Sweet Science."

The footman didn't show any surprise, though murmurs spread through the onlookers. She risked a look at Daniel Miller, who had resumed his conversation with the two men in uniform. She threw her shoulders back, knowing it would give her the posture of an athlete and not a lady. But this was business, and well, she was covered in butter and vegetables.

* * *

"Are you thoroughly mad?" Roger hissed, while Max did his best to give an elegant gesture to show Ruby Jackson the way to the ladies' retiring lounge.

Max shoved the now-emptied tray at Roger and whispered, "Take that back to the kitchens, please."

Ruby Jackson followed his directions, smelling for all the world like roasted parsnips.

"More than a thousand apologies, miss," Max said as she swept by him.

"A mistake, I'm certain." She slowed, clearly unsure where to go.

"This way, miss." He gestured again with his white-gloved hands.

Pristine and clean, unlike her gown. He couldn't imagine what she'd spent on that frock, and he'd utterly ruined it.

His stomach twisted. He'd been so shocked to see her approaching Daniel Miller, to see two incredible fighters, right there, in the flesh, and he'd stopped short, not thinking of what he carried—and what he carried had continued its momentum right onto the sunset-orange gown. It was a wonder she didn't knock him down right then.

She followed him, holding her dripping skirt off the floor. He was going to need to clean the parquet as well—couldn't have guests slipping.

"I've seen you fight, actually," Max ventured, peering back at her with an impertinence even he cringed at. "Against Nanny Gent."

Ruby Jackson studied him with interest. "What you think about that set-to?"

"I think you got a lot of bottom. You took so many wallops, but in the end, you knocked her out. It was impressive."

"You win any money on me?"

Was she pleased about his admission? About the compliment? "No, my employer wasn't betting on the women's fights. He waits for the men."

Her expression smoothed to one of almost boredom. Probably not the first time she'd heard that. "Next time, tell him to bet on me. And if you do too, you can pay me back for covering me in butter."

Max considered himself an honorable man. He was. Prided himself on how well he treated his ma, his sisters. But when he heard *butter* out of Miss Ruby Jackson's mouth, all he could do was picture her without her frock, covered in it. He almost walked into a column.

"Ladies' lounge is marked there with the potted palms," he directed.

"Don't forget, Mister ...?" She watched him expectantly, all shame erased.

"Vaughn. Maximillian Vaughn." Did he have any spit left? Why was his mouth so dry?

"Mister Maximillian Vaughn. With a name like that, you must have some coin. I'm a safe bet. Bring your paper." Then Ruby Jackson—who knocked out Nanny Gent—who went two hours in her bout with Ann Fielding—*winked* at him before striding into the ladies' lounge.

Max drifted over to the servants' stair in a daze. Ruby Jackson had winked at him. Told him to make wagers. He'd find a way to get the whole bloody world to risk coin on her.

CHAPTER 2

TWO WEEKS LATER

*B*ess Abbott grabbed Ruby's face and held it firm. "You keep
focused, you hear me?"

"I'm focused," Ruby insisted.

"Yer eyes are darting about the room like flies in chicken shite. Pay.
Attention." Her trainer straightened and scrutinized her adopted
daughter Violet, who wasn't fighting tonight. "Oi! Wot you getting up to?"

Ruby took advantage of Bess's distraction and scanned the crowd
again. She could see the Fancy coming together off in a corner. Even
though they tried to dress down, their ragged clothes were too well
cared for to pass as common. But Ruby was searching for Maximillian
Vaughn. She'd said his name every night since the Grand Mistletoe
Assembly. She'd repeated it so often that the other day, Violet had
looked up from her porridge and asked Bess who Maximillian Vaughn
was. Ruby kept her head down, successfully hiding both her embarrassment and knowledge when Bess admitted she had no idea.

Of course, at the ball, Maximillian Vaughn had been wearing his footman's white powdered wig, and Ruby didn't know exactly what he might look like out of uniform, except he was very tall. Was Mr. Pearler the sort to bring his footmen in livery? Not many did so anymore, but that didn't mean it never happened.

Unable to spot him, Ruby gave up and stretched her arms in front of her and then in back, loosening up her shoulders. She cracked her neck from side to side and thought about her breathing, steadying herself against any nerves she might have in meeting Bruising Peg in the ring. It wasn't much to fight for—two guineas to the winner and a pint of gin—but it was more for the chance to say she'd won. To show off her quick footwork and strong uppercuts. To prove that after all that unlucky business early in her life, Ruby could come out on top. She could work hard and win. Even if she worried she'd say something wrong to Bess one day and they wouldn't let her stay in their house anymore. Even if Violet suddenly decided she hated Ruby, at least there was this she could hang on to—she could fight, and she could win.

* * *

"I CAN'T TELL you who, sir," Max insisted to Baron Stone as they descended into the basement. "But the odds are very good."

"You don't make real money betting on small stakes." Stone pursed his lips and let out an annoyed breath. "But if it's a sure thing, and you're betting your own money, I'm willing to listen."

Max grinned at Roger, who kept his distance. They were lumped together, both hired at the same time, both the same height, both second footmen. But after Max's clumsy hands at the Mistletoe Assembly, Roger didn't want anything to do with him. If the Pearlers sacked Max, they might sack Roger too, and Stone might not have the blunt to hire both of them.

"I brought every spare coin I have." Max patted the internal pocket of his own waistcoat. Not wearing livery made it feel less like work and more like he was out on his own; like he was a sort of up-and-coming gentleman who had easy money and free time. When, as a second footman, he had neither.

The room was crowded, and the children's fights were already underway. Two rail-thin boys, all elbows and sharp shoulder blades, swung wildly at each other, not even bothering to check if their fists connected—less technique and more street fight. There were always boys like that. He'd been one himself. But he knew quick enough that he wasn't much for hurting others. Even in the ring, where they were supposed to.

Stone dove through the crowd, not bothering to wait for Roger or Max to clear the way for him. They hustled behind him, jostling away any probable cutpurses, until they arrived at the safety of the Fancy in the far corner of the room. Max recognized many of the members— regular watchers of the fights. Mostly they spoke to each other, backs turned to the rest of the room, footmen guarding their pockets or placing their bets.

Stone put his hand on Max's arm. "Let's hear more about your so-called tip." He hailed Lord Andrepont, who was speaking with a crowd of a few noteworthy men, including Corinthian John.

Max kept a straight face, knowing that Stone had picked the one group of people who would support Max's claim that betting Ruby Jackson versus Bruising Peg was a sure win. They elbowed past the merchants, who never bet on anything but the main bout. As working men, they weren't truly a part of the Fancy, but they were wealthy and had footmen, so they stood nearby, hoping to be welcomed into their fold.

The women of the Fancy, who didn't care to discuss the Sweet Science, stood closer to the wall. Most often they were the aristocrats' mistresses—women who couldn't necessarily go to a public event like the opera, often because they were in the performances—and the sweaty, crowded rooms gave them a chance to be seen with their sponsor of the moment. Behind them hovered the men who had more money than Croesus and more power than Zeus. These were the men who ran the British Empire. And these were the men who had sentenced Max's drunken father to transportation.

While Max should get on his knees to thank them for pushing his father off to the other side of the world, that kind of power made him nervous. Among that group, fighters and former fighters hobnobbed. They were broader than the bluebloods by at least half, their professions writ across their features, in some cases crippling their bodies. Max wondered if that would happen to Ruby. He gazed past the ring where the scrawny boys bled and windmilled their arms, to the back of the room where that night's fighters typically gathered. He could make out her dark hair, braided and pinned away for safety.

His stomach flipped. Would she remember him? Or would she be mad at him for cutting her time at the party short, ruining her dress, and making a fool of her? He winced. Talking to her was a terrible idea.

Stone returned to Max's side, purse in hand. "The Ruby Jackson bet is considered all but a certainty in that corner. Let's see if your information proves correct."

"Shall I put it all on her, or would you like to bet on particular rounds?" Max asked, already knowing Stone's habits.

"Half on the end outcome. Who knows if she'll go three rounds or ten? Let's keep the other half in reserve, just in case."

"Of course, sir." Max took the purse. Even at half the amount, that was still a good return. Max gave Roger a cheeky grin, then waded into the crowd to find the umpire. The boys were almost done, and after they finally gave it up, Ruby would be next. Max needed to get the bets placed before the match to get the best return.

A tall, gaunt man who went by the name of Basil took the coin, and Max made sure the man remembered him to give him his return. Once that was confirmed, Max surveyed the crowd and spotted Ruby bouncing on her toes, trying to keep warm. Bruising Peg was in another area, well over a foot taller. He hoped Ruby knew what she was doing.

Returning to the Fancy's corner, Max crossed his fingers for her—and for himself. If Stone lost half his purse on this, Max would be out on his arse.

"That's her," Lord Andrepont said behind him, no doubt to Stone.

Roger peeked at Max, and Max gave him a confident grin. More confident than he felt. Ruby Jackson made her way up to the raised platform. Bruising Peg did the same on the other side.

"You absolutely certain?" another man asked, his voice low, his accent scratched from the docks. It had to be Daniel Miller.

"She is," Corinthian John said. His accent was easy to spot—even though he sounded all plummy like the rest of the bluebloods, there was something about the way he pitched his words that conveyed imitation, not breeding.

"Let's see how she do against that Amazon," Miller said.

"She's quick," Lady Andrepont said.

Max eyed a street urchin who drifted, too casually, alongside the wealthy. He curled his lip in warning, and the boy skittered away. Basil took to the center of the ring and began spewing his pre-fight nonsense. Hardly anyone in the room took notice, as the next fight was the women's mill. In the next hour, the room would crowd even further, ready for the main set-to.

"I don't see it, mate," Miller said behind Max. "I mean, who'd she say her mother was?"

"She doesn't know," Lady Andrepont said, and Max could hear sympathy in her voice.

"Some chit says I'm her da 'cos she fights? I'm sorry, mate, but that's right daft. I'm not saying she ain't mine, but I can't in my right mind claim her, neither."

"Just watch her," Corinthian John murmured.

The fight commenced without the crowd noticing, and Bruising Peg's long wingspan cuffed Ruby on the ear as she danced away. But Ruby recovered well, shaking off the initial connection.

"Listen," Miller growled.

At this point, even Max was getting upset with the man. Would it kill him to actually watch a women's mill? Ruby danced inside Bruising Peg's reach and delivered a couple of hard blows, causing the larger fighter to fall back, while Ruby danced out of reach again.

Max stifled the urge to turn around and crow about Ruby's prowess.

The fight continued for only a few more minutes, Ruby darting in, delivering blows, while Bruising Peg lumbered about the ring. Then, without warning, Bruising Peg's foot fell through the floorboards.

Bruising Peg's kneeman jumped in front of his fighter to protect her from opportunistic hits. But Ruby didn't attempt any. Basil clambered back in the ring, and Ruby's kneeman came forward as well.

Each of the kneemen were former or current fighters as well— Max could see it in the off-angled noses and the telltale shorn hair. Each had seen his fair share of fights, but where Ruby's kneeman kept the corner tidy, able to keep one knee up and one knee down for Ruby to rest on for those brief thirty seconds between rounds, Bruising Peg's kneeman had to go onto all fours to provide a bench for the tall lady fighter to sit on. Still, both men were up and able in the wake of Bruising Peg's accident, asking questions of each other and their fighters, trying to iron out what happened and next steps.

Bruising Peg cursed and swore. She extracted her leg, and it had a long bloody gash in it. The surgeon was pushed up from the crowd and into the ring, plastering over the cut, but all agreed that the bout couldn't continue.

"She's probably a good fighter, but what do you want out of me?" Miller asked.

"To greet the girl. To see, up close, if she looks like she might be yours. Just give the kid a chance. You remember how it was, don't you?" Corinthian John said.

"I dunno, mate. Maybe next set-to. Night's over, what with the ring in need of repairs, and I don't want to be stuck in this crowd forever." The man shouldered past Max, heading to the doors now that the events had stalled. Max confirmed he was Daniel Miller, the fighter he'd seen at the Mistletoe Assembly as he'd spilled butter and vegetables all over Ruby.

Max's heart went out to Ruby. What was worse, not knowing your father, or knowing he was a right shit?

Stone touched Max on the shoulder. "Get them to refund the purse. Meet Roger and me at the tavern two doors down."

Max made his way to the ring. The crowd would give him an

excuse to talk to Ruby Jackson. His mouth went dry as he elbowed past the merchants, sailors, and tradesmen. What would he say to her?

He found Basil and talked the man into a refund for himself and Stone, promising to renew their bets when the rematch occurred.

Task accomplished, Max continued over to Ruby's corner. He offered a brief smile to the pale little girl who stood there with a sour look on her face. "Excuse me."

A tall woman, whom Max knew from other fights was Bess Abbott, stepped protectively in front of the little girl. "Wot?" Even without her tone, her sheer physicality was a clear threat. Nearly as tall as Max, her face told of the cost of a lifetime of fights, with a broken nose and misshapen ears.

Max's mouth opened and closed, unable to speak.

To his eternal gratitude, Ruby Jackson turned around and recognized him. "Maximillian Vaughn," she said.

This earned him a sharp look from Bess Abbott, and a curious one from the girl.

He bowed, feeling surprisingly clumsy for someone who bowed daily. "At your service. I'm sorry about the default tonight."

"I would have won," Ruby said.

"I know," Max said. "I got Lord Stone to bet on you."

Ruby stepped closer. "Did you bet on me?" Her hazel eyes swirled with all types of colors. Max didn't know his art, but he knew regular-folk beauty, and she had it.

He nodded, his mouth completely dry.

She grimaced. "Sorry I couldn't win you anything."

"Next time," he croaked.

Ruby gave him a faint smile, and a nod as if to dismiss him. But he didn't want to be dismissed. He glanced at Bess Abbott, who was staring. A very large man with very large arms came and stood right beside her. Ah yes. He'd heard the gossip that Bess Abbott was in fact married. The man was a giant. He folded his dark arms, and Max got the point.

"Er, I must be off, but"—he took deep, steady breaths—"well, ah, would you allow me to call on you on Sunday afternoon? It's my only time free."

Bess Abbott scoffed, or maybe she coughed, or maybe she laughed. All Max could hear was a high-pitched droning sound in his ears as his entire body seemed to collapse in on itself.

"Sunday's your free day too," the girl said to Ruby.

Ruby glared at the girl, but then fixed her gaze on Max. She was considering it. "That's all fine, then." Ruby narrowed her eyes, as if he were a type not to be trusted. "Meet you at the Pig and Thistle in Paddington?"

"Paddington?" It wasn't that far from Mayfair, but on his day off, every hour counted.

"Can't manage Paddington?" Ruby taunted.

"I'll be there." Max gulped and backed away, his hands shaking. She'd said he could call on her.

CHAPTER 3

*R*uby poured another draught and hollered at Miz Penny to bring out more pasties from the back. Whatever these people called 'em, Cornish pasties, not-Cornish-just-pasties, it didn't matter. It was a steaming packet of meat and veg wrapped in a pie crust, and Miz Penny could crank them out, delicious and perfect, day in and day out.

Ruby sent the ale down the bar and pocketed the coin in her apron. She glanced at the prized clock over the mantel. Maximillian hadn't set a time to visit, but every tavern knew when servants got their half-days. The crowd should be in soon. Ruby yanked at her dress under the apron, hoping everything was laying right. It was a new dress, or at least, new to her, from one of Lady Andrepont's acquaintances. At least, that's what she'd said, but Ruby would bet all her teeth that not another woman had ever worn this dress. It was perfectly tailored for her, and while it wasn't satin or silk, it was a pretty woolen print in the same deep orange she'd loved so much on her ballgown.

Miz Penny floated out with a tray of pasties, steam venting from each half-circle of pie. To bite into one of these would scald a person from tongue to tummy. But these hungry fools would do it anyway.

Miz Penny pushed off the hot food with her bare fingers and slid them into their appropriate slots for beef, rabbit, and chicken.

"The lad here yet?" she asked. Her fine white hair flew about her head as if it were an angel's halo. She was never flustered, never out of breath. Over the years, she baked, chopped, served, and poured, and took all manner of coin and abuse. If only Ruby could learn the same even-temper.

Ruby eyed the door. "Not yet."

Miz Penny wiped her greasy fingers on her stained apron. "He knows you train?"

Ruby told her he did, that he'd recognized her. It was flattering, really, if she thought about it.

"Then you've naught to worry. He'll be along when he gets a hold of his nerves." Miz Penny took her tray and headed back behind the curtain.

Ruby folded some old newspaper to hold the next few pasties ordered.

"Miss Jackson."

Ruby glanced up, and even knowing he would be there, knowing he wanted to see her, he still surprised her. He was handsome, she could admit that. Especially now, when he wasn't stiffly representing another household. He was himself, shoulders relaxed, dark hair softer, not slicked back with pomade, or worse, hidden under a wig.

"Mr. Vaughn." Before she could think of something witty or kind or interesting to say, her hands were already untying her apron. She could hardly wait to go out walking with him despite the nearly winter chill.

He was still bundled up in his scarf and overcoat, clutching his hat in his hands. "I had no idea you worked here."

"It helps when the fights dry up." Ruby turned and called back into the kitchen, "Miz Penny, I'm done for today."

Miz Penny peeked her wispy head out from the curtain and gave her a wink. "Of course. Have a lovely time, my dear."

Ruby shoved the apron into the basket on the floor and gave Miz Penny a look that let her know Ruby was onto her. Miz Penny hadn't poked her head out to be polite—she'd wanted to see what sort of young man Ruby had ensnared. Miz Penny looked right back at her, as if to say, *got yourself a nice pull in that one.*

By the heavy wooden double doors, Ruby slid on her overcoat and wound her scarf around her neck. Maximillian watched her don her bonnet, his gloves on, ready to escort her outside. Once she pulled on her mittens, he leaned against the great weight of the door and eased himself into the chill.

"Since you've got a few weeks until your rematch with Bruising Peg, I don't suppose your trainer would mind if I plied you with sweets," he said.

Ruby walked past him and paused for him to catch up. "I suppose that would be fine."

"The best place I know that's open on a Sunday is a bit of a walk from here. Do you mind?" Maximillian gestured at the sky, crisp, clear, and windy.

Feeling generous, Ruby leaned toward him a bit. "Part of my training is to do a bit of walking on my off days. So I don't get all cramped up."

"Then it works out," he said. "You get sweets, your trainer gets the walk."

"And what do you get, Mr. Vaughn?" Ruby asked, admiring the people in their scarves and hats pushing against the wind.

"The pleasure of your company." Maximillian puffed out his chest. "Not every day I get to escort London's lady champion."

"Oh, go on now. Don't let Ms. Abbott hear you say that. She's protective of her title."

They walked until Ruby felt her toes go numb, but she didn't complain. She liked hearing Maximillian's stories of service and his antics with his footman friend Roger. So she regaled him with stories of her own about other fighters, and throwing the drunks out of the Pig and Thistle every so often.

Maximillian indicated toward a vendor they approached. "Do you like roasted chestnuts?"

Ruby's eyes were near glassed-over from the chill, and the idea of warm chestnuts sounded heavenly. He paid for two packets and handed her one. They stood against a building to block the wind. Ruby held her packet up to her face to feel the warmth.

"Oh, bollocks, I'm sorry. Are you cold?" Maximillian asked.

"A little? If we keep moving, I'll warm up." Ruby didn't want to complain, but was pleased he noticed her shivering.

He shoved off the wall. "Then let's be off. Sweets await."

By the time they arrived at the chocolatiers, Ruby was frozen solid. But it was worth it, since he'd made her laugh and, in turn, laughed at her jokes. Made her feel downright witty, he did.

They stopped in, had a chocolate so thick and bitter that it felt like it coated her teeth, and he told her all about life at the Pearlers'. She liked hearing about all the people serving a great house as if they were their own sort of family downstairs. And it sounded nice to know that you'd always be warm.

"I suppose I should walk you home," Maximillian said finally. The windows outside the shop showed the gloomy cold day darkening further.

They stood, and he helped Ruby into her overcoat. "Though I'd walk you all the way to Liverpool if you'd let me."

Ruby laughed, pulling on her mittens. "And what about Mr. Hastings? I'm sure he wouldn't want you so far away when he expects you to be up with polished shoes tomorrow morning."

"Hang 'em all."

They walked out of the shop and into the cold. Ruby fought every urge to hunch over against the cold. But she wanted to look at Maximillian Vaughn, who was much more charming than she'd thought he'd be.

He stopped her just in time from walking right into a puddle, though it did look iced over. "Being in service is like this ... You can tell this puddle is iced over, and a part of you thinks, if I step there, my foot will get wet. But it doesn't, because the ice is a barrier between the water and your foot. Living downstairs is like that. My gloves are my barrier. I handle all their things, but not really. I never touch them.

I never touch their plates, their shoes, their luggage. My gloves do. As if no matter how close I get, I'll never touch them."

Ruby studied him for a long moment. "You know my favorite thing about this kind of puddle?"

He gave her a sly grin. "I think I do."

Ruby held out her foot and gently tapped on the ice. She increased the pressure, tapping harder and harder.

Maximillian grabbed her hand to steady her. "Break it open, Ruby."

The ice cracked and splintered below her boot, like a soft-boiled eggshell. "That is ever so satisfying."

"It's like a dream, living there. Not touching anything with my own hands." He didn't let go of her hand, and Ruby made no move to pull it from him. "Can I ask an impertinent favor?"

"Might as well." Her heart leapt to her throat. Would he ask to kiss her here in the street?

"May I hold your hand? Without our gloves? Just so I know I'm not dreaming, because this would be the best dream I've ever had." Maximillian gazed at her, his brown eyes earnest and needy.

Ruby tried to pull her hand away. "These aren't lady's hands, Maximillian. They won't be soft and white and fine. Let's just not."

He didn't let her go. "I know who you are, Ruby, and I know what boxers do to their hands. Does Ms. Abbott let you wear mufflers to protect your knuckles?"

Ruby snorted. "Only in practice with younger girls. It's supposed to remind me to pull my punches, so I don't hurt any of 'em."

"Then would you take off your mittens? Would you touch me with your ungloved hand? My hands aren't fine and soft either. They're calloused and hard from polishing and hauling and fixing and whatever else they have me do."

Ruby stared at her shoes, a lump forming in her throat. The afternoon had been so perfect.

Maximillian pulled off his glove with his teeth, still capturing hers with his other hand. He took his glove from his mouth and shoved it in his pocket. "I see you, Ruby. I want to make sure you see me."

His words felt like a bell, clanging about inside her, rattling her, changing her, not just knocking down her guard, but annihilating it completely. Something about them made her understand how he felt, that need to connect, that desire to reach out, hoping the other person would be there. She acquiesced, and he released her hand. She took off both coverings and shoved them in her pockets, afraid all the while that her hands were shaking.

Maximillian reached out, his hands bare, and she laid hers in his. His thumbs wrapped around her palms and ran along her calluses. "You're real."

Ruby's heart pounded, and she was no longer cold. "So are you."

They stood there like that, staring at their intertwined hands, letting skin touch skin. The hour chimed from a nearby church bell, startling them both.

He laughed and let go. "I suppose that's God reminding us not to dilly-dally."

Ruby blushed and pulled her mittens back on. They didn't say another word all the way back to Marylebone, where Maximillian walked her to the front door of Mr. Worley and Ms. Abbott's home.

"May I call on you again next Sunday?" he asked, his eyes on his shoes.

"I'd like that."

When she said it, Maximillian peered back up at her and smiled. "I'll take you back for more chocolate. Don't tell Ms. Abbott."

The door opened, and the tall prizefighter stood there in the flesh, bare-headed, and wearing a pinafore as if she'd just been cleaning. "Don't tell me wot?"

Ruby shooed Maximillian off the doorstep, laughing. He walked backward down the street, waiting for her to shut the door.

CHAPTER 4

"*A*gain," Bess commanded.

Ruby could barely see through the salty sweat that dripped into her eyes. But she obeyed and hit the straw dummy in the same combination. Left uppercut, right cross, left uppercut, right uppercut.

The rematch with Bruising Peg was in three days, and Ruby preferred to think about Bruising Peg instead of her bruised heart. Maximillian Vaughn had not shown up at the Pig and Thistle on Sunday. And he'd sent no word. She'd imagined the worst—him sick or hurt—but Bess Abbott's thin-lipped grimace and Mr. Worley's inability to meet her gaze at the breakfast table told her what they thought. Maximillian Vaughn hadn't appeared because he didn't want to see her.

Ruby's handwraps were fraying at the edges. She needed to make some new strips; they smelled of sweat and something foul. Something foul, indeed—hope and laughter and roasted chestnuts. She threw random jabs at the straw dummy, unleashing herself with no particular plan.

The world fell away, and all Ruby could feel was the burning of her upper back muscles, sweat, and the tight wound deep inside that Maximillian's absence inflicted.

When Ruby finally exhausted herself, Bess put her hand on her shoulder. "Get some water, girl." Bess's words might have offered advice, but Ruby heard what she meant: *I'm sorry he didn't come.*

Ruby caught her breath. She wanted a small beer instead. She wanted tankards and tankards of beer. She wanted to be one of those loose women who sometimes came into the public house and draped themselves across patrons until someone bought them a drink. The women that Miz Penny frowned at. The women who didn't care if one man rejected her because there was always another.

* * *

Every time Max thought of Ruby Jackson, his mouth went dry, and tonight it felt like every ounce of moisture had been sucked out of his body and put right into his sweaty palms.

"You all right?" Roger asked as they elbowed a path in the packed basement.

There were no boys' fights tonight. Just rematches. It was already overfull of impatient patrons, and no one was in a mood for conviviality. Some nights had an air of liveliness, as if everyone understood it was all just in good fun. Tonight though, tonight was tough and mean and all about money.

Max shook his head. He'd been unable to see Ruby last Sunday, after he'd promised he would. Mr. Hastings had taken ill, and then the first footman took ill, and then half the staff surrounding him fell to whatever was careening through the house. He couldn't even manage to send her a note, what with all the cleaning and washing he was having to do just to keep the men's rooms from smelling like a night-soil cart.

She'd be furious with him, and well she should. If it hadn't been the very worst of luck, he would have been there to take her somewhere. Anywhere.

"Oi, you hear me?" Roger said again, over the shuffling crowd. "You've gone white."

Max shook his head. "Fine, mate."

Roger gave him a concerned look as they deposited Baron Stone into the clutches of the Fancy.

"Same bets as before, my lord?" Max asked.

Stone shook his head as if changing his mind. Max pleaded internally for the man to bet on Ruby Jackson.

Fortunately, Lord Andrepont clapped Stone on the shoulder and welcomed him into the fold. "Should be a good one tonight. Ruby Jackson is faster than any boxer I've seen. Any."

Stone didn't even look at Max as he handed over the small purse. "Same as before, if you will, Max."

Max accepted the purse and made his way to Basil, standing ringside. He spotted Ruby across the room in her corner, swinging her arms, deliberately keeping her eyes on the floor. He willed her to look up until Basil snapped at him.

"You betting or gawking, sir?" the thin man said.

"Begging your pardon. Betting on Ruby Jackson for the win." Max laid both Stone's bet and his own.

Roger shouldered his way over. "And mine, too, if you will."

Max clapped his friend's shoulder in thanks.

"She won't even look at you, mate. If this will get your mopey chin off the floor, it's worth the coin."

"I thank you both, good sirs, as I'm sure the lovely Miss Jackson does as well." Basil tucked the coin into a purse and scratched some numbers onto a paper. "Any specifics?"

Max thought about it. How best could he prove to Ruby that he believed in her? That he thought she was the most magnificent person he'd ever seen in his whole miserable life? "For that small purse there" —Max pointed at his contribution—"put it all on Ruby Jackson to win in the first round."

Basil stopped his scratchings and surveyed him. "That's quite the bet, young sir. I don't normally discourage flights of fancy, but you know Bruising Peg is favored."

"I do. But that's because no one pays attention to a girl like Ruby Jackson. They think she's pretty enough to not be serious, and small enough to push around, but they don't know how fast she is, how smart she is, how perfect she is."

"You wanta lay a bet or propose marriage?" Basil asked.

Max blushed. "Ruby Jackson to win in the first round."

Basil resumed his scratching. "You'll be a rich man if she comes through for you."

"I'll be a rich man if I can come through for her," Max corrected, looking past the scrawny man to Ruby in the back corner. He ached to go to her.

"C'mon, we need to get back," Roger said, pulling at him.

"I should go talk to her." Max couldn't take his eyes off her. In profile she was beautiful, the harsh cut of her nose, the upward taper of her eye. Recalling the animation of her face when she laughed, she was more than beautiful, she was stunning.

"You'll throw her off," Roger warned. "Don't put thoughts in her head. She needs to concentrate."

Max agreed but couldn't help wanting to go to her. To apologize and explain. He'd never willingly be absent from her. He wanted to spend every day with her, and every day that he couldn't made him impatient and sometimes furious.

"Those cutpurses won't throw themselves out," Roger said, nudging Max.

They returned to the Fancy, where Daniel Miller was once again in conference with Lord Andrepont and Corinthian John. The prizefighter was trying to deny whatever Corinthian John was proposing, but Max couldn't hear their words. Given the last conversation Max had overheard, it was likely to do with Ruby Jackson. Max's whole life had revolved around Ruby these past two weeks. If only she'd look at him. He shuffled closer to listen in.

"John, please, we've known each other a long time. How would you feel in my position?" Daniel Miller asked. "I'm not going to say I'm her da on account of newspaper clippings."

Max wanted to turn around and yell at him. What would it cost him to speak to a young woman? Why was it such an imposition?

"I'm not asking you to. What I'm asking is allow me to introduce her to you. No admission, no discussion of involvement. Just meet her. Congratulate her on the set-to."

Daniel Miller protested again. "But—"

Roger clasped Max's forearm, which made Max realize he was tensed into fists. Roger shook his head. He was right. No good would come of Max's anger. All he wanted was for Ruby to meet a man who might be her father. He assumed Ruby wanted this. If her sponsors were insisting, he imagined she did. They might have discussed it on Sunday if he'd been able to go to her. If Mr. Hastings hadn't vomited all over Max's shoes.

Basil jumped into the ring, hawking the fighters to gather more wagers. He managed a few, and then the women joined him on the raised platform. They stayed in their corners, Bruising Peg closer to the Fancy, which meant Max could see Ruby's face.

Both women took their arms out of their sleeves and tied the fabric around their waists. It was clearly a practiced gesture for both women, neither of them bothering to preen and prance the way male fighters did. Max supposed it meant something different if they acted that way. But still, he'd love to see Ruby having fun up there, enjoying the pre-fight as much as she enjoyed the bout itself. Max watched her eyes, hoping she might look his way, but she never lost sight of Bruising Peg, watching her like a hungry dog watches a scrap of meat.

Neither of them wore their stays, and while Bruising Peg's shift was worn thin, Ruby's appeared new. He gave silent thanks to Lord and Lady Andrepont for sponsoring her and giving her what she needed.

Basil screamed for them to toe the line, and both obeyed. It appeared an unfair matchup due to their height difference, given Bruising Peg's reach was so much longer than Ruby's. But, Ruby had done well in the last set-to, if only Bruising Peg's foot hadn't gone through the floor.

Ruby leaned back, all her weight thrown behind her, as if she would dart away as soon as possible. That had been her strategy in the last fight, yet Bruising Peg had still managed to cuff her ear before her retreat had been complete.

Basil rang the bell.

Ruby shifted and near sprinted inside Bruising Peg's reach, pummeling her belly before dancing sideways. Max's jaw dropped. Bruising Peg was already doubled over. The crowd was silent a moment, trying to figure out what they had just witnessed. Ruby darted in again, Bruising Peg not yet righted, and gave her shots to the kidney and kicked her knees out from behind, forcing her taller opponent to the ground.

The crowd whooped and hollered. This was a brutality rarely seen in any set-to, even in the vicious men's fights.

Bare-knuckled as she was, Ruby Jackson gazed straight into Max's corner. Whether she sought Max, or her sponsors, or the man she believed to be her father, Max didn't know. But Ruby Jackson sunk a sickeningly hard facer into Bruising Peg.

The fight was over.

It hadn't lasted five minutes. Men who'd bet on Ruby Jackson clapped each other on the back. Roger cuffed Max on the shoulder in celebration, but Max couldn't move. He couldn't breathe. The fight had been surprising, swift and decisive, no attempts at entertainment, only domination.

It also meant that Max, Roger, and Lord Stone made a large sum of money. A ridiculous amount of money for Max.

Ruby thrust her hands into the air in victory, as Bruising Peg lay prostrate on the floor of the ring, her kneeman trying to revive her. Max threw his hands in the air and hooted. That was his Ruby. Ruby, who seemed less disheveled than when he'd taken her home from a long walk. Ruby, who let him buy her warm chestnuts.

She looked to him then. Really looked, not just in his direction. Max didn't care what his duties to Baron Stone might have been in that moment. He charged through the crowd to get ringside, wanting to celebrate, to congratulate. She watched him approach, her expression turning from triumphant to wary.

He made it to the ring and thrust up his arm in victory. They locked eyes. This was her moment. He knew that, but he also wanted her to know he was there for her. That he wanted not to take it from her, or even share it with her, but rather he wanted to amplify it. Make her triumph even bigger.

She stepped closer to him, the room still a deafening roar, and grasped his hand, thrusting her free hand into the air, letting out a roar of her own. Max let the euphoria in the room subsume him in a surge of victory.

* * *

RUBY HAD enough heat in her body to rival the sun. Although she'd planned to beat Bruising Peg, she felt stupefied. How did such a simple maneuver actually work? She'd managed to not only win but to escape without a scratch. Bruising Peg's men took her up and off the platform, nursing her back to awareness. Ruby let go of Maximillian's hand, still surprised that her gambit had paid off. Basil jumped into the ring to divvy up the winnings, and Ruby drifted back to her own corner, distracted by how long it took Bruising Peg's team to bring her back round.

"That's it, that's how you do it!" Bess Abbott helped Ruby down from the ring, crowing to everyone about Ruby's success.

Violet threw herself into Ruby's arms for a hug.

"You all right, girl?" Mr. Worley asked, his deep voice resonating in her chest. He gripped her shoulder to steady her.

She couldn't think. Someone shoved a small beer into her hand and helped raise it to her lips. The coldness of it helped shake her back into herself. Bess Abbott held her on one side, Mr. Worley on the other. They cared about her. Not just for the money, or the success. They actually cared for her as a person. Behind Bess, Maximillian Vaughn peered down at her, his dark brows coming together.

Bess kneaded her shoulder. "You know, it was you who knocked out Bruising Peg, not t'other way 'round."

Laughter bubbled up inside Ruby. Mr. Worley seemed concerned, but Bess looked relieved.

"There she is." Her trainer stopped massaging, noticing Maximillian lurking nearby. "Oi. Wot business you got here?"

"I wanted to speak with Miss Jackson." Bess didn't move, looking eye to eye with him, and he swallowed hard enough that Ruby could hear it over the din of the crowd. "Please."

Bess put her hands on her hips. "Last I knew, you made a date to see her and didn't show up. Not a gentlemanly thing to do."

Ruby saw the anguish on Maximillian's face. She'd grasped his hand on the side of the ring. She could feel that he was sorry. But then, Bess had a point. Maximillian had not actually apologized or explained his absence. Mr. Worley released Ruby's shoulder, likely so he could hold back his wife if need be.

"The whole household was sick." Maximillian held up his hands, his words tumbling out too quickly. "Really sick. Puking and shitting —oh shite. I'm not supposed to say that in mixed company, am I?" He blanched, his eyes as big as saucers. "But it's true. Mr. Hastings, the butler, he was the worst, and I had to polish his shoes after he—you know—all over them."

Mr. Worley began to chuckle. "Bess, love, that's enough toying with him. The poor boy just wants words. Ruby, do you want to speak to this young man?"

"How do I know he ain't lying to cover his undependable arse?" Bess countered, not taking her eyes off of Maximillian.

"Ask Roger, the other footman. Or Baron Stone. They would never lie for me. I'm not that good of a footman," he pleaded.

"Mr. Vaughn can talk to me if he likes," Ruby said. "I think I believe him." She'd felt the heat in his hand, the emotion in his face as he'd reached for her just after she knocked out Bruising Peg.

Bess moved aside, allowing Maximillian to step toward Ruby and take her hands.

"You were amazing. More than amazing. I've never seen such a decisive fight in my life."

Ruby preened. "Did you make any money off me?"

He grinned. "A king's ransom. So did Lord Stone. And Roger, too. But I made the most."

"Because you bet the most?"

"Because I bet everything I had that you would put her down in the first round." He squeezed her hands. "Don't you know yet? I believe in you, Ruby Jackson."

Her eyes pooled with water, but she gripped his collar and hauled him down to her level so she could kiss him proper. Although surprised, he didn't pull away. His lips were soft and warm, and she tried to be gentle. She was supposed to be gentle. But then he wrapped his arms around her, and she twined hers around his neck and pressed into him.

Ruby didn't care who saw or who judged what she did. This person in front of her believed in her and showed it in the clearest way—he put his money on the line. Maybe he hadn't shown up last Sunday when he promised, but if he truly was coming from a sick house, she wouldn't have wanted him there anyway.

"Oi, break it up, you two, or I'll throw cold water on you," Bess said. "Ruby, you've rounds to make to the Fancy. Don't forget who pays your bills."

Maximillian lifted his head but kept his arms around her. "May I escort you over?"

Ruby flushed with pleasure. "Please."

She followed as he cut a path through the crowd, his dark hair distinctive and his intimidating height easing the way. He held his arms out to maintain the space, making her feel more than wanted— special, prized. That she was worth more than the five quid and pint of gin she'd just won.

Maximillian presented her to Lord and Lady Andrepont, and they applauded her. Exalted, Ruby took a fine curtsy. Lady Andrepont came to her side and guided her by the arm over to where Corinthian John stood with the prizefighter and her could-be father, Daniel Miller, leaving Maximillian to resume his footman duties for Lord Stone. Ruby wished Maximillian could remain at her side, but his time was not his own tonight.

Ruby's stomach clenched. The joy of her win melted into terror.

"May I present to you, Miss Ruby Jackson, the prizefighter Daniel Miller."

Daniel stuck his meaty fist out to shake her hand. Hands clasped, they surveyed each other. She took in the arc of his dark brows, the shape of his clean-shaven head, the roundness of his eyes, and the shape of his nose and ears.

"Pleased to meet you, sir." Ruby let her hand fall away from his.

"Pleasure is mine. Quite a fight. Congratulations on a knockout." Daniel Miller narrowed his eyes at her.

"You're looking at me strangely." Ruby's heart tripped and stuttered all over again. She'd need a stout drink after this night was over.

"I'll confess, before tonight, I didn't think women belonged in prizefighting. Seemed all a bit ..." He seemed unsure how to put it politely.

"Whorish?" Ruby suggested. Taking down the tops of dresses did rile men.

Daniel Miller shifted his blocky jaw. "Didn't seem to have a purpose, other than to give a peep show."

"You've never worn stays, then," Ruby said.

Daniel Miller chortled. "I have not."

"So, you don't understand how restrictive they can be when you need more breath for an athletic competition."

Daniel Miller rubbed his hand over the short bristles on his scalp. "I didn't think about that."

"Nor, likely, how the sleeves on dresses often don't allow enough range of motion for a cross-body block or jab."

Daniel Miller frowned. "Well—"

"So, all in all, you made judgments about how you felt watching women engage in prizefighting, not how the women felt engaging in prizefighting?" Ruby kept smiling, even though this topic made her want to tear her hair out. This was not a new argument for her. "But you might take offense to someone telling you how it feels to be in the ring if they've never been in there themselves."

His expression darkened. "No one knows how it feels to be in there, unless you've done it."

"I agree."

Daniel Miller smiled, showing off a chipped tooth. "And no one can know the pleasure of a knockout, either."

Ruby grinned. "Nothing like it."

"Like it was ordained by God." Daniel Miller clapped his hand on her shoulder. "And executed by the devil himself."

"Gives more credit to the devil and less to me," Ruby countered.

Daniel Miller threw his head back and laughed.

Corinthian John stepped back to them. "I see you're getting along just fine."

"Just a couple of fighters talking the Sweet Science." Daniel Miller put his hands on his hips, as if he were marveling at her.

"We're adjourning to my house after the last fight if you'd like to join us," Corinthian John said. "You too, Ruby Jackson. I've already invited Bess and Os."

She bobbed her head, pleased that Daniel Miller expressed his willingness to go as well.

"Splendid. I'll see you both there. Now, if you'll excuse me, I need to place some bets on this next match."

Ruby caught his arm. "Please, sir, I don't know what's proper, but I've taken a liking to one of Lord Stone's footmen. I don't suppose we could invite his group along? The one called Maximillian Vaughn."

"*That's* Maximillian Vaughn?" Corinthian John laughed. "Bess has been at me for weeks about who that might be. I can't make Stone do anything, but I will certainly invite him and his footmen."

Ruby watched the men confer, and was delighted when Baron Stone agreed to bring his footmen along. She knew they could sneak off to the kitchens while everyone else talked in the drawing room. Footmen were not allowed to speak with guests, and if Ruby snuck off for a bit, who would notice?

CHAPTER 5

A YEAR LATER

*L*ady Andrepont poured Ruby another cup of tea. "Thank you again for allowing my maid to try different coiffures on you. I wish I had your hair."

Ruby felt the unusual configuration of her hair, pinned and plaited and adorned with a gold ribbon snaking through curls. She tamped down the urge to shrug. "My pleasure. I don't get to have my hair played with like this anymore. Violet doesn't seem to care."

Ruby and Violet had grown so close over the last year that they felt more like sisters than odd roommates. Ruby helped Violet with her technique, since she had a tendency to drop her elbows at inopportune times. And Violet, well, Violet thought Ruby could do no wrong. After spending her life being criticized for every little thing, it made Ruby start to feel like maybe Violet was right. Maybe Ruby was a right good fighter, and pretty, and stylish, within reason, of course.

The butler entered the drawing room. "A visitor, my lady."

Lady Andrepont raised her brows expectantly. "Send him in."

"A Mister Maximillian Vaughn," the butler announced.

Ruby's jaw dropped. What was a former-footman-turned-wine-distributor doing calling on a viscountess? Surely any of her wine deliveries would be arranged through the butler down at the servants' entrance.

Maximillian entered and bowed to Lady Andrepont. He carried a large garment box under one arm. His hair had grown longer than when he was in service, and Ruby thought it suited him well. She liked to run her hands through it when he gave her an opportunity, which wasn't often. But one day last summer, they had managed to lounge in Hyde Park as if they belonged there.

"My lady, thank you for allowing me to call. Miss Jackson, I see you are looking well."

Ruby felt strange having him address her as such after their year of walks and picnics and conversations. "Mr. Vaughn. I'm surprised to see you here."

He raised his eyebrows at Lady Andrepont as if asking permission, and the viscountess dipped her chin. "Tonight," he said, "as you know, is the Pearlers' charity ball."

Of course she knew that. That was why she was here, helping Lady Andrepont choose a coiffure for the evening. Tickets were frightfully expensive, and it wouldn't do to waste a social event with inferior fashion.

Maximillian sank to one knee in front of Ruby. He placed the garment box on her lap. "Last year, my mistake humiliated both me and you in a room full of strangers. That night, you told me to make it up to you, and when you winked at me, I lost my heart."

Ruby looked aghast at Lady Andrepont. "I did not wink."

Maximillian laughed. "You most assuredly winked. It was the best thing that ever happened to me."

"I would not wink at a footman." Ruby was no longer sure. Did she wink at him?

"You winked at this footman. And I did as you directed—I bet on you, I made my money. I left service to create a different life for myself, and most importantly, I'm here to make it up to you. Miss

Ruby Jackson, would you do me the honor of attending a ball with me?"

Ruby's mouth was hanging open but no words would come out.

"Before you tell me that you've nothing to wear—" Maximillian opened the garment box, and a beautiful silk dress the color of burnt oranges and gold shimmered in the light. "I wanted to replace the one I ruined last year."

Ruby's fingers trembled as she reached down to touch it. The silk was cool and fine against her fingers. It was so much more expensive than last year's frock. "How can you afford such finery?"

Maximillian smiled. "I bet on you every time. You've never let me down."

A lump formed in her throat. She didn't want to cry for fear that she would ruin the silk.

"Is that a yes? You'll go to the ball—"

"Yes!" She flung her arms about his neck.

"Shall I have my maid steam the dress, and you can ready yourself here? We can share a carriage."

Ruby tore her gaze from Maximillian. "You knew about this?"

Lady Andrepont kept her sphinx-like smile and rose to ring for her maid.

Ruby cradled Maximillian's clean-shaven jaw in her hand. "Thank you."

He searched her eyes. "You know there's a bigger question I have to ask you."

Ruby swallowed hard. Violet had predicted this very thing. They'd giggled about it under covers and talked about whether or not Ruby would keep her stage name the same, like Bess Abbott, or change it.

"What is it?" Ruby asked, near breathless.

"Do you have better dancing shoes than those?" Maximillian asked, pointing at her feet.

She cuffed him on the shoulder. But he leaned forward and planted a kiss on her cheek. "I don't like stolen moments. I want to whisk you off your feet, and I plan to make your heart melt." Maximillian sat on the settee beside her. "I make good money now, Ruby. I can provide for us, set up a nice household. Can even ask Violet to be your roommate again, if you want."

Ruby cuffed him again on the shoulder. "Full of jokes today, aren't you?"

"Anything to make you smile as much as you make me smile, Ruby Jackson."

In spite of herself, she giggled.

Before she knew it, Ruby was whisked upstairs by Lady Andrepont to dress with her and her sister-by-marriage. They talked and laughed, drank sparkling wine that Mrs. Arthur claimed was better than she expected it to be.

As she descended the staircase after Mrs. Arthur and Lady Andrepont, Ruby felt gratified to see Maximillian as she came down. The dress fit perfectly, no doubt Lady Andrepont knew her measurements, and the subtle gold threading and simple accents fit Ruby's tastes. She felt her name for the first time, a jewel in its own right.

They arrived at the Pearlers' home, and as Ruby and Maximillian descended from a carriage with Corinthian John and Mrs. Arthur, and Lord and Lady Andrepont, she was struck speechless. Who was she, to be cavorting with such fine company, in a dress like this, at a house like that?

Their party entered the Pearler household, and then splintered off in separate directions. Maximillian steered her out to the veranda and down into the back gardens.

"I loved being in these gardens when I worked here," he admitted. "This tree was a particular favorite."

Ruby gazed up at the massive oak, its gold and red leaves gently rustling in the breeze, lit only by the moon and the glow of the party inside. "It's beautiful here."

"This is where I wanted to take you. The ball because you missed it last year, but in all of London, this tree, in this garden, is the most beautiful place I could show you."

He took her roughened hands covered by supple gloves. "Since I've met you, my life has only gotten better. I've found a direction, taken chances that played to my favor, and found more contentment in my Sunday afternoons with you than any other time in my life."

She squeezed his hands, his also in white gloves. "I never had anyone who believed in me no matter what. Any support I had before felt like it might evaporate on a whim. I'm not sure many men would understand wanting this life, a fighter's life, but you never questioned me. Never thought I was strange or odd or unwomanly for doing so."

Maximillian grinned. "The Sweet Science is a part of you, and I love you, Ruby Jackson. All of you." He dropped to his knee. "Would you do me the honor of being my wife?"

Ruby nearly cried, so full was she with emotion, but she couldn't help but give him one last jab. "If Violet is to remain my roommate, then no."

"I would haul her out by her great, oversized feet if she tried to stay in our bed."

Ruby laughed, pulling him to standing. "Yes, Maximillian Vaughn. I will be your wife. Now, let's go dance before you spill a tray of buttered parsnips on me."

Maximillian slid his hands on either side of her jaw and pulled her lips to his. Ruby closed her eyes and pressed herself against him. She kissed him with every emotion she'd ever felt, letting the flow of disappointments and pains ease out of her, evaporating in the darkened sky above.

"The banns cannot be read fast enough for me," he said.

Ruby winked at him one more time. "Me neither. Now let's go dance."

AFTERWORD

If you enjoyed that peek into the world of women's boxing ... and want to know more about Lord and Lady Andrepont, John Arthur, Bess Abbott, and the goings-on at The Pig and Thistle, read **When the Blood Is Up** series:

A Lady's Revenge, featuring John Arthur and Lady Lydia

The Boxer and the Blacksmith, featuring Bess Abbott and Os Worley

A Lady's Finder, featuring Lady Agnes and Jack About Town

A Viscount's Revenge, featuring Pearl Arthur and Lord Andrepont

ABOUT THE AUTHOR

Edie Cay writes Regency Historical Romance about women's boxing. Her debut, A LADY'S REVENGE won the Next Generation Indie Book Award for Romance, and the Golden Leaf Best First Book, and was a finalist for the HOLT Medallion. The next in her series, THE BOXER AND THE BLACKSMITH won the Hearts Through History Legends Award as an unpublished manuscript in 2019, was a Discovering Diamonds Book of the Month for May 2021, won the Best Indie Book Award for Historical Romance in 2021, and was a finalist for the Chatelaine Award. The third in this award-winning series, A LADY'S FINDER, is a finalist for a Lambda Award. The fourth, A VISCOUNT'S VENGEANCE, just came out.

She obtained dual BAs in Creative Writing and in Music, and her MFA in Creative Writing from University of Alaska Anchorage. As a speaker, she has presented at Jolabokaflod PDX, Historical Novel Society North America, Sunrise Rotary, Regency Fiction Writers, the History Quill, Chicago-North Spring Fling, Northern Hearts conference and the Historical Romance Retreat. She is a member of ALLi, The Regency Fiction Writers, the Historical Novel Society, and a founding member of Paper Lantern Writers.

Once a month she interviews other authors on the Paper Lantern Writers YouTube channel! Follow her on social media for pictures of the latest baking project with her toddler @authorEdieCay.

... Really though? Set a timer for the steep on a cup of tea and she'll show up with a book in hand.

CAPTURED AT THE BALL BY SARA ADRIEN

Spice Level 🩶🩶

PREFACE

'Captured at the Ball' is a prequel for the *Check Mates* series and incorporates the characters from the *Infiltrating the Ton* and *Diamond Dynasty* series.

Told from the perspective of the villains, it gives a glimpse of how much antagonism the Jews faced, the same characters readers love to root for in Sara Adrien's other books. The prejudice against Jews is not the author's opinion but has been included to paint an authentic picture of the villains. Their misguided morality, combined with their tendency to choose the wrong paths, lead them to be cruel antagonists. Hopefully, you'll love to hate them and witness their battles against the heroes of the existing and forthcoming series.

It is important to understand how deep antisemitism ran and how calculated the opposition for the Jews and their friends, like Greg Stone, was. The hurdles have been—and often are to this day—insurmountable and shape every thought, deed, and moment in the lives of the Jews and other minorities who experience such injustice. Simply put, they have to be stronger to overcome such strong antagonism, which makes for interesting drama and page-turners and teaches important life lessons.

Although Sara Adrien speaks from experience in facing antisemitism, this story paints a comprehensive picture of the villains, with their faults but also emotional and physical pain. Even though they are on a mission, they are personally invested in putting the Jews down. In the books that follow this prequel, we see how the Jews and their friends rise up against these challenges and even find true love on the way. Stay tuned for how Greg Stone will take on Baron von List and Sophia in the first book of the Check Mates series, *Baron in Check*.

Meanwhile, if you enjoy the love stories and wonder what if Jews had mingled with the *ton*, then the *Infiltrating the Ton* and *Diamond Dynasty* series are perfect for you.

CHAPTER 1

*This is the story of the villains in all their evil glory. It serves as a **prequel** to the 'Check Mates' series and shows how much antagonism the Check Mates heroes will have to overcome. The union of the villains in this story amplifies their menacing power, setting the stage for a monumental clash with 'Check Mates' heroes. Join their beginning as they face the first hero of the Check Mates series, Baron Gregory Stone, before you see these villains from the heroes' points of view in the Check Mates series. Rest assured, the villains will be defeated and wrongs will be righted in spectacular fashion in the forthcoming books.*

LONDON, 1820

olfgang rolled his eyes at the carriages driving through puddles along Pall Mall as he closed his umbrella and shook off the rain. Nasty weather here in England, with unpredictable rain showers that would span days. Days! Like the heavens opened and cried every time Wolfgang wanted to set foot outside in London. Had the weather no respect? Back home in Prussia, the weather was more predictable. Everything had its place, including the rain. Specifically, in autumn, the gloomy time of year. But that was all right because it was when the vintners brought him wine to taste, the butcher delivered pickles and roasted pigs, and the harvest gave a multitude of distractions to a country gentleman. The question was how much longer he could occupy this role. All Wolfgang had was his father's ultimatum—either produce an heir or lose the title and his inheritance.

And that's what Wolfgang was, the lord over several hectares of agricultural land near Althof along the rivers Pregel, Inster, and Angerapp. His breweries traded in some of the most coveted beers in the empire, the dark ones with a malty aftertaste that had been boiled until they turned Maillard brown, and the acidic ones with more hops to give just the right fogginess to their color. Wolfgang always thought he'd pleased his family with the output of his lands, and they'd let him reign freely around Königsberg.

But it had all changed when the Crown Prince Frederick William of Prussia injected some funds last year and his father had renovated their baroque family seat. "The only son we can spare," Father had said. His two brothers had moved to their own seats, founding families and raising their status, but there had been nothing left for him. Wilhelm and his wife, a princess of Modena, Italy, were in Breslau, Silesia, tucked away in the country where he could enjoy his mistresses. He must have brought five or six children to Christmas last year. Wolfgang was not interested enough to count. His other brother, Johann, was in Schleswig. He'd married one of their first cousins, Maria Luisa, a Swedish princess with quite a zest for life. Always busy at the university, Johann was a prolific scholar of literature by day and a merry host for lovers of art and wine by night. His wife seemed to play along and entertained prominent guests nearly every day. Exhausting.

Wolfgang preferred to stay home in Königsberg, East Prussia, in the most lavish castle. His parents rarely knew whether he was home or not. They'd never reserved any niceties for him. As the youngest son, his mother called him the runt of the litter. On good days, he was her *Nesthäkchen*, the nestling.

Also not reserved for him was a princess. His brothers and older cousins had snatched away all the eligible candidates to marry. At age thirty-four, all Wolfgang was looking for in a bride—not that he'd ever find one—was a complacent wife who would never speak up against him or otherwise interfere with his affairs. "*Komm mir nicht in die Quere*," don't get in my way, was his favorite catchphrase. At least one thing the British got right was *laissez-faire*, let me be, borrowed from the French.

Whom he couldn't let be, however, were the Jews in England, a problem that had caught on like a forest fire in July. Some of the Jews in Prussia had gotten wind of the connections made in London by a certain Pearler family. They had a virtual diamond dynasty of jewelers, footholds in the countryside, and sway in Parliament. If nobody stopped this madness, the Jews would soon be naturalized. Just like the slogans he'd seen in the papers, silver etchings of peasants, arm-in-arm, marching along the Champs-Élysées in Paris and screaming *liberté, égalité, fraternité*. Liberty, equality, fraternity. Preposterous.

Father had been right. This had to stop before the disease spread. The people had no respect anymore. No appreciation for the noble elite and aristocratic bloodlines, almost as if society were turning into a meritocracy. And where would that lead? Surely, all one could expect from a country in which virtually anyone could ascend in society through hard work and riches was doom. "*Da wird einem ja die Hölle heiss*," he'd be on hot footing indeed, he mumbled in German.

Wolfgang handed the doorman his umbrella but followed him with his eyes. He didn't have enough money to purchase another umbrella, so he wanted to know in which metal bucket his was placed. They all looked the same in London, black with wooden sticks. Walking canes were almost superfluous in England. It rained so often that a sturdy umbrella was more useful.

"Ah, Baron von List," said Mr. Colthurst, the club's host.

Brooks's. A private club at 49 Pall Mall, neighboring the infamous Almack's. A sort of aristocratic meat marriage mart. Wolfgang needed a wife and had been to a few balls. He needed to bring a baroness home and succeed in his mission, or else he'd lose his inheritance. The runt of the litter, indeed. And he had to produce an heir for his title before he succumbed to his condition, or the Barony von List would revert to his cousin's line, and Wolfgang couldn't have that! The Bavarians had plenty.

Wolfgang proceeded to the back room. He'd gambled enough, but chess was his game of choice. The matches were longer, the stakes higher, the opponents smarter, and he loved strategizing for hours. His brothers enjoyed boxing and other sports of brute force, but Wolfgang could evaluate a certain chess move for hours. Even memorize games from books he'd read about the game.

"Ah, Baron von List, please join me, will you?" A stately Brit walked toward him and reached for his hand to greet him. "Everyone else is"—the young athletic man cleared his throat—"rather inebriated and not quite able to strategize as I hoped."

"Say no more, Lord Stone. It would be my pleasure to play a round." Wolfgang didn't like Baron Gregory Stone, a member of Parliament. He was young and had led a privileged life, even though his family was only recently ennobled. Converted Jews. Wolfgang tasted acid. As if a mere baptism could redeem their bloodline and earn the pope's favor. They weren't Catholic here anyhow. But as unholy as Baron Stone was, he was a pretty fantastic chess opponent, and Wolfgang itched to outman him on the checkered board. Maybe he could manage it today.

"What are we playing for tonight?" he asked, pulling out his coins.

"I'm afraid I lost all my money for the day against an old friend. Would you be willing to take something else?"

"No, I play for money."

Stone rifled through his inside pocket. "I have something that has become rather valuable in London these days, but it wouldn't be right to play for it."

That captured Wolfgang's attention. If it wasn't right, it was perfect for him indeed. "What is it?"

"A ticket for two to the Grand Mistletoe Assembly. I don't suppose you were planning to attend the ball?"

Wolfgang blinked incredulously. This was the ideal opportunity to dive into the lions' den and examine his targets, the Jewish hosts of the charity ball. He surely didn't want to stay in England longer than necessary to accomplish his mission of resolving the Jew question, as Father had called it. But attending a Christmas ball in their house? It lacked all manners of good taste.

"When is it?"

"Next week."

"The Christmas ball is *before* Christmas?" Wolfgang rubbed his chin. It was absurd. Back home, the markets were bustling with excitement before the holidays, the firs were hung with ribbons and alight with candles, and there were no Jews throwing society balls before the holiday even started. Oh, he'd rather be home sipping some *Glühwein*—mulled wine—and tumbling the local peasant girls in the stables.

"It's for a good cause, as you know. To support a foundling home."

"Well then, I must attend, mustn't I?" Wolfgang ventured as he turned to the chessboard. He always played white. Always.

"Only if you beat me, Baron von List." Stone gave him a sly smile and ordered a drink. "I know from the hosts personally that this is the last ticket. And winning it wouldn't be very charitable."

But Wolfgang wasn't after charity, anyway. The Jews were his targets. His goal was to diminish their influence, eradicate it if possible, to set an example for their continental counterparts. They should keep low and not cause any more irritation than they already had.

* * *

AN HOUR LATER, Stone blundered with a move of his bishop. Instead of sharp whiskey, Wolfgang had asked for some good old-fashioned beer. The British brew was, to his regret, quite a valid competition for his beloved *Weizen* back home. It must be all the rain the hops got in England, for the ale tonight was rather good. They were on their fourth serving, and Wolfgang's stomach rumbled. He was ready for a glazed and roasted piglet by now, but he couldn't interrupt the game. Stone slurred his speech, which made Wolfgang chuckle. The title of an aristocrat did not make Stone a proper drinking pal, especially not with a slow-sipping ale that was a little too warm and a lot too flat. The perfect kind to get someone drunk quickly.

So, Wolfgang found himself with a strong white king ready to jump to e6 to deliver the winning move. Stone was in an absolute pin, unable to move his pieces to protect his king.

Stone blinked his hooded puppy eyes. "You wouldn't accept a stalemate at this point?" Beautiful men were nauseating.

"How would that translate in terms of the ticket to the ball?" Wolfgang asked.

"We could split it, one for you and one for me."

"And you'd want me to wear a pink gown and hold your arm, too?" Wolfgang joked.

King on e6. Checkmate.

"Argh," Stone growled, "here you go." He threw the tickets on the chessboard. "I hope you'll find a good companion."

"I shall," Wolfgang said, although he had no idea whom to ask.

In England, a dance with a debutante meant something. Two dances meant even more. After the third, the vicar was called. Well, at least the *ton*, England's aristocracy, cherished their traditions.

"I warn you, List. Read the requirements. You have to auction something off, something valuable. And that means something to the Pearlers because they are invested in the charity rather than the social event."

And with that, he left Wolfgang pondering his bittersweet victory. Wolfgang didn't have anyone to accompany him, nor anything of value for an auction. But it was November already, and he had to take this chance to get to know the Jews. It might be his only chance to get into their lavish home, which was financed through their business as crown jewelers and all sorts of treasures they got their fingers on. An opportunity to see how he could make their diamond dynasty crumble before the *ton*.

CHAPTER 2

$\mathcal{S}$ophia didn't mind cowering in an alley between the elegant shops on Regent Street. She was on the prowl, waiting for her target to arrive.

Sofia Rosomakha. What a name. Not a single person in England had pronounced it correctly. Rosomakha meant wolverine. And it was a damn apt name for Sophia! She'd been hunting alone in life. Terrible experiences turned her into a predator. Better to eat than to be eaten, she always told herself.

Meanwhile, she opened her papers again, just to remind herself of the fake birthdate. Sophia Roche was born twenty-four years ago, a tender and imaginary Brit shelved by the *ton*. Pah! If anyone knew what Sophia had truly seen in her eight-and-twenty years, they wouldn't dare shelve her. What she'd done far surpassed the inexperienced debutantes at the usual balls. She was an expert pickpocket, an excellent shot, and danced like a prima ballerina.

In all her life struggles, her dream of becoming the prima ballerina at the Bolshoi Theatre had not come true. At her age, it was too late, she was a poltergeist at the ballet academy by now. Young dancers had come and gone, but the head, Michail Lopatin, had kept her there. She'd worked off her debts to him years ago after training the young dancers and entertaining Michail in any manner that he or his friends wished. And one of his friends was the great Vasily Gorsky. He could have gotten her into the Bolshoi. Well, he did. Except not as Sophia had hoped. He'd taken her backstage to meet the Tzar Alexander. Gorsky had told him of her many talents and her knack for languages. Instead of giving her a solo that season as she'd hoped, they'd shipped her solo to England.

And here she was, carrying around an umbrella all year and living on the pittance they deemed a fair salary to spy on the Jews. Had they known how strong the Pearlers were, in number and riches, they would have sent a small army, not an English-speaking ballerina.

Now that she was here, she had to please the tzar. Or else ... Sophia preferred not to think about the end of her career and her life. Maybe she could win the tzar's favor after all. But first she had to succeed in her mission—taking down the Jews in England. At least bringing them down a notch so that they would no longer stir up politics and push for naturalization, civil rights for Jews, and all that nonsense. Why couldn't the British Jews stick within a certain geographic area like the Russian Jews? But no, the Jews here wanted to be equal citizens. Restricting them geographically had worked until they became ennobled through university degrees, growing wealth, and connections, like the ones in London. And their example inspired uproars among Jews in the Russian Empire. All of Europe, truly. How much damage one family in England could do made Sophia sick. The Jews should keep their heads down if they wanted to hang on to them. She'd internalized that lesson first-hand. Plus, there wasn't enough money and nobility around to share with her, much less with Jews. Why should they have what she'd gone without, a pure-bred Russian?

But this family had means and connections. Unlike her. And what was worse, all their connections would be at the winter ball. It was the week before the Grand Mistletoe Assembly, and Sophia had not yet acquired a ticket. But she had to get in. She bit her lips. How could a Christmas charity ball be hosted by a Jewish family? They were not even ennobled. Only because Eve Pearler, the matriarch of the dynasty of jewelers, supported the foundling home and called it a charity. The ball was everything but that. Hypocritical aristocrats and parvenus paid exorbitant amounts for a ticket just to dance at the grand house of the Pearlers. Sophia nearly choked at the thought of how many children could have been fed and clothed or sent to ballet lessons if there were no ball, just the donations and the money that was wasted on the ball. Nobody had paid for her to go to the ballet academy to train as a prima ballerina when she was orphaned. Why should other children be luckier? And now, she gulped, she had to dance at the ball at the Jews' luxurious home. The world was upside down. It was the event of the Season!

The cost of the tickets was another problem. The price was high. Impossibly high for Sophia. And since Parliament was still in session, the *ton* would all be there, all the nobility of England. She'd asked Gorsky for more support, but he'd returned her letter. Sophia was on her own.

Clack-clack. Horse hooves came to a stop. The swirly P crest for Pearler on the cabin door indicated her target had arrived. It was time.

* * *

HALF AN HOUR later at Mme Giselle's, the Pearlers' French modiste, according to Sophia's surveillance, Eve and Rachel were receiving near royal treatment. Through the corner of her eyes, Sophia saw their assistant had brought them cream tea with scones. From the back room, the poor dressmakers, exploited for their expertly tight stitching, peeked at the infamous customers. This was Sophia's chance. If she managed to take down the Jews, she could ascend in society herself. The tzar might even pay her pension for her old age. She filled her lungs with air and held out for courage to follow. Then she stepped onto the upholstered stool and admired her gown overtly, like a ballerina on stage.

It worked; the Pearlers were looking. It was a creamy white dress with a violet overlay and little embroidered flowers. The silk bodice felt like pure luxury on her skin. Even the puffy sleeves had tiny purple flowers embroidered on the rims. Her décolletage was not too deep, which pleased her. She preferred not to show her fine silhouette for free. It had only ever brought her trouble to be this pretty. Sophia was just like her mother in that regard. Too pretty for her own good.

When Sophia was still quite young, her father had drowned in the Baltic Sea during a British attack on Copenhagen in September 1807, just before Alexander formally declared war on the United Kingdom. Sophia, however, preferred to say her father had been a British soldier who died in honor, hence her knowledge of the English language. In truth, he'd been deemed a low-cost casualty, and her mother was forced into prostitution to afford food and clothes for Sophia. And tuition. It was not only Sophia's dream to become a prima ballerina but also her mother's, and they did anything to achieve it. Anything. Then her mother had died, too.

The current obstacle in her way was the Jewish problem, as the advisers to the tzar called it. Alexander I was liberal like his grand-mother, Catherine the Great, but he couldn't institute his dream of a Russian constitution if it applied equally to all people. Jews were not considered "people" but demanded such rights. They'd crawled their way into universities, trade, and even the ballet! It was Sophia's civic duty, as well as her mission, to stop this nonsense. And if weakening the English Jews was a way to set an example for the growing numbers of Jews back home, so be it. If nothing else, a few spots would open up at the Bolshoi, and her chances could improve if the Jewish dancers were forced back to the Pale of Settlement, the area Catherine II had designated for Jews. It was too bad that Jews could shop freely among the gentiles here in London. They were taking goods away from other citizens, who deserved more than to shop alongside Jews.

For now, she turned her attention back to the Jews shopping alongside her. Sophia twirled around, admiring herself in the set of three tall, wood-framed mirrors positioned so she could see even the bustled back of her gown. It was exquisite. And what she liked best was that she was decently covered—unlike her ballet costumes, which encouraged men to ogle her, making her most uncomfortable.

A young woman stepped onto another tufted stool right next to Sophia. "This is a charming gown."

The dressmaker kneeling at the woman's feet started to push little pins into the hem of her dress. Sophia sniffed; it should have been the other way around, with the Jewish woman kneeling.

"I'm Rachel Pearler. Pleased to meet you."

Sophia already knew who she was—Eve Pearler's darling daughter-in-law. She was soft-spoken with her children and seemed to tutor them herself. Sophia had seen them reading with their golden-haired father, Feivel Pearler, in Green Park for hours. They huddled together like bunnies in a burrow, smothering the children with tender kisses and caresses while reading leather-bound books to them. Probably epic fairy tales. The entire image made Sophia shudder. The Pearlers were like too much candy, so sweet they gave Sophia a stomachache.

And they had the most disgusting nicknames. Feivel Pearler, for instance, Eve's son, was called Fave—because he was everyone's favorite. Blah! Sophia knew all about them and hated all of it. They oozed sweetness like an overstuffed Piroshki pastry.

"I am Sophia." She gave a well-practiced smile to Rachel, who was fumbling with the bodice of her opulent gown. "Pleased to meet you, too!" Sophia knew how to handle girls' talk from years in the dressing rooms at the ballet academy. "For which occasion are you purchasing this beautiful dress, milady?"

"Oh, I'm not milady, just Rachel, please." She was not just beautiful, rich, and educated, she was so nice that Sophia couldn't think why she had to hate her so. But she did. "I'm attending a charity ball this month. My mother-in-law is hosting it."

"You don't say, the Grand Mistletoe Assembly?" Sophia feigned amazement, but she knew all too well, of course.

"Indeed. You've heard of it?"

"The whole Town is aflutter about it. I hear it's going to be lavishly decorated and quite scandalous for a charity event."

"Scandalous? How so?"

"Oh my, because of the mistletoes, of course. You are going to hang them, aren't you?"

"I suppose, yes. But we are Jewish, you see. We don't kiss under a twig," Rachel said to Sophia's mirror image.

Sophia flinched. Little did Rachel know that Sophia had seen her kiss her children. And even her husband that time when … Sophia's insides stirred. She preferred to witness acts of brutality over the procreation of Jews. It was sickening to think of a husband with such an appetite for his wife. Such tenderness as if she were a fragile doll. Ugh! Sophia was used to spying, never to be noticed. But that didn't mean that she had to stomach all she witnessed.

Back to the job.

"Oh, what I wouldn't give to dance at the ball and sway to the music, gathered in the strong arms of a handsome gentleman until he kisses me under the mistletoe," Sophia said with a well-rehearsed dreaminess that she'd observed in the naïve ballerinas back home.

"You're quite romantic, Sophia!" Rachel laughed and turned to her. "I wish I could give you an extra ticket, but we ran out. The house is at maximum capacity already."

"Yes, I'd heard there are no tickets left. Expensive they were, too."

"All the proceeds will go to charity," Rachel said self-gratifyingly.

Sophia shuddered. "What kind of charity, may I ask?" But she knew, of course. She'd been spying on the Pearlers for months now.

"A foundling home. Poor dears. I go there weekly to bring them fresh fruit, toys, and books. But nothing can take the place of motherly love."

Sophia knew that to be true. She'd missed her mother since she died of something she contracted in her line of work. If her own experience was any sign, Sophia knew all too well that the orphans didn't appreciate the gifts. They mourned their mothers' tenderness and cried at the loss when kind visitors left. Orphanages were waiting rooms for prison, death, or a life of sorrow. The latter had been Sophia's fate. She'd never stopped feeling sorry for herself and blaming the world for her misfortune. And if she couldn't be happy, then nobody else deserved to be.

Rachel hopped off the stool and thanked the seamstress. She wasn't like other members of the *ton* Sophia had met. She spoke kindly to the help. Maybe she secretly knew she was no better than a lowly seamstress. Jews didn't belong where Rachel Pearler was. None of her clan did. The only question was, how could Sophia get them all off their thrones?

"I wouldn't want to intrude, but may I see the decorations before the ball?" Sophia hopped off her stool and followed Rachel to a rose-colored settee.

Rachel took a biscuit, and Sophia followed suit. She didn't like the crumbly English cookies, but she hadn't eaten yet today. Beggars couldn't be choosers.

"You want to see the decorations?"

"I'd love to!" Sophia clutched her hands under her chin like the dull-witted dreamy girls did at the academy.

"I suppose that could be arranged." Rachel picked up a cup of gold-rimmed china and took a sip of tea. "Why don't you come for tea the day before the ball?" She crinkled her nose. "I promise to serve something better than this brew."

"Better than English tea?" Sophia thought she'd peaked her voice too much in her role as the chatty girl. If it didn't come from a samovar, it wasn't worth another thought of hers.

"Jasmine pearls, my dear. I'll let you try it."

And with that, Sophia had a foot in the door. And hopefully, the lions would be hounded out of their palace as soon as possible.

CHAPTER 3

Baron von List,
If you have any interest in the event of the Season, meet me at the Coffee
Room on Throgmorton-street at two o'clock. Look for a white rose.
A friend.

Sophia had been waiting in the coffee shop for an hour. Her tea was strong, but the clear liquid in the small glass on the table was stronger. A welcome jolt of energy. The custom of adding milk made her stomach turn; she'd been weaned a long time ago. Nobody gave her creamy desserts, and if she earned them, they had always been overpriced, costing her dignity. No milk for Sophia's tea, thank you very much. She liked hers with a pang of lemon.

She'd paid Mr. Colthurst at Brooks's enough to know that this baron had an extra ticket to the Pearlers' charity ball, and she had her eyes on it. The question was whether he'd turn into a new target or help. She had low hopes for anything good to come of liaising with a Prussian.

The wall clock struck two. All right, he was officially late. Sophia hated people who were not perfectly punctual. Just as she was growing uncomfortable and considering taking her leave, a man entered the front door. A stately figure, tall with broad shoulders tapering to a slim waist. He was in a dark olive morning coat, a plain single-breasted frock. His cream pantaloons were tight and stretched over his bottom, capturing Sophia's gaze as he turned to the waiter and received a beverage.

He walked toward the back where she sat, swirling an amber liquid in his glass. As he stopped to scan the people, she smiled invitingly. It must be him, for he looked Prussian and held himself stiffer than the Englishmen around. There was no doubt. He was close enough for her to see the metal buttons on his frock, depicting a hunting scene with a fallen deer. She touched the white rose in her hair and gestured for him to sit. He scanned her from top to bottom. His eyes were of such a light blue. Like water, they seemed colorless and reflected the green hues of his frock. The room was well lit, but there was a darkness to him that Sophia found instantly unsettling. He was perfect for the job, an intimidating figure.

He placed both hands on the table and scooted onto the wooden bench. "It's rare that a woman invites me to a blind meeting." No accent, as she'd expected.

He smiled, and she caught a reflection of gold in the far back of his mouth. His movements were swift, and she noticed the waistcoat of blue and white striped toilinette stretching over his chest. He was younger and more muscular than she'd expected.

He sipped his drink and hissed at the burn. Ah, whiskey, an aromatic spirit with about 40 percent alcohol. She preferred the clean burn of an 80 percent beverage, such as vodka, from her home.

She swirled her small glass. "The distillery next door supplies the spirits. What a shame they don't use all their good British rye for something as crisp as this."

He reached for her glass and sniffed, flaring his nostrils in a way that pleased her. Her reaction to him was most unsettling.

He crinkled his face as if to shake off the scent. "This isn't water with a splash of vodka, it's a full glass of vodka with a splash of water."

She laughed, and he rewarded her with an open-mouthed guffaw. He had a few gold fillings, the back ones rather large, but the rest of his teeth were bright white and impeccably clean. His overall appearance was rather clean. He had no stubble, smooth skin, and a crisp haircut. Only his top hair was slightly longer and fell in a wave that framed his forehead. He was dangerous and had an edge to his neat look that captured Sophia's interest.

"So why have you asked me here?"

* * *

SHE HAD the self-indulgent look of an avaricious woman, the kind List knew well. Yet there was something sad and beautiful, too, as if she carried a secret while her mien remained frozen. She'd be good at cards. But those games never interested him. He liked strategy games, even the ones that would span extended periods. He could lie in ambush with an ace up his sleeve for months. Victory would always be worth it.

"I hear you gamble," she said.

At least she was pretty. "Why do you care?"

"I don't, truly." Her R rolled tellingly. She had pretty lips, a kissable pout that would surely be soft. A profound appetite thundered inside, and he tried to dismiss it. "But I heard that you have a ticket—"

"You want to be my guest?" Oh, that's what she was all about. A social climber. The worst kind of woman, who'd sell herself for a position in society. The entire Prussian Empire was filled with the sort.

"How kind of you to ask." She gave a sly smile and bowed her head.

"I didn't ask you to go with me, I just—"

"Oh, but I accepted, and you know what they say about an offer that's been accepted."

"What?" His grumbled response bordered on rudeness, but the woman had only just met him and was already patronizing him. He had to get out of here.

"It's a valid contract."

"Das gibt's ja nicht, solch' eine Frechheit." Unbelievable, such audacity. He stood to leave and stopped to put some money on the table.

She tugged his coat. "Sit down." Instead of meeting his gaze, she looked at the spot where he ought to sit. She folded her hands and placed them on the edge of the table. Waiting.

Fascinated by her demeanor, he sat. She moved with elegant vigilance and seemed stronger than her slim figure let on. Her hair was in a loose bun on the side, peeking out from a felt bonnet held in place with a purple bow. Her hands were slim, her fingers long, and her nails trimmed sensibly. She looked rather more athletic than was usual for a lady.

"You have my interest but not my ticket."

"I don't believe you have a choice, Mr. List."

"Milord is the correct address in England, Lady ..."

"Sophia is enough. And I will call you Wolfgang."

He leaned back at her declaration and crossed his arms. "Who gave you permission to use my Christian name? And how did you find me?"

"The priest. Whose name you should tell me, so our stories line up when I am your baroness at the ball."

Now he wrapped his knuckles in the palm of his other hand and leaned forward. "You're mad. It's really a shame because you are so pretty, Sophia." He wanted to get up, but her death stare stopped him again.

"Have you met Eve Pearler yet?"

"I beg your pardon?"

"Well, I have befriended her daughter-in-law. She expects me for tea later this afternoon."

"Who's that?"

"Oh, come on." She waved the question away like a pesky fly. "She's your target and mine. We have to work together if we want to take her down along with her entire diamond dynasty."

How did the chit know that?

He plopped back against the wooden bench. There was more to her than met the eye. And even though she'd just outed his mission and stepped into his territory, he had a feeling he would quite like her intrusion.

* * *

AN HOUR LATER, after they'd left the coffee shop, she had her arm in the crux of his elbow. They must have walked like this for a long time, for his hand was growing a dull blue, and his nails had lost their pink. They'd been strolling along the gravel path in St. James's Park and had come to the duck pond. A few large-beaked birds with white feathers were sleeping on one foot at the edge of the canal that yawned along the park.

"Did you know these are Russian, too?"

"The ducks?"

"They're not ducks but pelicans. The Russian Ambassador gave King Charles II some pelicans as a gift, and here they are."

"And are you planning to stay here, too?"

She sputtered a laugh. "What a gift I would be, the ballerina spy."

"You're a dancer? So you are from Moscow, then?" He'd asked her too many questions already, and answering went against her reflexes to protect her cover. Her impermeable heart. But if they were going to pretend to be engaged, he might need to learn a few things about her.

Her heart dropped, and her gaze followed to the rough stones on the ground. Bits of shredded leaves and sand were mixed in, and some black-and-white substance she could only attribute to the birds. She bent down and picked up a decent-sized rock. It was almost oval. She weighed it in her hand, bumping it up and down. What should she tell the handsome baron, who was walking more elegantly with her than she probably deserved? She'd never had a solo at the great opera, but she'd been putting on a show for years. She swung her arm and flicked the rock into the water.

The entire flock of birds, ducks, geese, pigeons, and pelicans, took flight, unleashing a wave of wind from uncountable beating wings. A noisy endeavor that resembled a stampede in the air rather than the elegant taking of flight that one would expect from birds in the royal backyard of St. James's Palace. The pond was desolate within seconds. Some lost feathers tumbled through the air.

She grimaced. "Oops!"

He gave her a smile of surprising warmth, never letting go of her arm. "That was a rather impressive toss for a girl." Didn't he think she'd been mean to the feathery creatures?

"I'm a woman, not a girl." She thrust her nose almost as high in the air as the birds.

"Certainly not," he said, scanning her face.

Oddly, she didn't feel watched. She felt seen.

They found a picnic table with marble chess squares. A set of wooden pieces was in total disarray. Wolfgang sat on the bench and arranged them. The set was complete.

He inclined his head and invited her to sit across from him. "You're white. You're the bride, after all."

"And the bride plays *against* her groom?" She grinned. She was good at being bad. And she liked it.

"It's just a game. You play, don't you?"

She remained silent and made her opening moves.

White started. As usual. She moved a pawn to e4. Classic. Easy.

He mirrored her with his pawn on e5.

Then she brought her bishop to c4. Wolfgang eyed her suspiciously. "Il Calabrese?"

"Certainly. Greco's opening gives white forty-three percent advantage." She smiled as she made her next move.

"But twenty-one percent are draws."

She shrugged and took his knight. In less than fifteen moves, she had checked him twice and mated him in one with the queen.

"That queen's a problem, Sophia. She cleans up the board."

"Just like Eve Pearler," she mumbled, but he heard her and nodded.

"So how would this plan of yours work, exactly?"

"I'm not sure yet. There are a few obstacles I have to—"

"Like what?"

"Well first, nobody knows me, and I haven't been introduced to society."

"I could take care of that." He nodded. "What else?"

"If you bring me to the ball—"

"Wait." He froze and looked at her. "Sharing the mission is a high price to pay, Sophia. I don't even know if I can trust you."

"You cannot." She cast a dangerous smile, and he appeared to quite like it again. "But what is your plan once you are at the ball? How will you take the queen?"

"What did you say?"

"The Queen of the Jews, Eve Pearler. We have to get her off the board."

"She's not a chess figure they will sacrifice. She's worth too much."

"Agreed. But she's our easiest angle of attack. If we take the queen, we take down the entire dynasty. I befriended her daughter-in-law."

"It might take more than that, but I see your point. Let's find out who we're up against."

They spent the afternoon scheming and devising a plan to take down an entire family.

CHAPTER 4

wo days later, Sophia moved into Wolfgang's rented townhouse, not too far from St. James's Park. Like all the houses in this part of Town, it had a carved oak door, black rails on either side of the entrance steps, and a small receiving room next to the parlor facing the street. It would have been charming to come here as a loyal wife to a baron, even if he was an outcast, as he called himself, but Sophia knew this was only a show and would likely be over if their mission succeeded. Except, she wondered, what if it didn't? How long could she pretend to be the besotted bride of the handsome blond aristocrat who led her inside?

Wolfgang's small staff of three welcomed the new baroness in the fine German holiday spirit, with fragrant spruce and holly with bright red berries and spiky leaves. Apparently, they were made to believe the couple had married—or they were significantly more discreet than she'd ever known servants to be. They'd even tied juniper with dark blue berries and gold ribbons all over the wooden railing that led to the master's chambers on the first floor.

There was only one bedroom, which didn't please Sophia, but they had a plan and little time to implement it, so she didn't complain. The butler, who was also the footman and secretary for the frugal salary of one and a half people, followed Wolfgang and Sophia up the stairs, carrying Sophia's only bag to her new bedroom. He eyed her suspiciously as she halted in front of the young fir that was propped up in the bedroom. Not only was it positioned dangerously close to the mantel, they'd also decorated it with shiny glass balls and metal rings holding lit candles. On the very tip of the tree was the figurine of an angel holding a star. Sophia marveled at this monument to German Christmas tradition.

The butler smiled and walked backward to leave the room, his head inclined. Wolfgang clearly knew how to be stern with the help and put them in their place.

Wolfgang beamed at her. "This is a Christmas tree. We always had one, and I'm glad to have the chance to share one with you this year."

* * *

LATER THAT AFTERNOON, the allegedly newly-minted baroness placed her hand in Wolfgang's arm and walked with him to the Pearlers' house. Except she wouldn't call this a house at all, for it rose from the side of Green Park into a majestic four-story building.

"I wouldn't mind taking this house once we get rid of the Pearlers," Wolfgang mumbled to Sophia. He seemed to be himself around her, and she felt flattered by his honesty.

"We have to overthrow the owners first." Sophia righted her upswept hair before they ascended the steps to the large double doors. Even their entrance was imposing. Much more suitable for royalty.

Once inside, Sophia deflated. If the opulence of the anteroom alone was any indication of the Pearlers' wealth, she, and probably even Wolfgang, were out of their depth. Ming vases with intricate paintings, French tapestries, mosaic parquet inlays, and ebony side tables lined the first room she saw. And she had a sinking feeling, the ballroom and dining room would top this elegance with ease.

"Oh Sophia, dear, there you are!" Rachel Pearler approached her carrying a little girl across her hip, a small creature in a frilly gown and a collar of … was that Belgian lace?

"Oh, how adorable! Who's this?" Sophia feigned interest in the child. Little girls with fussing mothers made her sick, but she knew the way to a mother's heart was by complimenting her brood.

But Rachel busied herself with welcoming Baron von List. She was most attentive.

"I thought you hoped for a kiss under the mistletoe by a prince at the ball?" Rachel whispered to Sophia.

"I never said I hadn't identified my prince yet," Sophia answered with a sly smile. The kind that formed bonds between women. She had to take down Rachel, and this was but one of her opening moves. Hopefully, Rachel was just a minor piece.

"Oh, my sweet little darling," an elderly woman called as she drifted across the hall. "Granny has some rugelach for you. Come here." Clearly, this grandmother was smitten with the child at the expense of her manners. Her attention was on the bustle of the tiny person.

Eve Pearler. Sophia recognized her immediately. Her hair was pale but her coiffure impeccable. Her elegance irritated Sophia, who'd trained tirelessly to achieve a fraction of this allure as a dancer. It seemed to come naturally to the Jewish matriarch. How unfair!

* * *

"Oh Greg, join us!" Rachel Pearler waved when ... was that Gregory Stone in the hall?

Gregory peeked through the doorway of the drawing room and groaned. "Oh List, not you again!" He gave a boyish smile and reached out to greet him. "And you found your companion, I see?"

"Indeed, I have. This is the Baroness von List."

"I didn't know you'd wed since we last played." Stone placed a reluctant kiss on Sophia's outreached hand.

"Naturally, I wouldn't burden you with matters of the heart when you have to concentrate in a game against an opponent like me," Wolfgang said smoothly.

"You must tell me where your family's holdings are," Eve said. "I hear the Baltic Sea is marvelous in the summer. Are you quite home-sick and wish to return to the Holy Roman Empire with your new bride?"

"It's neither Holy, nor Roman, nor an Empire," Rachel said to Stone.

"I beg your pardon?" List turned to Rachel. "Were you quoting Voltaire for my benefit?"

She blushed and whispered to Eve in hushed *jüdisch Deutsch*, Yiddish, *"Er kukt aoys vi a valf. Es iz nit nor zeyn nomen."* He looks like a wolf. It's not just his name.

"Ich bin weder ein Wolf, noch ein Raubtier, seien Sie versichert." Rest assured, I am neither a wolf nor a predator, List added in perfect German.

"Entschuldigen Sie, ich habe nicht erwartet dass Sie mich verstehen." Excuse me, I didn't expect you to understand. Rachel responded in such polished German, it almost knocked Wolfgang out of his boots. He thought Jews only spoke their own dialect. But her German pronunciation was perfect. Natural, even. Her lilt native. He had a sinking feeling there was more to this woman than he'd expected.

She folded her hands primly and nodded at Eve. "Greg, if you're staying for dinner this evening, would you mind terribly if our new acquaintances joined?" Not a hint of German accent in her English. List humphed.

Stone bowed and called for the butler. He was oddly at home in the Pearlers' majestic home. This irritated Wolfgang. He was too close. Almost like a rook who had the queen's back.

"I'm not dressed for dinner," Sophia protested.

"Nonsense, my dear. It's just the family tonight. Best not to appear in all of your fineries," Eve said with a grandmotherly smile. "The children splatter a bit and crumble the bread."

"That's why they'll be upstairs during the ball tomorrow," Stone added.

"I'm sorry you won't be able to join the festivities, Baron," Wolfgang said mockingly. "If only you still had a ticket." He chuckled, glad to have said ticket.

"Oh, he doesn't need a ticket to be in this house, Baron von List."
Eve smiled. "He is practically family and always welcome."

"But you must allow me to make a donation for the charity, Eve,"
Stone said, continuing their friendly banter.

"I shan't allow it!" Eve put her hand on his arm and leaned closer.
"It would be unseemly for the treasurer to make a donation. You paid
for so many renovations already." She stepped out, presumably
headed toward the dining room.

Stone turned to follow their hostess, but Wolfgang stopped him.
"Wait!"

"Yes? Is something the matter, Baron von List?" Stone asked, as if
indulging Wolfgang for politeness' sake.

"How would Mrs. Pearler know the finances of the charity if you
are the treasurer and she's merely on the committee?"

Stone left him hanging without an answer.

CHAPTER 5

$\mathcal{E}$ ve Pearler was right. Dinner was an affair unlike any Sophia had ever witnessed. There were at least twenty little children and relations from every walk of life. Eve Pearler's daughter had married into an entire litter of nearly identical brothers with dark hair, eyes like those of pretty little fawns, and an appetite that shamed List to bear the name wolf, for he clearly couldn't eat a fraction of what those young Jewish men devoured.

Sophia was most uncomfortable with such a large and loving family. Even in her best memories, it had only ever been her and her mother since her father was usually at sea. And there had never been so much delicious food for a simple dinner—not even for Christmas! Frustrated with the laughter and merry chatter around her, Sophia eyed the wine glasses in front of her. There was a large, high-rimmed one, with etched swirls and hexagonal shapes that resembled snowflakes floating on the crystal. The smaller glass, with identical and equally nauseatingly beautiful etchings, bore white wine. There was no goblet for water, just another low crystal bowl with water and some slices of lemon. Convinced that drinking too much alcohol would risk her cover, Sophia drank the lemon-infused water.

"Mami, the lady is drinking from the *rince-doigts*," a little boy said.

The room instantly fell quiet. Sophia still held the crystal bowl to her mouth. It was easily one of the most embarrassing moments of her life. And to be embarrassed by Jews made it worse. She'd kill them all!

Later that night, Sophia paced the bedroom furiously. "How am I supposed to know that they put a finger bowl out for everyone to wash their hands? At the table?"

"The footman told you it was the *rince-doigts*."

"Yes, the one they called Max mumbled something. I thought he was trying to flirt with me!" Sophia scoffed. "And what the hell is that, anyway? Who puts French words in the middle of an English sentence?"

Wolfgang bent over laughing. "It is quite common, Sophia. How is it possible you don't speak French? Everyone does in Russia." His face wrinkled as he chortled heartily. At her expense. She hated it.

"I don't speak French. I didn't go to school. Only to the ballet academy. And there, they kept me hostage. I paid for my tuition, I can tell you that! With more than money. And now I'm stuck here in London, where I have to pretend to be your wife and let a bunch of Jews embarrass me!"

"You didn't go to school, I understand. But the way you play chess, you had some tutors?"

"No! I taught myself." She was ashamed when he gave her a look of pity. She hated pity. "Now turn around. I'm going to take a bath."

* * *

LATER THAT NIGHT, Sophia was still hungry, since she hadn't eaten the rest of the meal. She was too embarrassed, as though she might wash her feet in the soup or something like that.

She wandered around the townhouse and found the kitchen. A candle had burned low, but it cast enough light for her to find a sack of seeds. She took one, cracked it sideways between her teeth, and the kernel dropped into her mouth. It was nutty and tasted wholesome. Like the home she no longer had.

She carried the whole sack of roasted and salted sunflower seeds to their chamber, plopped onto the carpet in front of the fire, and cracked them one by one.

* * *

CRUNCH. *Snap.*

She chewed lightly and smacked her lips.

Crunch. Snap.

Again and again.

Wolfgang got off the armchair and looked at the bag. Still half full. "Are you going to crack and eat all of this tonight?"

She shrugged. "Perhaps."

Crunch. Snap.

"You hate those seeds, don't you?"

"What?"

"You hate them. They're being punished for something. You're quite aggressive about it, too. And I'm trying to read here. It's outright killing my nerves."

"Eh." She looked back at the fire.

Crunch. Snap.

Wolfgang had endured enough. This had to stop. He grabbed the bag and tied the string to close it. "You're going to tell me why you hate the seeds so much. And then you'll let me go through these ledgers."

"First, I don't hate the seeds. It's not their fault they stem from the middle of those huge yellow heads with frayed petals. Pah!"

He sat. This was going to be fun. A prima ballerina pretending to be his wife, who spoke with a heavy rolling R when she was angry. And she hated sunflowers. He laughed.

"Sunflowers aren't funny!" she scolded him.

He sobered and covered his mouth with his hand. "Oh no, they're quite serious, indeed. Those evil round things with green leaves and … why do you hate them so much?"

"You can make many delicious foods out of them. Bread, oil, even sweet pastes." She was flushed and her hair hung loosely around her face, the ends still wet and curly from her bath. She was rather beautiful and smelled of soap and something sweet.

"That's atrocious because ..." he nudged her on.

"Because they were chasing me for days, and I was hungry. When I finally hid in a field of sunflowers, not one of them was ripe. Do you know the pain of hunger, Baron?" She emphasized the last word, mocking his noble status.

"I'm sorry." He walked to a bellpull near the bed and pulled the string. "I rang for some food. Not sure what we have in the house, but the butler will bring you a tray soon."

* * *

"THANK YOU." She warmed to him and thought that was more dangerous than scheming and even living with him. This strange Prussian baron. "Why aren't you married, Baron?"

"Stop calling me Baron. We've been over this. Wolfgang, please."

"All right, Wolfgang. I understand you're stubborn, but surely that's not the only reason you aren't wed?"

He turned his gaze to the flickering in the mantelpiece. The bedroom was comfortable enough, but there was only one enormous bed and they hadn't discussed who'd sleep in it tonight. He was leaning on one arm, and she noticed his hand had turned bluish-purple.

She nodded at it. "Is it because you're unwell?"

He straightened and rubbed his hand. White spots appeared on the flesh where he'd pressed the purple away. "I haven't gone to bloodletting since I arrived in England."

"I see. Are you dying?"

"No! Do I look like a man on his deathbed?"

She looked him over, and her gaze lingered on his muscular chest and colossal frame. She shook her head.

"I'm going to bed." He stalked to the bed.

Sophia's heart sank. She'd hoped that at least once in her life, a man would treat her as a lady and let her sleep on the soft down pillow. With a sigh, she rose and pushed the settee toward the fire for warmth. At least she didn't have to sleep outside tonight.

"Thank you, but I can manage," Wolfgang said, a woolen blanket in his hand. He'd removed his boots and wore fuzzy woolen socks.

Confused, Sophia folded her hands and stared at him. She'd learned a long time ago not to ask dumb questions. Especially not when she was alone in the room with a man who was stronger than her. He didn't look that sick.

"Please, just blow out the candle on the night table when you are ready." And with that, Wolfgang sprawled on the settee with one leg on the back and the other on the armrest. He was altogether too long and looked like a bird that had outgrown its nest.

But to Sophia, it was the most beautiful picture she'd ever seen. A gentleman. Never had a man given up sleeping in a soft bed for her.

She walked over to the bed and shrugged off her shawl.

* * *

HIS EYES FELL to Sophia's slim silhouette under the covers. Her shoulder and hip formed two perfect curves, and her lovely legs an elongated flare. He'd peeked at her body when she sat like a tailor before the fire cracking her little seeds. He chuckled. It had only been a day, but already, thinking of her made him warm in a way he hadn't felt in a long time. Or ever. And yet, she was a dangerous spy who might pose many risks to him.

He twisted and turned, but it was most uncomfortable on the little settee. He moved down to the floor, not too close to the fire. The carpet smelled a bit like a wet dog, but he could tolerate it if he closed his eyes and focused on the smell of the Christmas tree only a meter away.

Another glance at the bed and those perfect ballerina hills and valleys. His breeches stretched uncomfortably, and he faced the fire. What should have been soothing heat felt like the flames of purgatory.

Touching her was taboo. She just wanted to sleep, and he barely knew her. It would surely complicate their mission. Bad idea.

Wolfgang pulled up the knitted throw, making sure his erection didn't stand up like a tent pole.

"Stop moving so much, I'm trying to sleep," she mumbled from in between the soft bedding.

"It's the stupid tea. It's going to keep me up all night. But I'll be quiet. My apologies."

She sat up, pulling the covers over her breasts—although he could imagine them just fine.

He shuffled, trying to get comfortable. "I'm used to having a *Kirschwasser*, cherry schnaps, at bedtime. They don't have that here."

"I don't know about cherries, but I have something that might help you sleep." She got out of bed and rummaged around her valise.

He could see her arms, shoulders, and the silhouette of her middle under the transparent white fabric of her shift. She came back with a flask and stood over him, the light from the fireplace illuminating her figure. Her breasts were perky, and her nipples poked out hard under the thin material. She looked like an angel aflame with her hair wildly cascading down her shoulders and framing her face. She handed him the flask, which he took and unscrewed, speechless at the sight of her. She must not have noticed how the fabric had stretched over her thighs and risen just enough to give him a perfect view of ... He pulled the cover up again, checking that there wasn't a tent situation.

"It's my last, so enjoy it."

He took a sip and cherished the violent burn that tore through his throat. "Ahh!"

"Good, eh?" She smiled brightly and reached for the flask. "Did you finish it?"

"In one gulp? Of course not! This is strong."

"What? This?" She smiled slyly and shook the flask. The liquid splashed around and sounded like water. But it wasn't water at all. "It's ninety-six percent, the best you can get." She smelled it, then tilted her head back and tried to pour the liquid directly into her mouth—without touching the metal to her lips.

Wolfgang's mouth went dry. Her lower jaw bones were beautifully angled. She'd parted her lips in anticipation of the clear liquid, and he stretched his neck and saw into her mouth. His hand flew to his cock, to control and hide it. But he'd want to do something else entirely as soon as she fell asleep.

Plik, plok. Just one tiny drop came out of the bottle and wet her lips. She licked the fluid off and leveled her head. "You finished it."

"Sophia," he croaked like a green boy. He knew his gaze was hooded. She must have put on that show deliberately.

"If you had touched the flask to your lips, you might just as well have kissed me."

She bit her lower lip and frowned. "I have never been properly kissed, Baron. I don't do that."

His heart lurched, and he sat up. "You've never been kissed?"

She shook her head. "I never wanted anyone to. They only ever hurt me."

He tasted acid. How could anyone hurt such a beauty? She was like the white rose she'd worn in her hair the first time he saw her.

A moment of silence passed between them, and he noticed her gaze fell to his mouth.

"Are you not curious?"

"About kissing?"

He nodded. His gaze on her mouth and the lovely neck swept with dark amber hair. He reached for a strand and wrapped it around his fingers. "If I were truly your husband, Sophia, I'd show you how a man kisses a woman."

She swallowed and knelt beside him. "Can you show me now?" She leaned in, her lashes batting expectantly. She was as innocent as a newly-hatched viper, but she was growing on him.

"Are you sure?"

She nodded, her gaze still fixed on his lips.

* * *

Sophia's heart pounded with something she first mistook as fear, but she felt safe expecting his touch. He drove his hand deeper into her hair until he held the back of her head. His other hand took hers. He was close to her, his eyes locked with hers. She felt his breath, sharp and clean. Some of his hair had fallen onto his forehead.

"Sophia, I'm not the prince you might hope I am."

"I have long stopped hoping for one, Baron."

"I mean … Don't fall in love with me, all right?"

She nodded.

He touched her lips ever so slightly. She trembled with the sheer surprise of the contact, his lips fleshy and hot. Then she felt the slight stubble of his beard. A light scratch.

She took a moment to reconcile how intimate the contact was. Her mother had been right to warn her. But she wanted him now. Not just his mouth, but all of him. So, she opened her mouth a little.

He pulled her closer. And parted his lips wider. His movements were gentle but deliberate. Controlled and clean, just like everything else about him.

But Sophia wanted no more of that. She'd crossed a line, now she might as well enjoy it. She pushed her mouth onto his, tilted her head to give him access.

And he took it.

CHAPTER 6

The afternoon before the Grand Mistletoe Assembly charity ball, Sophia couldn't muster the energy to open her eyes anymore. She'd collapsed after being tumbled in an avalanche of passion. Her private parts were sore, but she wanted to spread her legs and ask for more. It was a good sort of pain, like after a breakthrough training where she gained new strength. Oh, but the memory of last night was nothing like training. It had felt like that famously raw emotion she'd been specifically warned about, the one that would make her more vulnerable than even poverty.

Sophia touched her neck, where the sweat from lovemaking had dried. She called for a bath and dressed for dinner. Everything would be different now. They had crossed a threshold that spies should never ... but she hadn't felt like a spy then. For the first time in her life, she'd felt safe in the arms of a man. Cherished. Admired. With him, she could be more than a pretty doll. No longer would they pawn her off or blackmail her for her favors.

Sophia found a large box with a big purple bow on the table next to the bed. A little note was wedged into the side of the bow.

Merry Christmas

- W.

It was the first gift she'd received since her mother had died. Sophia eagerly opened it and found the white dress with purple lace that she'd ordered at Mme Giselle's. She held the flowing fabric against herself to look in the mirror. But when she twirled, her eyes fell on the books that Wolfgang had been studying at night.

"*Chort vozmi,*" the devil may take him, Sophia muttered in Russian.

He'd stolen them from the Pearlers' house. She shouldn't have trusted him on this mission, for he was bound to get caught. But she'd been swept away by his tender kisses for the last day and had pushed her worries aside. She was alone in the bedroom for the first time since they'd … She had no words for what they'd done again and again. But what she hadn't done was check these books.

She opened the top one and turned to a page he'd marked with a strip of paper.

"*Sukin sin,*" son of a bitch, she cursed.

The book detailed funds received and allocated for costs for the foundling home, and this page showed a log of medical expenses for a physician from Harley Street, no less, where only the most prestigious and expensive doctors offered their services. The next marked page listed materials and labor for roof repairs and the addition of a second bath-room.

Sophia took the quill and added the numbers on every page.

The door opened, and Wolfgang entered. "You are not dressed yet? Has the gown not arrived?"

"Why didn't you tell me you took the ledgers for the orphanage?"

"What a lovely thank you. Aren't you a sunshine today?" He grinned as he came to wrap his hands around her waist. "I expected you'd be in a more mellow mood after last night—"

"You lied!"

He stepped back. "Which time?"

"To me! You lied to me! You said we'd take them down together, and yet you took the ledgers. What are you going to do with them?"

He shrugged, dropping his hands from her waist. "Use their

evidence against them, of course." He sat at his desk and laid the ledgers out on the marked pages.

"I looked them over, and they all add up. Every page!"

"Yes, they do. That irritated me at first. But tell me, what else do you see?"

Sophia bent over him, and her breasts rubbed against his back.

His hand weaved behind him, and he clasped her thigh. "You feel so good. I don't know if I can wait till after the ball again."

She wanted to move away but pressed herself into his hand instead. Something about him made her crave his closeness.

And then she noticed it! "Do you think that's enough to overthrow Eve Pearler?"

"It depends on her defense, doesn't it?"

Sophia smiled at the chess term. "We're just as powerful attackers as the queen, only her mobility is different. She's rich and well-connected. Everyone at the ball will know her."

"Yes, she's the most mobile and most valuable piece besides the king. That's why she's worth the most if we attack her ... ahem ... if you attack her, as my queen."

"An early queen attack only works if she's not protected." Sophia dismissed his plans but tingled with excitement that he'd called her his queen.

"Exactly! And why would they defend her in her own home? At a charity ball that supports such a good cause?" Wolfgang gestured with grandeur and smiled mischievously.

"Let's go and get their queen!" Sophia clapped her hands together.

* * *

A QUARTER TO EIGHT. Time to go. Wolfgang took his hat and glanced at his reflection. It wasn't obvious that he felt sicker every day. Tall, broad-shouldered, ramrod straight was the image of the man who stared back at him. And a new spark of élan in his eyes, probably because of his beautiful fake baroness.

The bedroom door upstairs opened and closed, and when he looked up, a demure ballerina in a silky white gown descended slowly toward him. His heart skipped a few beats.

She gave a shy smile over her shoulder, and the butler came to hold her coat out for her.

"You look stunning, my queen," Wolfgang whispered, and she blushed, which he found immensely pleasing.

When he entered the Pearlers' house with Sophia on his arm, he was struck dumb with pride. The glitz of the ball only added to the glow of her beauty. Chandeliers, crystals filled with fizzing wines, and London's aristocracy gave this night a magical feeling.

The Pearlers had formed a receiving line with their king and queen, Gustav and Eve, at the head.

Gustav Pearler placed a tender kiss on Sophia's knuckles. "What a pleasure to meet you, Baroness."

Wolfgang didn't like it, a Jew touching his woman. His baroness. But she wasn't truly his, was she? It was a ruse to take down their hosts.

Eve Pearler had donned a blinding diamond *collier*.

"Your necklace is exquisite, Mrs. Pearler," Wolfgang said with the refined hypocrisy he'd honed his entire life.

"Thank you so much, Baron. It's my husband's design, and my entry for tonight's auction," Eve responded. "Baroness von List, are you entering the pearl comb?"

Sophia gulped. "I-ahem ..."

Wolfgang steadied her by placing his hand on her back. "Certainly, Mrs. Pearler." He nodded gallantly and pulled Sophia away.

* * *

THEY FOUND AN EMPTY ROOM, probably a study.

"What was that all about?" Wolfgang asked. "Did she already win an attack before you even moved a square?"

Sophia became blotchy, tears welling in her eyes. How could such a simple question fluster her so? It was unlike her. "My mother's comb ... it's from my grandmother. It's all I have left of my family."

Wolfgang sighed. "Then why did you put it on tonight?"

"B-because I wanted to be pretty for you. Worthy of a baron." She slumped lower.

"I'll prove that you're worthy." He led her to the ballroom.

CHAPTER 7

Sophia's stomach tensed when she laid her mother's pearl comb on the auction table.

The same footman she'd seen before, Max, put a little card next to it. "It'll be item number six, milady."

"I'll bid for it and get it back for you before the night is over. I promise," Wolfgang said as he pulled her onto the parquet. A crowd had gathered, and the orchestra played a waltz. "May I have this dance?" He bowed and offered his hand.

Sophia's heart flip-flopped, and she felt herself turn crimson. Between Wolfgang's kindness and the stakes of their scheme, she'd become unexpectedly flustered and lost her composure.

"I've never danced a waltz," she admitted. The music had started, and pairs were swirling around her. She watched their steps, but there was no rhyme or reason to their forward and backward sways.

"Allow me to lead you." Wolfgang placed her hands in position and pulled her along with him.

Within a moment, Sophia was breathless. His legs were scandalously close to hers, giving her direction. Everything melted away, and she felt as though she was floating among the sparkling chandeliers. Large wall mirrors augmented the lighting effects, and Sophia's heart nearly burst with joy. She tilted her head back and let her senses take in the heady euphoria of dancing with her baron.

* * *

WOLFGANG HAD NEVER BEEN SMITTEN with a girl, much less danced with a prima ballerina. But in only a few days, after giving her her first kiss and showing her pleasure, he feared he'd probably lost his heart. He tightened his grip and looked around the ballroom for a private place to lead her. She was pliable and responsive, the perfect waltz partner.

A hand landed on his shoulder. "May I have a dance with the bride?" It was Stone.

Wolfgang froze.

Sophia's eyes darted to his. He gave her a nod. This was why they were here. Attack and capture. So, he reluctantly handed her over to Stone and walked away. He couldn't watch the newly enabled member of Parliament dance with his bride.

But she wasn't his bride, was she? She was his partner, a spy.

Faster and faster, Wolfgang pushed his way through the crowd to the auction tables.

Oh no! The latest bid was for a small fortune! Wolfgang wanted to kick the table and throw the ledger in the fire when he saw Stone's name next to the number. The same handwriting as in the ledgers. The amount was more than he'd pay for the townhouse all year, an engagement ring for Sophia, and his passage back to Prussia.

"Oh no!" Sophia's voice came from beside him.

She was slightly flushed from waltzing with Stone, and Wolfgang's stomach churned. Never again would anyone lay a hand on her.

He picked up the quill and scratched a number. Double Stone's bidding.

Sophia gasped and her hand flew to her mouth.

Wolfgang tore the page out of the auction ledger, picked up the comb, and grabbed her arm.

"Where are we going?"

"To confront them!" He glanced down the hall outside the ball-room and … Oh!

He stopped. A sprig of mistletoe hung over the door to the study where they'd been earlier.

"Sophia." He took her hand and placed it on his cheek. "Under ordinary circumstances, I'd court you, buy an engagement ring, and —" She whimpered, and he smiled. "Will you accept your own comb back instead of an engagement ring?"

She sniffled. "It's better than a ring by the Jews."

"Please be my baroness in earnest," he almost begged. That was how much he wanted her to say yes.

He didn't give her time to answer for fear that she'd say no, that she wouldn't want the damaged and scarred runt of the litter. She looked into his eyes, and he took her mouth. After all, mistletoe hung over their heads.

She parted her lips as if to say something, but his tongue darted into her mouth. He had to show her how he felt, for he couldn't explain it himself. The icy walls around his heart were melting. She made his insides boil with desire.

"In earnest?" a voice thundered from behind them.

Wolfgang broke the kiss, startled that someone had overheard them.

Eve Pearler and Stone gazed at him from the threshold of the study.

"I beg your pardon?" Wolfgang said.

"How can you propose to the baroness if she is your wife already?" Eve asked sternly.

Wolfgang squared his back. "The same way you have your ledgers filled out by someone other than the treasurer." In position.

"You mean the ledgers you stole?" Stone said.

"The ledgers you forged," Wolfgang countered. Attack.

Sophia stepped back from Wolfgang and took the comb from his hand. She slid it back into her hair. And straight as a stick, as the queen that she was, she said, "I recognized Mrs. Pearler's handwriting on several of the pages."

273

"So what?" Eve asked.

Wolfgang gave an evil chuckle. "So, the treasurer here let a woman alter the numbers. It looks like embezzlement to me, fraud, and probably theft. Have you commingled the orphanage funds with any of your own? Maybe let the foundlings pay for the diamonds you're auctioning off tonight? Doubling your profit on the same piece?" Capture.

"Step in here." Stone signaled for them to enter the study.

They followed Eve and Stone inside.

"Baron von List, I don't know what your game is here, but it's not working. Eve has helped me with my responsibilities as treasurer. I have a lot to balance, believe it or not. A member of Parliament is rather busy during the Season and when Parliament is in session."

"It's a crime to let a woman balance your accounts," Wolfgang said.

Stone shook his head. "It would be a crime not to let her! She's been running a fortune for decades and knows this town better than any of us. And she's invested in making sure the charity is properly financed."

"*Paperlapapp.*" Nonsense, Wolfgang sputtered in German.

"Baron von List, I don't know what you're after or why you're trying to catch me making an error. But I won't allow you to taint my good name at my ball."

Wolfgang scoffed. "A Christmas ball with Jews. Who's ever heard of such a thing?"

"Ah, so that's what this is about." Eve opened the door and left.

Stone stared after her, agog. "Is this why you got me drunk and gambled for the ticket?"

"Gambled? I won it fair and square," Wolfgang snarled.

"Maybe I let you have it? Maybe I wanted to see what you were after?" Stone paced the room and then halted. "What are you after? Do you want to be treasurer of the foundling home yourself, Baron von List?" Why hadn't he thought of it himself? It was rather ingenious, truly. Masking his sheer hatred of the Jews as jealousy, taking on the role of treasurer to grab them where they hurt the most, their money.

"That would be a start, yes."

"I have another start right here." Eve Pearler returned with a man who was a foot shorter than her and a decade older. "This is the archbishop. He can wed you now."

Sophia gasped, and Wolfgang turned to Eve. "I beg your pardon?"

Eve stepped uncomfortably close to him, and he felt the heat of her breath as she said, "Baron von List, you have been captured at the ball. I call your little scheme."

"Whatever do you mean?" Wolfgang met her gaze, unintimidated.

"I mean that I know your kind. You waltzed into my home, questioned my integrity, and sat with my family with a fake baroness. Time to right your wrongs."

"If you two wish to be Baron and Baroness, here is your chance." Stone led the archbishop to the center of the room.

The irony was not lost on Wolfgang. The bishop's defense of the queen and her knight.

He reached for Sophia's hand. "Will you be my baroness tonight?"

CHAPTER 8

Sophia watched List in their dark bedroom, lit by only a candle on the small desk in front of him. He pushed a chess piece off the wooden board.

She nestled into his lap and pushed the chessboard aside. "Why do you think the Jews are so strong?"

"I don't think they are, actually. They don't deserve the air they are breathing."

"But they usurped power here in England—"

"And the risk stands for all the Jews in our homes, on the entire Continent."

"Surely the Pearlers are a bit more than merely poor examples?"

"They are a disease. A pest. And we must eradicate the pest."

"Except that we failed to do exactly that."

"Wer mir in die Quere kommt, muss dafür büßen." Who gets in my way, will pay, Wolfgang warned in German. A deep frown creased his forehead, and his disheveled hair appeared almost like horns on his head. "Sophia, with you by my side, I think I can do this." His hands came to her shoulders and slowly ran down her upper arms. "We rushed because of the ball. I thought I'd take their queen and go back to Königsberg—"

"But now you won't?"

"If you stay with me in London, I won't go after the hanging piece again. When we attacked the queen, we triggered her protections."

"I don't understand."

"We will go for the free pieces."

"Who?"

"I'm not sure yet, maybe Stone. I have to take time to consider the best angle of attack."

"You will lurk in the shadows until you find a free piece?"

"Yes. We need to take a few points first. You from Rachel's side. I will check out the boys, maybe the unmarried lads who ate at the Pearlers'." He leaned in closer. "But let's do that after our honeymoon. This will be a long game."

"My favorite kind, Baron." She licked her lips.

"You know what it does to me when you dart out your little pointy tongue?" He picked her up and carried her to the bed.

"But Baron, so naughty!"

"Oh, I am just getting started."

* * *

The Check Mates series continues with Baron Gregory Stone as he plays for love and honor. Read his story in Baron in Check because in love and chess, every move counts!

277

AFTERWORD

Would you like to find out how the villains, List and Sophia fare? The series continues with Baron Gregory Stone's story in Baron in Check.

Sign up for Sara's VIP Newsletter to be the first to know about new releases. Find out about her books at saraadrien.com

* * *

INFILTRATING THE TON

- Margins of Love
- The Pearl of All Brides
- A Kiss After Tea

DIAMOND DYNASTY

- Instead of Harmony
- In Eternal Love
- In Tune with His Heart

AFTERWORD

- In Just a Year
- In a Precious Vow

CHECK MATES

- Baron in Check
- Love is a Draw
- Brilliance and Glory

ABOUT THE AUTHOR

Bestselling author Sara Adrien writes hot and heart-melting Regency romance with a Jewish twist. As a law professor-turned-author, she writes about clandestine identities, whims of fate, and sizzling seduction. If you like unique and intelligent characters, deliciously sexy scenes, and the nostalgia of afternoon tea, then you'll adore Sara Adrien's tender tear-jerkers. She is the author of the series Infiltrating the Ton, Diamond Dynasty, Check Mates, and Miracles on Harley Street, and more.

Sign up for her VIP newsletter to be the first to hear about new releases, audiobooks, sales, and bonus content at saraadrien.com.

BALLROOM WHISPERS: BONUS BOOK DOWNLOAD

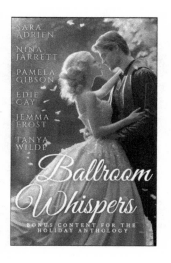

Download this special companion book which includes deleted and bonus scenes from The Grand Mistletoe Assembly.

But hurry! The download is only available between September 21st and October 1st 2023.

https://dl.bookfunnel.com/swkuoezgkn